The Newsagent

Kevin H. Hilton

To Jackie

For finding me that job

Prologue

Following orders, barked through the slot in the door, 'Big Ben' McGregor got up from where he was sitting on the edge of his bunk to stand against the back wall. Waiting there to be cuffed he noticed a splash of blood on the wall next to the other bunk which had been missed during the clean-up after the latest incident.

The heavy cell door clanked open. Two warders strode in and were none too gentle snapping the cuffs on, hands forwards.

He ducked slightly and turned sideways as he stepped out onto the landing. Then as the threesome headed along the third floor to the stairs, Ben's neighbouring inmates made themselves scarce.

'Psycho!' echoed around.

'Ooo *he's* in trouble *now.*'

The wing seemed to erupt with gorilla grunts, which failed to intimidate Ben, serving instead to bring a half smile to an otherwise bored expression.

'Knock it off you lot!' shouted the thinner of the two warders.

'They're like dogs that bark bravely when you're moving away,' Ben did nothing to disguise his Geordie.

'You can shut up as well, Morton,' the other warder snapped. 'I knew you were trouble from day one, as soon as I spotted that missing little finger and that scar on the side of your head.'

'Hey, I told you, they're just paper-cuts I got at the library.'

'Except, I know for a fact, you can't read.'

Down the stairs they went. Finally, Ben turned his back on D-wing.

'Bye-bye Barry! The showers won't be the same without you!'

Ben didn't even consider a response, trying instead to place the voice. It could have been the wannabe who had slipped on the soap, *repeatedly*.

On he went, through Processing and Transfer, where he was passed to two transport guards. They were busy signing paperwork in order to take him away.

Secured in the rear of a prison truck the journey took a while. Ben power-napped, like in the old days, until the transport stopped and the back door was finally reopened.

He was led into a police station and processed once more.

'Name?' the desk sergeant sounded bored.

Ben looked at the guards either side of him expecting them to handle all the paperwork. When it was clear they were not going to he responded 'It's on the sheet, mate.'

'Name?!'

Ben sighed. 'Barry Morton.'

With a nod the desk sergeant ticked some boxes and signed the bottom of the sheet. Ben was then escorted to a cell where he hoped he wouldn't have to wait long. He might be hard pushed to power-nap there with its strong odour of urine and vomit.

A little later a woman in civvies who he had never seen before, in her early thirties, with long shiny dark brown hair and big brown eyes, entered his cell. Ben watched her place a change of clothes next to him; some casuals. Without comment she then removed his cuffs.

'Thanks luv,' Ben beamed a smile as he rubbed feeling back into his wrists.

No return smile, no introduction. She just turned to leave.

'Hey, aren't you going to stay and watch me get changed?'

'Don't be a prick McGregor.' Her accent was smooth Aussie.

She closed the cell door but left it unlocked.

Sometime later *Aussie* stood in the doorway. Ben remained seated on the bench. Her eyebrows raised in a questioning expression. Ben was tempted to say something smart but this time thought better of it, at least until he knew who he was dealing with. She was certainly fit, he thought, a real head-turner. He smiled again, hoping for rather more amiable words.

'Get a *fucking* move on McGregor, we haven't got all day.'

He followed her through the station, to get processed yet again. Finally he was handed a clear zip-lock plastic bag containing Barry Morton's drivers licence, wallet and other possessions, then he was led out the rear of the station to a black Range Rover with tinted windows.

Aussie opened the rear door for Ben to get inside. Then she got into the front with the driver, who wasted no time in pulling away.

Ben was all too familiar with the older woman he found waiting on the backseat.

Shoulder length silver hair, thin rimmed bifocals, and cruelly thin lips.

'Cynthia,' he left his greeting devoid of any *so nice to see you* formality, wanting a break from lying.

Cynthia Cartwright reached into her Burberry jacket and brought out a zip-lock bag similar to the one Ben was still holding. Handing it to him, she took the other.

'What's this?' he opened it to examine the contents. 'You promised it would be *my* op next, if I sorted that last mess for you. My *major* op,' he tapped his scar, where the source of his cognitive issues lay.

'And so it is. That's why we are in a rush. The team of specialists is ready to go. They don't have much of a time-window to work together before they all need to be back where they came from.'

'I see...Thanks...So what's *this* for then?' he jiggled the contents of the new plastic bag.

'It's your next cover, for when you get out of the clinic. I suggest you to get into character while you are recovering.'

'You think of everything Cynthia,' by which he meant she never stopped thinking of things she needed him to sort.

'One does try, especially for those who go the extra mile.'

Opening up the new wallet and checking the name on the driver's licence, his immediate thought was that maybe this was just some sort of pre-op wind up, but then Cynthia didn't do humour.

'You've got to be pissing me!...This isn't a *cover*. It's a *porn star*!'

1

Six months later

Chance Dare still did not sit well with Ben but that was the legend Section 13 had prepared for him.

He had barely had time to get settled into village life of Sevensands, near Curston, when he was sent to inquire after a specific job vacancy. It was nothing grand but it would afford him time for his *other* commitments.

The vacant position was part-time store assistant at Sevensands Village Store and Newsagents. This was his first visit since he had moved in, not being one for a daily paper. However, arriving for the interview he discovered that the shop was more than he had expected. It was also the bakery, sweet shop, post office, filling station, social hub, and general notice board, all crammed into something not much bigger than a garden shed.

The manager, Harry Garrick, was polite and up front from the outset, making it clear that no one else had applied. Harry took pride in showing Chance the range of products. The first impression of Harry was that he was like some reincarnation of Albert Arkwright from Open All Hours. Harry didn't ask for a CV or ID, just Chance's NI number and contact details. It was obvious to anyone, from the rather laid back chatter that this was not a real interview, rather just a tick box formality for appearances.

Chance was asked to start at nine the next morning, but in future would be required to work from seven. That suited him fine, he was no stranger to early rising, or long days.

Finally Harry told him that once he was confident that Chance had learned the ropes, maybe in a couple of weeks of working with other staff, he would sort out his regular shifts.

Ben headed back to his accommodation, a house which was only fifteen minutes on foot, up a bit of a hill. It was a sandstone barn-conversion. He had yet to meet his neighbours properly, but he could tell that they both had young teenage boys who by the sounds of things enjoyed a kick-about and a fight.

Before entering the house he glanced over his shoulder. The jungle of a garden needed some serious sorting out. There had been a lawn under there once. It looked like a job for Time Team never mind Ground Force.

The interior looked like it could have done with a make-over too. Nevertheless it was fit for purpose. On colder days the whole house could be heated by a solid fuel Rayburn, with a back boiler, oven and hobs, which had seen better days. Maybe he would get that sorted, maybe he wouldn't. In the meantime it was good to know he had a place to destroy confidential paperwork quickly if he was compromised.

He made himself lunch. Pulled pork with fresh mixed veg, none of that frozen stuff which tasted like wallpaper paste run through a 3D printer.

After lunch, he went for a stroll, a route that he had already jogged a couple of times since he had moved in. This route took him up the lane and over the hill. Then he cut through the disused sandpit where he guessed the village got its name from.

Left to its own devices it had filled with water, plants and wildlife, to become something of a nature reserve, or at least it would have but for the fact that the *lough* was the property of the rather preoccupied landowner.

There was a well-worn path there but no public footpath signage. The far end connected to a track which led to a church yard, of the oddly Welsh St Gethin. He was to find that some non-congregation locals referred to this as *sin to get in*. From there it was possible to follow what the locals called the *Arrow* back into the village.

The Arrow was the main road that connected Curston with Strayden, Sevensands, and further along Strawford. *The Arrow* was also the name of the local newsletter, an old copy of which Ben chanced across at the back of a cupboard.

Given a cursory read, as a break from unpacking the only two crates of Chance's possessions, *The Arrow* was found to contain a local history article. It described how the main road had originally been constructed by the people of Strayden. This feat of engineering had been undertaken when the mud track no longer sufficed for heavy quarry traffic between Curston and what became Sevensands. The improved road was initially unfenced single-track with marshland to either side. The article went on to claim that at the Curston end there had once stood a sign, warning folk to *Keep to the Strayden Arrow.*

Some locals however claimed the sign was just scaremongering to ensure that quarrymen and other travellers paid the toll to the landowner. Nevertheless, over the years, a number of people and their carts went missing, as a result of venturing off the beaten track. There was much speculation as to whether they had been lost to the marsh or to the landowner's musket.

Coming into Sevensands, there was the local pub, the Quarryman's Arms, known to locals simply as the Quarryman. It was the only pub left in the village.

The Arrow Inn, on the Curston side of Sevensands, had been closed down for some years pending the present landowner's planning application to convert it into a bunkhouse. The animosity almost divided the village, as the local newsletter described, under its headline of: The Arrow Inn Experience.

Reaching the Quarryman's Arms, Ben called in for only the third time since his arrival in the village. It was a nice layout inside, with lounge bar and a restaurant. There were a couple of nods from still unfamiliar locals as he strode to the bar. He ordered a Guinness from the young woman with the head of red curls he'd not seen serving there previously.

'Be passing through?' her west-country accent was broad.

'Not if I can help it.'

The woman burst out laughing, surprisingly loud. 'No, silly. I mean *you*…not your pint.'

'Yeah…Still, I'm not passing through, no. I just moved in up the road.'

'Oh that's nice,' she left the pint to settle. 'I'm Gloria, pleased to meet you.'

'Hi Gloria. I'm Chance.'

'Chance? What sort of name is that?'

'I know, right. What can I say…The product of bad parents.'

'Well it makes me think you was considered fated then…or maybe…you was just an *accident*.'

'Cheers.' He could hardly believe this woman's bluntness.

Prompted by his reply she topped up his Guinness and handed it to him, taking his five pound note and giving him little change. He turned his back on her deciding it might be a good idea to go and enjoy his pint outside. However, she called after him before he could reach the door, like she had just had a great idea that simply had to be shared.

'Hey, Chance….Good job you're not fat then, innit?'

The pub erupted with howls of laughter, which could still be heard after the door had been closed tightly behind him.

Shaking his head, Ben started across the road towards the three beer benches in the shade of trees by the village green.

Those to left and centre were empty, but the bench to the right seated a rather nondescript woman in her late twenties or early thirties, with a blonde bob. She appeared to be engrossed in a paperback.

However, she lowered the book and looked at him with a puzzled expression, watching his

13

eyes dart from one table to the next. 'Would you like to join me?'

'I thought you were reading?'

'I only read when there's nothing better to do.' Her smile seemed to light up her face.

'I see.' He sat in front of her.

'Besides, I read this last week.'

'Really?' Ben couldn't help wondering if all the women in this village might be showing signs of inbreeding.

'Yes, it turns out it's one of those books with a twist at the end which makes you want to read it all through again, immediately.'

'Wow.' He tilted his head. 'What's it called?'

The woman raised the book. 'Breakfast's in Bed.'

'Full of typos is it?'

'No, why? Oh, no, that apostrophe is quite important, I assure you.'

'Fair enough.'

'It's rather puerile, but very funny. You can borrow it if you want…When I finish it again.'

He frowned. 'How do you know that I'm not just *passing through*?' he affected a west-country accent for the last two words.

She smiled like she got the reference. 'I'm, shall we say, a little more *inquisitive* than some, Mr Dare.'

He was immediately on his guard.

She could see that she had made him uncomfortable. 'Sorry. My name is Jill Selkirk. I'm a writer.'

'Fiction?'

'Some try to claim so, but I write freelance for the media.'

'That must be interesting.'

'It has its moments. So what are you doing here Chance?'

The guarded feeling returned. 'I urr, well, I just got the job of store assistant at the local newsagents.'

'Right…I wouldn't have figured you as a shop assistant. You look more…Never mind it's none of my business.'

'No, go on. Stereotyping can be fun.'

'I was thinking ex-forces.'

'Wow really?' he shook his head. 'You couldn't be further from the truth. Nothing quite so exciting I'm afraid, though I did get to travel round the world a bit…I used to hold a middle management position at a university until they brought in consultants to feed the fat cats through persistent asset stripping. I was one of a number whose *ass* got stripped. *Voluntary* severance,' he scoffed with a couple of air quotes for good measure.

He prepared to respond to an anticipated comment about his bitterness, which never came.

Instead she simply pointed out, 'It's happening up and down the country. You shouldn't take it personally.'

'That's what *they* said. But it makes you feel worthless, the speed they get rid of you.' He forced his previously prepared line in there with a growl.

Suddenly though, it dawned on him, this disappointment was actually coming from the heart. The real him, Ben McGregor, actually could relate to this cover story, having not that long ago faced the option of being RTU'd, Returned To Unit from the SAS to the Paras.

That feeling had continued on through his job with the post office. That was probably what had him going a bit off the rails, with a group of lads, pulling mad pranks on people.

'Are you okay, Chance?'

'Urr yeah, fine.' He noticed her empty glass, and saw it as an opportunity to get to know *her* a bit better. 'Can I get you another, Jill?'

'Thanks. A tonic water please.'

'Gin?'

'No. Ice and lemon would be just fine.'

With a nod he got up and crossed the still quiet road with a smile, feeling a bit more relaxed now.

He noticed a man in his eighties sitting outside the front door smoking. His completely bald head desperately needed some sun cream on.

As Ben drew close, the old man caught his eye with a wink then looked from him across to Jill and back as if with a knowing smile.

In rather garbled west-country, he uttered 'Oyvaddur.'

2

Ben got to work for eight fifty-five the next morning, to be greeted by two massive pallets of goods, like tank-stops at the doorway. It seemed to him that whoever had ordered all this has been under the mistaken impression that this garden shed was in point of fact the Tardis.

Inside he saw a lad serving behind the counter who he had not met the previous day.

'Hi, I'm Chance, meeting the boss here at nine.'

'Ha. You'll be lucky if he turns up until *after* all of that order out there gets brought inside. You must be the new guy. I'm Eddie by the way.'

'Hi Eddie.'

First impressions of Eddie were that he looked like a cage fighter, with tattoos down the length of his arms and up round his neck. Ben knew he should not jump to assumptions but there were also missing teeth and a number-one crew-cut which would make hair-pulling impossible.

'Whilst there are no customers I should introduce you to Rosie, who does the bakery side of things. She makes cakes, pies, and hot sandwiches to order.'

'Rosie. This is the new guy, Chance.'

'More staff? At the shop?' she frowned. 'Chance would be a fine thing.'

'Let's hope so.' Ben considered how Rosie was possibly the least appropriate name for this frail looking woman, with her black hair and pallid grey complexion.

'Customer,' Eddie nodded toward the door before heading back to the counter. 'You might want to start bringing that stuff in from outside, Chance. I'll give you a hand between customers.'

Ben looked round for a storeroom and spotted a door between two fridges. His first thought was to put everything in there out of the way, to sort through later. However, he was surprised to find it was only a broom cupboard, stacked almost to head height with pop bottles, which blocked access to the shelving at the back filled with beer and packs of something unlabelled.

There was only one thing for it, he decided, the goods would have to be placed as near as possible to their related shelves, on the floor of the already narrow aisles.

Outside he struggled with unwinding the industrial cling film from the pallets, realising a little too late that if you unwound all of it at once there was the risk of goods toppling to the ground. Half a dozen ready-meals made it to the grit of the forecourt with all the finesse of an overturned car transporter. Ben began to wonder how much of this job was going to be learned by trial and error rather than training.

Entering the shop with another load of pop bottles and taking it round towards the fridges, Ben heard a softly spoken voice saying 'I'm looking for beans now.'

Pausing for a quick glance, Ben spotted them, 'They're there,' he struggled to point with his arms full.

'I know,' the man said in a near whisper.

Ben smiled politely and got back to what he was doing. By the fridges he thought it best to stack the packs of pop in front of the shelf of toilet rolls, and hoped that in the time it took him to ever find shelf space for all these bottles and cans the village didn't come down with dysentery.

As he passed the whispering man he heard him say 'I'm looking in the chiller for cheese slices.'

Ben left him to it, grabbing three more packs of pop before returning to hear the soft muttering was continuing.

'The cool air is going down my shirt as I reach for the top shelf.'

Putting the pop on top of the previous load, Ben went round to the counter.

'Hey, Eddie. Is that guy okay?' he nodded towards the chiller, worried that the shopper might be about to have a turn and fall, which he imagined would take all the shelving down like dominos.

'Oh that's just Winston. He says he's got something called Socd.'

'Socked?'

'Self-report Obsessive Compulsive Disorder. He's fine.'

'Right.' Ben had never heard of such a thing. With a shrug he continued with the pallets of goods.

As he made a start on the second pallet, having shifted the empty one away from the doorway where it had been left, Winston was just leaving.

'Bye Winston.' It occurred to Ben that it would be a good idea to try and learn as many of the villagers names as he could with this being a small community store.

'Good bye,' Winston whispered with a nod. 'I've just said good bye to the giant and now I'm walking across the forecourt towards the post box, which is still red.'

Eddie came out to help Ben, and as they worked their way down through the stack they came to trays of bread. Ben guessed that Rosie was far too busy or there really wasn't space and time in this Tardis for her to be baking bread in addition to all the rest she was on with.

The top trays of bread, not having the protection of a tray above, contained a number of squashed loaves, because whoever had packed the pallet at the wholesalers had thought it fine to put pop bottles on top.

'These are going to have to be returned, I guess,' Ben pointed.

'They might bounce back, with a bit of shaking and bashing.'

'Shaking and bashing?' he laughed, imagining Eddie in a cage fight with a loaf, crumbs going everywhere.

'Or we see what Harry says when he gets in.'

'Right.'

A disgruntled customer made it known with huffs and groans that she wasn't happy about the remaining pallet being so close to the store entrance.

She pushed past Ben and Eddie with her pram, struggled up the ramp and in through the single door. As Eddie took a tray of bread inside, Ben could hear the volume of the huffing and groaning increase. Then as Ben entered with the last tray, passing behind her as she tried to squeeze onwards between a chiller and stacks of dog food, she went ballistic.

'How the fuck, am I supposed to get my fuckin baby round the fuckin aisles in this fuckin shop with all this fuckin shit on the fuckin floor?!'

'Sorry,' Ben forced an apology. 'I'm new here and didn't know where else to put them.'

'Well *you could* try putting them on the fuckin shelves for a fuckin start, and if there ain't no fuckin room, you can shove it right up your fucking arse for all I care!' the young mother blared up into Ben's face.

Ben was somewhat amused to hear that her vocabulary did stretch to a second offensive word. Though sadly it did leave him wondering which would be the baby's first word.

Turning away, abandoning the pram near the first chiller, the young woman took the only wire basket and got on with her shopping, dropping more of her favourite expletive as she shuffled round in her Crocs. Her complaints about having to hunt for things and then the pricing, could be heard clearly from outside as Ben and Eddie continued with unloading the remaining pallet.

'That's Celia Trent,' Eddie explained once outside. 'She gets called Celia Trap, for obvious reasons, though since she had the kid, with no one admitting to being the father, I've heard a few people start referring to her as Celia Trench.'

'I'm guessing *she* has Tourette's.'

'Ha ha, no. Just parents who taught her everything they know.'

'So, she's fine with either name then?'

'Are you kidding?'

'Yes.'

'Ha. You had me going there for a moment. Oh it looks like she's heading for the till.' Eddie went inside with boxes of sweets.

Bringing more sweets in after him, and placing them with the others on the floor of the confectionary aisle, Ben noted the contents of Celia's basket. There was one pack of baby wipes, two pot noodles, and three bottles of wine.

Standing there hands on hips and chest out, Celia demanded Eddie give her a bottle of gin and three packs of rolling tobacco. With those in hand she turned her attention to chocolates placing handfuls into the basket, like a crane at the amusements but which actually did reach the chute before dropping everything.

'Is that all you want today Celia?' Eddie checked before turning his attention from the till to the card reader.

'What are you fuckin inferring by that, you little shit?!'

'Nothing...Paying by card?'

'You wanna watch I don't shove this card right up your arse!'

With her bag of purchases soon forced under the cradle of the pram, Celia reversed her chilled baby out into the sun, with further huffing and groaning. Then, as she pulled away, she shouted 'I heard that!' to some imagined slight.

Eddie helped shift the second pallet to one side with the other. 'And now is the real challenge, of putting stuff away. You just need to pull the older stuff out first, you know, stock rotation. Just make sure all the old stuff will fit back in front. The spare stuff needs to be stored away, someplace.'

'Right. Sounds easy enough.'

'And as you do that I will need you to give me one item from each pack to scan everything onto stock at the till. I'll show you how stock entry works next week, if Harry doesn't think to show you first.'

'Fine,' Ben got on with shelf packing.

Later in the morning, workmen began coming in and ordering hot sandwiches from Rosie. Ben heard two of them over by the chiller.

'I know that some of the guys bring their dog's to work but there has to be a law against Steve bringing in his Chimp,' the shorter of the two complained.

'I took that as a Gibbon.'

Ben laughed, attracting attention, kneeling on the floor.

The taller man turned to look at Ben as he sorted out the pet foods. 'Say one for me while you're down there.'

Ben smiled at the comedian's comment. 'Anything in particular you want me to mention?'

'Yeah…Quieter laughter at the pub…Gloria's quarry blasting requires ear defenders once I get going with my wisecracks.'

At mid-day a woman came in for a chat with Rosie. Ben couldn't help but listen in as he continued to pack shelves. The gist of it was that there had been some shocking news.

Last night, in Curston, there had been three stabbings. The one surviving victim described being mugged by two young men. The description was a very close fit to two dead bodies found in Wrap Park. However, it would seem that those young men had themselves been robbed.

3

Ben finished his first shift at three in the afternoon and headed home, making a mental note of a good place to park the car in case he needed to drive to work.

As he drew close to the school he saw an obese woman shuffling across the road from the school gates towards the car park by the playing field. She was urging her daughter to get a move on; not to linger on the road. The infant already looked well on her way to following in her mother's footsteps though.

Then Ben noticed the old west-country man, who he had seen outside the Quarryman. As the old man passed the obese woman and her child he smirked, which tilted his cigarette up. When he crossed paths with Ben seconds later he said 'Oyvaddur.'

Ben wondered whether this was the only sound the old man could make, or was he actually claiming the child was his.

After his evening meal Ben decided to go down the pub to celebrate his first day at work.

As he came around the corner of the pub he saw an old couple get out of their Range Rover and make for the front door. Outside, on his favourite bench, was the old west-country man again. As the couple reached the door Ben heard 'Oyvaddur.'

The old couple paused to look down in disgust, the man clearly contemplating saying something but thinking better of it. They opened the door and went in with Ben right on their heels.

There were two people serving at the bar, a young man called Peter who Ben had seen there on a previous occasion, and Gloria Blunt as Ben now thought of her. As Peter served the old couple, Gloria finished serving one of the local farmers and turned to Ben with a cheeky smile.

'What you gunner *Chance* today?' she enquired and exploded.

With a wince, Ben replied 'Pint of Guinness please, Gloria.'

'Coming right up. And *before* you say anything, I don't mean that in a vomity sorta way.' She had another of her explosions of laughter, making the old couple next to Ben jump a second time.

'No I didn't think you did...By the way, there's an old guy who sits outside, he seems to be of the opinion he's had sex with all the women in the village.'

'Cedric? At is age? I specked ee as.' She exploded once more.

The old couple, now with drinks, moved well away from the bar, for what little difference that would make.

'Well I think he needs to watch what he's saying or someone might take offence.'

'Oh no, not with Granddad, ee's armless.'

Gloria finished topping up Ben's pint. He took his change and moved away from the bar too. Spotting one of the workmen he'd seen in the store, the comedian, standing with another local whose name Ben had yet to learn. He decided to go and strike up a conversation. However, before he'd even reached the comedian the man had launched into a joke with a nod to Ben.

'Did you hear about the scouse that went back to their dentist to complain about their new false teeth? He says "Yous lot overcharged me for these things, dintures? Dintures?!"'

Ben chuckled along with the other man, but taking a breath in to introduce himself he was beaten to it by the comedian launching into another joke.

'Did you hear about that guy who was caught snatching a doll from a kiddie in a pram? Those who knew him said it was only a question of time. His name was Robert Oddler.'

Again Ben and the other man laughed, but before the other man stopped laughing Ben started with 'My…'

'Did you hear about the three men who got stabbed?'

'Police described it as a blade-ing nuisance?' suggested Ben.

The other man laughed again, but the comedian gave Ben an odd look. 'Oh, you're a dark one mate. I'm being serious.'

'Sorry. I thought it was another of your jokes. I'm Chance by the way.'

'I'm Mikey. Some call me Spikey Mikey on account of my sharp wit I guess. And this is Herman. Well it's Bruce really, but he's a hermit, so the locals call him Herman.'

'I'm not a hermit,' protested Bruce.

'Well what do you call someone who lives on their own in the woods without a road or any other services?'

'Blessed,' Bruce insisted.

'If it wasn't for that ruin you call a cottage I'd have said you were homeless.'

'It's not a ruin, it's a *project*. I'm doing it up. I've been trying to get round to asking if you know where I could get my hands on some stone tiles, on the cheap?'

'I'm a brickie not a roofie Herman.'

'I know, but I just thought…'

'You *do* know the difference between a brickie and a roofie, don't you Herman?'

'Of course I…

'Brickies make memories while roofies take'em.'

Ben frowned, wondering whether Mikey made this stuff up as he went along.

The next morning, as Ben got up he reflected how he was a little disappointed that there had been no sign of Jill at the pub last night.

Standing in front of the bathroom mirror before getting in the shower, he marvelled once again at what the clinic had been able to do.

The plate in his skull was gone. There was no longer a trace of a scar on the side of his head. In fact all of his scars had vanished, even that self-stitched knife wound on his thigh from years ago. He had been in an incident on the Metro outside Newcastle Airport. His nose too was now straight, and his teeth had never been healthier. However, the most striking

28

change to his appearance was the little finger on his left hand. He had managed to grow a new one.

Who would have thought that someone would find a good use for the Crown of Thorns starfish, which was continuing to decimate whole coral reefs? It had been explained to Ben that in conjunction with stem-cell and gene-therapy sciences, medical research was now onto a breakthrough in nerve tissue regeneration. Finally there looked to be a way of healing those with spinal injuries.

However, the way it was spoken about in the clinic, as still being early days, it made Ben feel like a guinea pig. The memory and other cognitive problems he had lived with since the bad accident no longer appeared to be an issue. Yet he couldn't help but wonder whether he should expect some side effects.

4

Ben turned up for work at six fifty-five as Rosie was opening up, and was promptly shown how to switch the store's alarm off, then how to sort the newspapers.

He had never realised that papers could be so complicated. Some required names of customers to be written on them, to then be held inside for collection. The rest went outside in their bins. Some customers would have vouchers, while others had accounts. Then on weekends he was told there would be masses of supplements to sort through and correctly add to each paper first, before working through the book of regular customers names.

Ben couldn't believe there was such fuss over what often amounted to a dozen sheets of paper filled with fake news and ads, at questionable prices. Especially considering you could hear the same crap being spouted on the TV, the radio, computer, and not to forget the smartphone.

Rosie also showed Ben how to use the till which looked overly complicated, with its temperamental scanner, layers of screens for different goods, all of which required Ben to learn where to find things. He was certainly thankful that his object recognition issues had been fixed.

In that first half hour, customers were coming in expecting everything to be ready for them, though papers and things were still being sorted out between interruptions.

'Why don't we sort things out at six-thirty, to be ready for seven?' Ben asked when the store was empty of customers.

'My predecessor used to come in for six-thirty just to get things ready, but then the customers wanted in and got irritated if they weren't allowed to shop early too. So Harry rationalised the opening times to seven till seven, now we all have to make do.'

A smartly dressed elderly man came into the store with a paper tucked under one arm. He selected half a dozen of the extra large eggs from the wicker basket by the door then went to the chiller for two litres of semi-skimmed milk. When he came to pay he had difficulty slipping his card into the reader.

Ben removed the card and saw that it had two bad splits in it. 'You need to contact the bank about getting a new card.'

'But that's the third one I've had this year.'

'Well there's only one thing for it then.'

'Change bank?'

'No. Quit with your break-dancing.'

'Ha. Very good.'

Ben finally managed to get the machine to read the man's broken card.

'My name's Chance by the way. I just started working here yesterday, so I'm still getting to know people.'

'My name is Ken. Ken Dough. I'm visiting a friend who is poorly. I thought I'd sort breakfast and a paper for him.

'That's very thoughtful of you.'

'I've driven across from Curston early. Good job it wasn't further.'

'Oh?'

'I don't want the police catching me.'

'I see,' said Ben, frowning because he didn't.

'The optician told me last year I mustn't drive anymore. But when so many of your old friends need your help what else can you do?'

'Get a bus?'

'Public transport? When I have a perfectly good car?'

'Let's hope it stays that way.'

As Ken left, Mikey came in, grabbed milk, coffee and sugar then placed an order with Rosie for two bacon rolls, after which he came to Ben at the counter.

'Morning, Chance. It must have been some heavy night we had. I woke up this morning feeling rubbish, 'cos I found myself in a skip.'

Ben laughed as he scanned the goods and rang in the bacon rolls. 'That old guy you passed as you came in. Do you know him?'

'No,' Mikey shook his head as he swiped his card over the reader as soon as Ben entered the figures.

'Said his name was Ken Dough.'

'Maybe he's a baker.'

'Or a Samurai.'

'I don't get it.'

'Like Kendo.'

'Yeah, nice…That reminds me of a posh do I went to. One of those where the MC calls out the names of people as they arrive. One woman was announced as Miss Elaine Eos.'

'Sounds like some random bystander.'

Mikey nodded with a grin. 'Did you read about those ants they've had up in the International Space Station?'

'No. I don't read the papers.'

'Well, with the experiment finished they brought them back down and have been selling each of them off for charity.'

'Really? Single ants? What would anyone want with an ant?'

'To brag to people that this ant has been in space, I guess.'

'I suppose.'

'Anyway, one guy paid twenty thousand pounds for his. Can you imagine it? Twenty thousand? He called it Ex-Orbit-Ant.'

'You're rolls.' Rosie called from the kitchen, curtailing another joke.

Just before Ben was due to knock off at two having started at seven, he looked up from the till to see a familiar face, standing in the doorway with her head of long dark brown hair. It was his handler.

While he had been at the clinic they had had a number of meetings. He learned that her name was Veronica Coultard, but by then it was too late, he had already settled on a name for her.

'Aussie.'

She didn't complain. It was as good a cover name as any. 'Just dropped by to see how you're settling in.'

'I'm off in a couple of minutes.'

'I know. I'll wait out there for you and we can walk together.'

'Okay,' Ben nodded then turned his attention to the till-float for the next day, which he had been shown how to prepare. It only needed the notes adding now that there were some spare. With that done he put the zip bag away in the safe. Then he told Rosie, who was just about finished in the kitchen, wiping down surfaces, that he was off.

'Here, take this bag to the bins on your way past.'

'Will do.'

Out of earshot down the road, Veronica prompted, 'Well?'

'Well Aussie, you and Cynthia have placed me among a bunch of head-cases. Any one of them could be your man.'

Ben had been briefed whilst still at the clinic. This was to be an anti-vigilante operation. He wasn't keen on the idea at all, and said so. It seemed to be a waste of his energy, tracking down someone who had been cleaning scum off the streets. He had even tried his hand at that, more than once before, like what he did to the guy who made the mistake of abducting his sister Marion.

'They might not be in Sevensands,' Veronica reminded Ben. 'They could be anywhere in the region.'

At the clinic Ben had been shown a large number of images from different scenes of crime, in the region. The vigilante had been very thorough in removing evidence however, with relevant security footage always erased. Nevertheless, one partial print had been found so far, which did not match any of the deceased. Unfortunately it turned out not to be on any police or intelligence database. Ben wondered whether this might be the same individual who had saved him and Adam Underwood from a gruelling death at the hands of Frank Chesney and his eager audience. What a massacre that had turned out to be.

'More recently,' Veronica continued, 'there have been two domestic shootings, without forced entry, suggesting the killer was known to the victims. It looked at first like gangland killings but the two people who died don't have criminal records, or appear to have known one another. The weapon used was the same though, a Glock 9mm going by ballistics. The weapon has not yet been found, so investigations are ongoing.'

'From what I was shown at the clinic, the man we are after kills by a number of different ways and means, which will make him more difficult to track. But all victims appear to have got what was coming to them, so there must be a criminal link which has not been found yet.'

They both fell silent as a jogger in fluorescent pink sweatshirt and trousers was making her way towards them. For all her effort she seemed to be almost running on the spot. The strangest way of running that either Ben or Veronica had ever seen.

'Hi Jill,' Ben greeted as she passed.

Jill did little more than grimace back though, as if she couldn't speak for fear of losing what little breath and rhythm she had.

Before she was out of earshot, Veronica said, 'I see what you mean about these fuckwit villagers.'

Ben hoped Jill hadn't caught that.

'Who the hell was that? Barbie?'

'No that's Jill. She's okay, though that running is a bit of a worry.'

'I'll say. Looks like she's heading for a heart attack...Anyway, as I was saying, there have been a number of unexplained deaths in the area, the latest has been two young men in Wrap Park at Curston, whose ID was removed. They are believed to be illegal immigrants possibly with criminal records, who had set upon a transgender male around midnight. That victim positively identified the dead bodies, from photos shown to them at the hospital. He knew nothing else though. Said he'd seen no one else around. Certainly no one had come when he had first called for help. Took himself to Curston hospital because when he phoned for an ambulance and said he'd been stabbed, the call centre started asking him what he'd had for breakfast, and what colour his shit was.'

'No change there then.'

'He'd have been dealt with better asking for the police, as many people do. But that's the state of the underfunded British emergency services for you, having to run the gauntlet of a tick-box check list before they take you seriously.'

'I blame the service design consultants.'

'I guess they've designed the process to make people hang up and find help elsewhere.'

They reached the Quarryman's Arms.

'Fancy a quickie?' asked Ben.

Veronica's face showed her lack of appreciation for the double entendre, 'I can't. I have to get off, but before I go, I've put a parcel in your log stack.'

'It's a bit early for Christmas.'

Ignoring him she continued. 'You are a keen photographer of urban nightscapes.'

'Am I?'

'So you better get the manuals read, and get out observing the area. Oh and join the Curston Photographic Society while you're at it.'

'Why? Are they involved?'

'No you idiot, for your cover story!'

Ben watched her get into her Mercedes SLK which she had parked outside the pub. As she drove off towards Curston he waved with a smile at her scowl.

'Wow. They do say good can come of bad. Even with her face scrunched up she looks cute.'

Ben's last handler, Harriet Wallace, had sadly died at the hands of interrogators, after only her third visit to see Ben at the prison. Someone had been overly keen for answers as to why Ben had been transferred to their boss's place of detention.

5

Ben was holding something, but his arms felt so heavy. He tried to focus his eyes. What was he holding? Was it a newspaper? He tried to focus on the words.

Transphobic attack by immigrants, read the headline. He tried to look down at the text below. The text swam in and out of focus. Why couldn't he read? Had his cognitive issues returned? He remembered the period of his life when, following the accident, road signs and vehicle number plates had all appeared to be in a foreign language. However, the clinic was supposed to have fixed all that. He groaned.

Alex Robinson, 26, was attacked by two men of Eastern European origin wielding something something 'Hot Spotted' something in Curston. Alex reported something something something deserted high street in front of him, just after 1.00am. They something something. Then something something, before stabbing Alex three times then running off. Something something something. The next day Alex positively identified from photos, two dead bodies found in Curston's Wrap Park, something something something.

The alarm went off.

Reaching out to return peace to his room, Ben remained in bed for a few moments, rather than getting straight up as he would normally. Why, he wondered, was he dreaming about the resent stabbings. Maybe his subconscious had pieced together gossip heard in the store and the pub to prompt him that something crucial was being missed in locating the vigilante. Or maybe it was just nonsense. After all, he was sure no one had mentioned the name of the night club to him, or the time that the first stabbing took place.

Saturday morning at the store, Ben could hear two young lads turning a discussion into a full blown argument over by the fridges.

'Classic coke is the best.'

'No. Diet coke is.'

'No way!'

'Anything diet is better for you.'

'Not if it's diet erribledeath!' called Ben, creating a hush.

Harry arrived. 'What's the shouting about?'

'Just a couple of kids there blowing off steam, boss.'

'Oh...well I've got more important things to worry about. We need to revise our food ingredients list to come in line with changes in food safety laws.'

'Right,' Ben acknowledged, as the two, now quiet lads, paid for their cans.

'We need some way of highlighting the allergens for customers.'

'Best get an allergen lamp then.'

'Can you get such a thing?'

'Doubt it but you could get a *halogen* lamp.'

'Oh I see,' he didn't laugh.

The phone rang and Ben picked it up. The line crackled badly but he launched into 'Sevensands Village Store and Newsagents.'

The voice at the other end seemed to say 'Huloo. I wis jes wundrin who much y'charge f'your sexy legs?'

Ben half laughed, taking this as a wind-up call, and repeated the last bit. 'My sexy legs?'

Harry turned with an amused smile but wrinkled brow.

The woman at the other end laughed. 'Ach noo.' She raised her voice and tried saying it more clearly. 'Y'saxa lorgs!'

The penny dropped. 'Sacks of logs are six pounds.'

'Eee that much? That'd be lake burnin money.'

'It *wood* that…Especially in such warm weather.'

'Aye but there's a fair chill of an evenin. I'll heff me a think on.'

'Aye you do that.' Ben hung up.

'Becoming something of a porn star are you now Chance?'

'Well boss, you make ends meet however you can.'

They could both hear the freezer cabinet door hissing like a blizzard as it was opened and then closed again repeatedly.

'What's going on over the back there now?'

'I'll go check.' With no customers at the counter Ben went over.

An old man stood by the freezer opening a door, not reaching in for anything then letting it close again, causing the fan to suck the door shut with a hiss, until he opened it once more.

'Are looking for something?'

'The sound that your freezer makes is reminding me of the Artic Warfare Cadre.'

Surprised by the remark, Ben asked 'You were in the Royal Marines then sir?'

The old man gave Ben an odd look, 'Good lord no. It was on the History channel yesterday.'

Ben headed back to the counter, just in time to serve a woman he had met before but could not yet remember her name. 'Morning…It's Margaret isn't it?'

'Mavis.'

Ben heard Harry groan, as Ben started scanning the shopping through the till.

'That's twenty eight pounds ninety.'

'How much?'

'Twenty eight pounds ninety.'

'Oh dear.' Mavis drew a card from her purse. 'Do you do contactless?'

'Yes we do contactless but it still hurts.'

'Does it?'

'It's a joke. The price doesn't change.'

'Oh I see. Very good.'

After Mavis had left, Harry said, 'You shouldn't do that.'

'What, a bit of a joke with the customers?'

'No. Trying to learn their names. The guy who had your job last tried doing that. It was really embarrassing, with all his mistakes. There are some people in this village who are the spitting image of one another. I've given up trying to work out who's who.'

'Maybe it's the inbreeding.'

'The what?'

'Never mind.'

Ben looked up to see a woman in a smart suit and skirt get out of her silver Honda Civic and begin to fuel up. It was Jill. He couldn't help but notice through the tight skirt that she had a fit ass, and good legs. Either she naturally had a tidy figure, or that crazy running thing of hers actually worked.

'Morning Jill,' Ben greeted her as soon as she came inside.

'Hi Chance.'

'I was wondering what you were doing tonight? Whether you fancied meeting up at the Quarryman, or somewhere else even?'

'Sorry I'm going to be working.'

'Oh, okay.' Ben was extra-jabby punching the numbers into the card machine. 'That's forty pounds.'

'Are you working tomorrow Chance?'

'Until twelve thirty.'

'I could meet you at the pub at say one?'

'Great.' Ben made a complete hash of tearing the receipt from the machine, and had to print a second one.

That afternoon Ben's clumsiness seemed to be on a roll. As he made to pass a customer their Curston Gazette with their name written on, from behind the counter, the top sheet separated from the rest. Reaching down to recover the rest of the paper, Ben's heart began to beat a little faster and his eyes widened as he noticed something surprising on page three.

Transphobic attack by immigrants.
Alex Robinson, 26, was attacked by two men of Eastern European origin wielding knives, near the 'Hot Spotted' night club in Curston. Alex reported that the two men came out of a dark alley onto the deserted high street in front of him, just after 1.00am. They began by robbing him of his wallet, mobile and watch. Then they turned abusive, saying they knew that he was a she, before stabbing Alex three times then running off. Alex, unable to get help made his own way to Curston hospital A&E. The next day Alex positively identified from photos, two dead bodies found in Curston's Wrap Park, as the men who had stabbed him.

6

Ben picked up the 102 megapixel mirrorless DSLR. The camera was both lighter and quieter than some of the older DSLRs which needed to move a mirror out of the way each time a shot was taken.

He had read the manual previously but there wasn't much he didn't already understand from years of OP surveillance.

Removing the bayonet fitting cover from the front of the body he connected the 18 – 135mm f3.5 zoom lens. It wasn't as fast as the f1.2 50mm standard lens he had been supplied with for low light conditions but the zoom would be very good for what he had planned that Saturday afternoon.

The kit bag had also come equipped with a 100-400 f3.5 telephoto zoom in case there was call for longer distance surveillance. The kit would have cost a tidy sum, but with new kit coming out every six months, there was nothing in the kit bag that would set him aside from a keen photographer.

Previously he had been checking out Google Maps. He looked at both the street maps and satellite views, for an overview of Curston, his first area for familiarisation.

He was thinking like the vigilante, which meant working out the CCTV surveillance camera points and coverage around town, and both the high and low footfall areas. Also the bolt routes for when on foot or with a vehicle. In addition there was the question of where the vigilante's future targets might show up and where would make good ambush points.

The difficulty was that according to the briefing, this particular vigilante was very successful in both taking out his targets *and* not getting caught, because he was less predictable as well as highly skilled.

Ben thought he should start photographing the streets around the town centre then work his way out towards the industrial estates.

Putting some snacks and water in the side pockets of his back pack which contained other items of equipment that he might need, Ben headed out to his car.

He had had a silver Skoda Fabia signed out to him. It looked ridiculous for someone his size. He had to have the seat right back to fit his six foot six in but it actually had more head room than a number of higher 4x4s had.

Despite appearances, this Fabia was more like a cheetah than even a wolf in its sheep's clothing. What was under the bonnet did not match the 1L get-about it was labelled as. It was even superior to the VRS rally version. This was typical of vehicles signed out to field agents from MI5.

However, Ben had to be careful handling it not to betray its power until necessity called. There were certain other unorthodox modifications and additions. It wasn't quite a James Bond car with any machine guns behind headlamps but it did have a small-arms case with a thumb-print lock under the driving seat, containing a Glock 9mm and extra magazines. There were also Night Vision Goggles, an NBC suit and gas mask in a safe box under the back seat.

So behaving like a newsagent heading to town in his little second hand car, he reversed off his weed-ridden car-standing onto the shared driveway and down onto the lane, checking for farm traffic or kids as he did so. At the junction with the Arrow, he headed for Curston. He kept to the thirty speed limit unlike most other users he had seen doing at least twice that past the store. Being in the security services was not a license to race around everywhere attracting attention to oneself.

In town Ben parked at the sports centre's free car park. He had no idea how long this was going to take. He was a fast walker, even without rushing, but there was a lot of ground to cover.

Starting at the market square by the remains of Curston castle he spiralled his way outwards like a Pac-Man in a maze, looking above shop fronts for cameras, and taking plenty of photos. He didn't need to worry about his camera's memory space as he had a 128GB card in it.

After he had photographed the church, and the park, with its recreation ground, band stand, and labyrinth of paths and bushes, he came out onto Curston high street.

Returning towards the town centre Ben passed the police station, two banks, three pubs, two night clubs, four restaurants and two cafes separated by a variety of shops. Further on lay the bus terminus and the hospital.

Turning off and circling back he passed the Hot Spotted night club, a builders merchants, train station and then he was back to the retail park where the sports centre was, with three of the leading supermarkets, as if one was not enough.

Beyond the retail park was the older of the two industrial estates. Ben hadn't even started with any of the housing areas and time was getting on.

This task was clearly going to take more than an afternoon, even with his long legs. It would likely take a few days in fact. So much for a quick daytime recce, followed by an evening's slow patrol, he thought. Nevertheless, he decided, he would get this industrial estate photographed then go and get something to eat at one of the restaurants he'd photographed earlier.

He hadn't been in the industrial estate long, but noted how quiet this area was on a Saturday. Then he noticed some unexpected and very fast movement, just as he came around a corner.

A figure, dressed in khaki mechanics overalls, with black boots, gloves, and balaclava, sped along the pavement in front of an old mill. They turned to look in Ben's direction then as if his camera might be a firearm, the figure leaped up grabbed the top of a seven foot wall then cleared it.

Ben dashed forwards, clutching his camera tightly, setting it to rapid-shots mode. He single-handedly jumped the wall to straddle it, bringing his camera to bear. There was no sign of the figure.

The other side of the wall was a stream, the opposite bank of which was a windowless back of another building, with a down pipe which

Ben would never have missed someone scaling. To either side, the stream led in one direction up towards some lower walling then a bridge not far from the entrance to the industrial estate. In the other direction, just below him, was a large culvert which went under the old mill.

Ben was tempted to go in chase, after all, the potential vigilante, or whoever it was, may only have gone just out of sight inside. However, the thought of going into the stream after him did not seem sensible. The camera could prove a liability inside the culvert. He could pack it away but there was no time.

He had to make the right move quickly. Ben felt caught in a dilemma. Either the guy was waiting for him to jump back down to the pavement before venturing back out, or was already heading down the culvert to come out the other end.

Ben decided the only course of action open to him was to come down off the wall soundlessly then creep off in the direction of travel of the culvert. Hopefully it might appear he was still on the wall waiting while he in fact he would be searching for the other end quickly. If the person in the tunnel was too nervous to come back out where they went in, it might force them to go through to the other end where Ben planned to be waiting.

By the time Ben reached the other end of the mill building he had already broken back into a run. He scaled the wall at that end but as he looked over he was confronted with car parking not stream, and further on was another building. The culvert clearly ran some distance.

Down off the second wall Ben sprinted along the pavement, to the far end of the next building, which was a road junction. The culvert went under the road.

On the opposite side of the road was some old warehousing. From the memorised map Ben knew that if he turned right the road would lead round to the car parking he had just seen but would otherwise be a dead end. If he turned left the road would eventually reconnect with the main road after a number of industrial unit cul-de-sacs. However, some way down to the left, on the opposite side of the road should be a footpath which would lead down to the river.

Ben bounded down the road and skidded round into the narrow footpath hoping he would not meet anyone coming the other way.

Beyond the warehousing there was fencing at their rear for more parking then the path came to a junction where he took a right. He tried to judge where the culvert would be coming out, looking to his left, trying to control his breathing. It would be no good to come panting to the end of the tunnel which would exaggerate his breathing like a megaphone.

There were glimpses of the river through the trees. This all looked promising, as long as he was there before the person came out. There was no sight or sound of anyone else around. Then he spotted the stone structure of the culvert's exit, like a bridge under the footpath just up ahead. Returning to a slow approach for stealth, listening out for any splashing and panting he closed in.

It was clear as he looked for tracks around the culvert's exit that his quarry had not yet come out. So he chose a good observation point close by and vanished into the bushes.

Ben waited patiently, but as time went on he began to wonder if the guy had not just waited for him to leave and come out of hiding at the start of the culvert. A while later he heard a car door close nearby. An engine started in what sounded like the parking behind the warehousing. It could prove to be a distraction but he had the urge to go check it out before it drove away.

There were no sounds coming from the culvert, so he burst from the bushes and ran to the fence at the footpath. He could not see through the bushes beyond the fence, only hear the vehicle pulling away.

He broke into a sprint again, in a vain attempt to get back along the footpath and onto the industrial estate in time to catch a glimpse of the vehicle. Whatever this person had been up to, it would seem that they already had knowledge of other ways of entering and exiting services like the culvert.

7

Sunday afternoon arrived and Ben sat with Jill in the snug. There was something about her that just seemed to connect with him, on some level. More so in fact than it ever had with Meg, his ex-wife, from what he allowed himself to remember anyway.

He had been surprised by her mention of him being sectioned and a therefore a threat to his children's safety. This had been cited as one of the reasons for the divorce. Meg had clearly got the wrong end of the stick, but since he had also been served a restraining order and she wasn't taking his calls there seemed little he could do about it. He had reluctantly signed the papers. On reflection he thought Meg, Robbie and Beth probably were better off without him.

Now however, he felt almost at ease with Jill. It was only 'almost' because he could not stop acting out his cover for even a second. He would like to be able to open up to Jill about Meg and the kids. He was sure she would understand, but Chance didn't have a family.

Peter, the barman, had served Ben with his usual plus the tonic water with ice and lemon Jill had insisted on. She had told Ben that she didn't drink alcohol when she thought she might be writing of an evening.

So now he knew not to expect much in the way of *action* this evening.

She had explained that she had once done some rather carefree editing after a few drinks. This was before submission of an article about why women really smoke, and she lost that job. She wasn't about to make the same mistake twice. Nevertheless, she had said she hoped there would be times she and Chance could share a bottle of wine.

'So how has your day been, Chance?'

'Oh you know pretty normal really. Some of the papers weren't delivered, customers got irate, that sort of thing.'

'Are you still enjoying your job as much as you claimed the other day?'

'Yeah. I'm certainly starting to feel like I'm becoming part of the community, working down there.'

'So what are you intending to do with yourself now you are settling in? I imagine you won't be down *here* all of the time.'

'Oh no. I'll be a regular, but I do have other interests.'

'The gym I bet.'

'That's not a bad idea actually.'

'There's the Curston sports centre.'

'Are you a member?'

'Yes, but I just go for a swim.'

Ben couldn't help but wonder if she swam like she ran. 'What's their gym equipment like?'

'I never looked. I can't be doing with any of that weight lifting stuff, far too strenuous for little old me.'

'Ha.' Ben took a mouthful of his Guinness. 'I was thinking of joining the Curston Photography Club. I enjoy taking my camera for a walk and it might be interesting to see what other people are doing.'

'Sounds like an idea. So what sort of photos do you take? Nature? Landscape?'

'I like urban photography mainly, especially after dark.'

'After dark? That sounds unusual.'

'Not really. Quite a few people do it.'

'But what's there worth photographing at night?'

'With extended exposure it enables you to get deserted shots of buildings in the dark highlighted by street lighting. A whole different character to how they appear during the day.'

'Right.'

'But still, I do like getting out for walks during the day as well.'

'Well this is certainly great walking country. I like to get out when I can. Maybe we could go for a walk together.'

'Yeah sure.'

'There are still lots of places I haven't visited yet. As I've said before, I've only been in Sevensands a couple of months myself.'

'How far would you normally walk?'

'Oh five or even six miles, at a push, if there aren't too many hilly bits.'

'Ha. Where isn't hilly round here?'

'True…So what about you?'

'Oh yeah, I'm up for it.'

'I mean what do you normally walk?'

He felt the urge to admit he had been able to cover seventy five miles in a day, but put the brakes on. 'Oh urr ten or twelve miles.'

'Wow.'

Ben was distracted for a moment. He spotted Veronica sitting at the bar. He hadn't heard her come in. She was making eyes at him, but not happy eyes. Her head tilted towards the door. Does she always turn up out of the blue, he wondered. What was wrong with a text?

'Mind you, if I'm using the camera a lot,' Ben continued 'that ten or twelve could take me all day. No sense in rushing right?'

'Absolutely.'

If it were possible, Veronica was now looking crosser. What did she expect him to do, just get up and go talk to her instead. That would kill his chances with Jill, dead. Their drinks were still half full, so there was no excuse to go to the bar. So instead he stared back at Veronica crossly.

With that, Veronica walked outside with her drink.

'Are you okay Chance? Was it something I said?' Jill not having noticed Veronica, too concerned with Chance's change in expression.

'What? Urr no. I'm fine. I just remembered a time when a guy with a shotgun refused to let me continue along a public right of way that went across his property, and I got my boots soaked taking a marshy detour.'

Ben's phone buzzed in his pocket. He could tell Jill had heard it. He pulled it out.

'Looks like it's the boss,' which technically wasn't a lie.

'What does he want?'

'No idea. But he better not be asking for me to come back in *now*.'

Checking the text it simply read 'OUTSIDE NOW!'

'I better call him from outside. The reception in here is really poor. Probably why he texted.'

'Okay.'

'I'll be back shortly.' Ben left his drink with Jill and went outside to see Veronica hoping Jill wouldn't see them together again.

She wasn't out front, but he located her round the side.

Without any pleasantries Veronica launched straight into 'What the hell are you doing wasting your time with that *fuckwit* in the snug?'

'Not *jealous* are we?'

'Of course I'm not *fucking* jealous! What *numpties* you want to shag on your own time is your business, but this is *our* time. You've got work to be doing.'

'Hey, I got a stack done yesterday afternoon *and* last night.'

'Well it would seem you missed a bit.'

'What do you mean?'

'A call centre was terminated.'

'A *whole* call centre?'

'Well, eleven people. A Caucasian manager and security guard, plus nine immigrants.'

'Well if they were cold-callers, they probably had it coming to them.'

'This isn't funny, Chance,' she kept to his cover name in case she was overheard.

'Well it doesn't sound like our lone vigilante. It sounds more like one of those covert black van teams that we hear about these days.'

'Agreed it would have been easier to explain if it *was* one of those, but no one appears to have been taken away, which is what *they* usually do, as you know.'

'Where was this?'

'On the old industrial estate in Curston, around mid-afternoon.'

'Broad daylight?...Wait...I saw a figure acting suspicious down there around that time. But they moved so fast I didn't get a shot of them.'

'What did they look like?'

'Average build, around five eight or five ten. They must have been bloody fit though. They cleared a seven foot wall to get away.'

'Why the hell didn't you go after them?'

'I tried, but the other side of the wall was a stream and...'

'What? You worried you might get your dainty boots wet?'

'No. The only place the guy could have gone before I had time to get to the wall and look over was into a culvert that ran under an old mill. I decided that rather than follow him in, it would be quicker if I ran to the other end of the culvert and waited for him to come out.'

'Sensible...And?'

'By the time I found the end, the other side of the industrial estate, near the river, he had either already come out, or there was another exit elsewhere.'

'Brilliant work. I thought you guys were meant to be the cream. Looks like I've been landed with the clotted cream.' Veronica shook her head. 'So when you were running around all over the place, like a prime arsehole, did you see anyone else, on foot or in a car?'

'I heard someone drive away, but wasn't in a position to get eyes-on.'

'Well it's highly likely that this is our guy. The attack was a mixture of slit throats and what must have been supressed nine millimetre rounds to the head and chest.'

'Double taps?'

'Yes.'

'So that could be someone with special weapons training.'

'No shit. Probably one of *your* ex-colleagues, gone rogue.'

'But why hit a call centre?'

'From what we have gleaned from the police IT forensics, they turned out to be running scams and other extortion activities, claiming to be HMRC and a number of banks and service providers demanding immediate payment to avoid legal action.'

'So the usual scams then?'

'Yes.'

'Is it possible that the two bodies recovered from Wrap Park from there too?'

'Possibly. We don't know yet. There were certainly no spare phone desks without corpses. But maybe the dead guys were immediately replaced.'

'I guess…From the briefing I got at the clinic could this have been the expected *big hit*? So this could be case closed for a while because the vigilante will have moved on?'

'Maybe.'

'I understand he tracks down everyone involved in a criminal organisation and kills them by whatever means. From the thugs all the way up to the big boss, the whole network. So I would have expected the big boss to be one of the ones now lying dead in the morgue, if that was the case.'

'We will have to see what happens over the next week, but yes we could have missed our chance here.'

'Right…Are we done?'

'In a rush to get back to that *woman*?'

'Well it certainly won't help to piss off the locals will it Aussie.'

Ben turned his back on Veronica and headed inside. The thought that this part of the mission might be over and he might have to move again was not very appealing this time. He was just getting settled in, and despite its quirky characters, he rather liked Sevensands.

'That was a long call,' Jill commented upon his return.

'Yeah, sorry. Harry couldn't find the till rolls. The till comes to a grinding halt without a roll of paper in the receipt machine, and I had to hang on while he found it. I'm wondering if he's just disorganised or totally clueless.'

'Ha.'

8

Ben was having a run of the mill week. He had continued the reconnaissance photography, both day and night when spare time permitted. However, there had been no more sightings of the balaclava figure, in or around Curston.

Vigilantes could go weeks, even months, between taking action. The team were not just waiting on Ben though. Behind Aussie, as his Section 13 handler, there was a whole intelligence machine. It would be constantly monitoring communications, internet searches, and such like, out of GCHQ in Cheltenham.

Nevertheless, Ben felt that his time in this rather odd village could be coming to a close sooner rather than later. It was bound to come at some point, as his attentions would no doubt be needed elsewhere, but he actually felt he would be sorry to put this cover behind him. He rather liked the quirkiness of it all.

Ben was looking forward to the walk-date at the weekend with Jill. She had suggested doing a section of Hadrian's Wall, one of the region's many attractions. Ben had lied in saying he had never done any of it. Some years back he had run the length of it in one day, from Wallsend to Bowness on Solway, with his mates from The Regiment. Admittedly they had followed the shorter truer path of the roman wall, rather than the 'official' Hadrian Wall footpath with all its 'points of interest' dog-leg detours.

Mikey came to the store for a paper, picking up a Star from outside on his way in.

'Haven't seen you for a few days,' Ben said in greeting as he input the paper on the till before Mikey had even reached the counter.

'Aye. I've been for a break, up in Scotland.'

'Was it good?'

'Not bad, but I got a puncture out in the middle of nowhere. Luckily I was able to change the tyre and go looking for a garage in the hope of a new spare. When I found one, not *too* far away, I said to the guy there, it was a pot-hole that had done it, pinched through the wall of the tyre. You people really need to get something done about your roads, I said. There must be some person in your council responsible for maintaining the roads. He nodded and said that a number of them had written letters of complaint to Noah Vale.'

'Urr,' Ben groaned, having been duped into thinking it was all a true story.

'After the tyre was sorted, as I was about to leave, I thought it best to fill up with fuel while I was there. When I came back in to pay again, I noticed a bloke come across the forecourt and lay down in front of my car. I couldn't believe it. And if that wasn't odd enough another half a dozen people came and lay down with him, resting their heads on his chest, tummy, and thighs. I asked the guy at the counter, what does he think he's doing with those people, protesting against my diesel purchase? He shook his head with a smile at my reaction, and says, no no, that's John, he's not protesting anything, he's a pillow of our community.'

'Mikey, your jokes are dreadful,' Ben laughed anyway.

'Thanks,' Mikey paid for his paper.

'Actually, while I think on, the till is running short on clinker already. Do you happen to have any coppers I can change-up?'

'What do you take me for, Chance? A police station?'

Mikey swapped a selection of ones, twos, and fives for a fifty pence piece and left.

Ben chuckled. Mikey was certainly a likeable character. In fact there was something about him that was rubbing off on Ben.

A number of workmen came into the shop during the day, for papers or other believed essentials, and many of them had hands black with oil or dirt. A regular came in, his face like his hands were as black as soot.

'Twenty Players Red please.'

'Sorry mate, I can't serve cigarettes to miners.'

The customer's eyes beamed like headlights with surprise then he laughed as the penny dropped. 'Ho ho. Very funny, Chance.'

Later on, another man came in, a retired gentleman, and he stood staring at the empty bread rack with disappointment for a wasted journey. 'You've got no bread left,' he stated the obvious.

'Sorry Sid. Some days it hot-foots it right out of here probably wearing loafers.'

Sid didn't get it, or at least didn't laugh.

'Anyway, I believe we only have that flat bread left.'

'Fine for some I suppose, but I live in a house.'

Ben laughed.

In the afternoon, after school was over, a girl came for a look around then came to the counter with toothpaste. She did not look very cheerful.

'My Nan is asking which is better for her gums, an electric toothbrush or a manual?'

'Does she not watch the adverts?'

'No, Nan only listens to the radio.'

'Oh well, the risk with trying to use a manual would be paper-cuts.'

'Oh is that why her gums bleed?'

Ben realised his joke was going wrong. 'No, it was a joke. Like manuals that you have to read to use equipment properly...Made of paper.'

The girl frowned at the idea of reading something on paper. 'I'll just have the toothpaste.'

As Ben scanned the box he suggested, 'If you're Nan's gums are bleeding she ought to go to the dentist.'

'I know but she says it's too expensive. I don't think she knows how to floss properly. I've heard mum shouting at her *'not to the bone'* a number of times now, but that might have been to do with her injections.'

'Right.' Ben decided this was probably best all left well alone. 'That's one twenty.'

'The girl gave him one twenty pence piece.'

'One pound twenty.'

'Oh.'

Next into the store was a mother of twins, looking like she was at the end of her tether. Going round the shop her boys were making a dreadful din, teasing one another. Eventually she approached Ben at the counter.

'Do you have anything that deals with the problem of chewing gum getting on trousers?' she span the lads round to show matching patches on their bottoms.

'There really is only one solution.'

'What's that?'

'Shove them in the freezer,' said Ben looking from one lad to the other.

The store fell silent.

Shortly after the woman and her sticky twins left, an old lady came into the shop and made straight for Rosie's cake cabinet, where she seemed to um and ah over what was left on display, whilst counting on her fingers.

Ben watched this for a minute or two then helpfully suggested, 'Including yourself, you have five mouths to feed.'

The old lady looked taken aback. 'How could you possibly know that young man?'

Ben pointed at the clock, 'It's four forty.'

She turned to look then frowned.

'Four...for...tea.'

'Well I never...I think I'll take the chocolate cake.'

'I'm sorry but the boss would rather you paid for it.' Ben's favourite joke.

She got that one, and burst out laughing, almost losing her false teeth.

When she had gone, Ben could hear muttering, and realised that Winston was in the store.

'I'm glad they've gone. I'm holding a bottle of pop and it's not very cool, because it's not been in the chiller.'

Ben was about to suggest that he get one from the chiller, but logic suggested Winston knew this already, so he left him to it.

'Checking the weights on the packets of crisps, to see which is best value for money.' There was a long pause filled with crinkling like an unwelcome cinema goer, followed by, 'Salt and Vinegar are the best value. But I don't like Salt and Vinegar. I'll have the shrimp puffs, even though they remind me of packing material.'

Winston came to the till placing the crisps on the counter first. 'I'm going to ask the giant a question now.'

'Yes?'

'Do these bottles of pop go in the fridge?'

'Yes, when there's room.'

'Good. There's plenty of room in my fridge.'

As he placed the bottle on the counter it tipped over.

Ben's quick reactions saved it from reaching the floor and going into shock-fizz, but in his haste Ben's thumb must have caught a splinter on the underside of the counter, because as he placed the bottle safely by the till he noticed he was bleeding.

With no other staff in the shop to take over this time of day, he sucked his thumb to prevent mess as he served Winston with his free hand. He tried to remember if he had seen a first aid kit anywhere. It wouldn't do to bleed over the customers and their shopping. He was likely to need a plaster for this one.

Ben still had his thumb in his mouth as Winston headed out of the store but by the door he turned back and Ben groaned inwardly, he just wanted him off the premises so he could attend to his injury.

'Don't worry Giant. You will grow out of your oral fixation one day. You just need a good woman.'

Winston had spoken so softly, Ben wondered whether he had heard him right.

Focusing on the injury Ben first went to the kitchen and ran the thumb under the cold tap, then inspected it. It was deep, but not bad enough to need a stitch. However it was still bleeding, so he wrapped it in paper towel then went looking for the first aid kit. It wasn't in the kitchen, or in the filing cabinet behind the counter. He was about to give up and just get a box of plasters from the shop when he found the kit in the cupboard next to the cabinet.

Soon he had the thumb out of the paper towel and safely sealed up with a blue plaster.

He looked at the clock. Not much more of the day to go before closing. He turned his attention back to the underside of the till, above the drops of blood on the floor. That would need cleaning up. He still had the whole shop floor to mop but first he would make sure that sharp edge got sorted with a sharper one. Ben reached for the container of pens, rulers, and allsorts, and removed the Stanley knife.

Later, at home, he got his dinner in the oven then with twenty minutes spare he went to wash the day off in the shower.

Plasters were meant to be waterproof but in Ben's experience they rarely were. As he bent his head under the shower he pulled the plaster off, thinking as he did so that it was going to be one of those mistakes people make when they're tired.

'I don't believe it.' He missed his chance to say it as a Victor Meldrew impersonation.

There was certainly blood soaked into the plaster. He stepped away from the shower into better lighting. Not only had his thumb stopped bleeding, it had almost completely healed.

9

Ben's arms were heavy. He could feel something in his hands. Was it the first aid kit? Was his thumb bleeding again? No, it felt like a book. He couldn't see what he was looking at properly. He tried opening his eyes further, blinking. Hadn't he done this already, a number of times? There were words there in front of him but he felt too tired to read. He just wanted to sleep a bit longer. Nevertheless, there *was* that urge to read. Just a bit, just so he could say he knew what he was not bothering with. He tried to bring it all into focus with his mind because his eyes clearly were not playing ball.

The Steel Rigg something something walk is one of the most scenic sections of Hadrian's Wall, suitable for the whole family, with views north from something where on a clear day you can see something something.

Something Gap, famous long before it was used for the something Costner film Robin Hood Prince of something, has become an icon of something something with many photographs taken of something seen hanging in a number of the local pubs.

Jill picked Ben up from outside the Quarryman's Arms in her Honda Civic to head out for their walk. He had offered to drive out in his car, but she won the argument on the grounds that this way if they went for a drink afterwards he would be able to have a beer or two.

Ben also suggested that Cawfields to Walltown Crags and back looked like it might be interesting, but Jill won that argument too, saying that east from Steel Rigg car park was said to be the best section of the whole wall.

However, they were not long into the walk when Jill seemed to be struggling up a section of steep path.

'Would you like a hand, Jill?'

'I'll manage…It's okay for you…with those long legs.'

'Well I'm certainly glad they *are* this long, or they wouldn't reach the ground.'

'I'd be tempted to say that was a lame joke, if that didn't describe me right now.'

'Well it *is* a steep section. Just take it easy. There's no rush.'

'True,' she puffed.

They made better headway when they reached the level on top of Steel Rigg but that wasn't to last.

'Hold on, Chance. I think I have a stone in my boot.'

Ben stopped and watched as she unlaced her offending boot and removed it. Turning it upside down he saw nothing fall out. Next she felt her sock then reached into the boot. Satisfied the stone must have gone she started putting the boot back on. Ben leaned against the wall and looked to the north.

When Jill was done, she mirrored Ben's posture, though the wall came higher up her chest.

'What are you thinking, Chance?'

'Oh how we've been lucky with the weather of late, though it might not last much longer. It's good to make the most of it. It's such a lovely part of the country.'

'Yes. My parents used to bring me up this way when I was a kid.'

Ben said nothing just nodded.

'Have you ever been married, Chance?'

'Ha, no. Never saw the point.'

'Oh. I thought you were going to say *Never saw the right woman.*'

'Well that too I guess. There's so much divorce these days marriage seems a rather pointless tradition.' Ben tried not to make it sound like it was coming from bitter experience. 'I just think people should make the most of what they have while it lasts.'

'I agree. Many people change over time, and want different things.'

'And what do *you* want Jill?'

'Good company and a bit of excitement I guess.'

'Well then, shall we continue?'

They walked on and down to the sycamore tree where they sat for a bit. Ben wondered whether Jill was up to doing more or would be looking to turn back to the car park. So he was pleasantly surprised when she suggested walking on to Housesteads and getting a tea and muffin at the café.

After their refreshments at the café, while Ben waited for Jill to return from the toilet he looked at the selection of books in the gift shop.

Picking up a tour guide for Hadrian's Wall he flicked through the photos till he spotted a picture of Sycamore Gap. Only when he began to read the text on the opposite page did he have that déjà vu feeling again.

This second bizarre experience now set him thinking of Adam Underwood, who he had once worked with. Adam was troubled by strange Flintstones that he kept finding. Ben was shown a number of these stones. Their chalky white surface was etched away to the glassy black beneath on one side. They provided cryptic rhymes relating to near future events.

Ben had been convinced at first that Adam was making them himself in his workshop but it wasn't Adam though. In the end it was all connected to a dreadful chain of misadventures which were finally solved with the help of the stones.

The Flintstones turned out to be planted by a woman they both met a number of times, called Dawn Summers. She was an odd character with something of a contact phobia, quite averse to any risk of contact as if concerned about contagion.

Since Ben's extended time at the clinic there was much he felt he had forgotten about Dawn. There was something disturbing about her. She possessed a rather fatalistic attitude, often leaving Adam and Ben little the wiser for her visits.

So, as Ben read the words on the tour guide a shiver ran down his broad back.

The Steel Rigg to Crag Lough walk is one of the most scenic sections of Hadrian's Wall, suitable for the whole family, with views north from the escarpment where on a clear day you can see well into Reiver country.

Sycamore Gap, famous long before it was used for the Kevin Costner film Robin Hood Prince of Thieves, has become an icon of Hadrian's Wall with many photographs taken of it, and seen hanging in a number of the local pubs.

How could that Dawn Summers woman be getting inside his head, if it was her? He wondered. Planting Flintstones was one thing, but this was a whole other Derren Brown style trick.

'Chance, whatever *are* you doing with *her* again?'

Ben turned around, surprised more by who he saw behind him than he had been by finding the text from his dream in the tour guide. 'Aussie? Are you tracking my every move?'

'Of course. You are a valuable asset.'

'How did you know I was here?'

'The asset tracer we had implanted in you when you were at the clinic.'

'You're kidding.'

She shook her head with a mischievous smile.

'Where is it?'

'You'll never find it without a scan,' she laughed, 'because there's not a scar on your perfect body.'

Ben did not look amused. 'What about my rights to privacy?'

'Oh don't be silly now. You lost those. After what we did for you in the clinic we *own* you now, and you are *my* property.'

'So, a bit like selling your soul to the Devil then.'

'Kind of like that sweetie.'

'Oh now I get your thing. *You* have a controlling, dominatrix complex. You think of me as your toy.'

'More like my *tool*.'

'Whatever. Look, Jill will be back any moment, you need to get gone. I don't understand why you needed to come here, now, unarranged, when I'm clearly not alone.'

'Just thought you should know that those two individuals found dead at Wrap Park, and those call centre employees, they all had connections to the same bank account. An account that still appears to be active via the Dark Net. So the vigilante may not be finished here yet after all.'

They both turned to see Jill coming back, and too late for Veronica to leave now without looking suspicious.

'What a coincidence,' said Veronica, swapping her hard tone for all sweetness and light. 'I was just visiting Housesteads when I spotted Chance from Sevensands Village Store, and now you are here *toooo*.' The last word didn't sound so sweet.

'Yes, just out for some fresh air. I'm Jill.'

'Hi, I'm Beth. So are you two…um,' Veronica left it hanging awkwardly, with her eyes saying *get your hands off my property*.

Ben sensed things were turning unprofessional.

'Just local acquaintances,' Jill replied with a half frown.

'Good.' Veronica's plastic smile said it all. 'Well I'll leave you both to it and go get my coffee.'

As Veronica turned away, Ben expected Jill to ask the obvious question. Instead she seemed disinterested.

'Strange woman…Well I'm ready to head back to the car if you are.'

'Sure.'

'Then we can pop into Twice Brewed for a drink.'

10

Not again, Ben found himself thinking as he struggled to read what was in front of him this time. He questioned why he was bothering. What was the relevance of these dreams? Was this a side effect of the clinic's treatment? This time the text seemed clearer.

DDT would have remained on the cab roof if the brakes had not locked the six tyres and sent him sliding into the water.

His head hissed with whispers in what otherwise felt like emptiness, as if his short term memory had just been forced out through his ears. He presumed he had fallen, but from where and what had he been doing? He knew he needed to gather his thoughts quickly. He felt the urge to mumble.

'Bobbing uselessly, my mind filled with those damned whispers, each giving differing advice for my present situation, the cab door opened with the driver getting out and I immediately noted the very attractive figure'.

Ben was almost blown to work, the weather had finally turned.

The pile of papers waiting for him were damp with the drizzle hanging in the air like low cloud. Unlocking the store and silencing the alarm system, he returned for the papers. As usual it took a few trips to bring them all in.

Checking the diary first for any notes left for him, he sorted through the papers thinking how unpleasant it would be to read a damp paper. He wondered about keeping them all behind the counter, but decided that he would just put the lids down on the paper bins outside, because there wasn't really room for two sets of papers behind the counter with all the other things that needed to go on there.

Not long after Ben had the store officially open, the heavens opened up and he was glad he had put the lids down on the paper bins. A woman dashed inside and shook herself over the large door mat. Dripping wet from the horizontal rain.

'No papers today?'

'Yes. They are in their usual bins.'

'Oh I thought with the lids on there were none.'

Ben didn't recognise her, not that he knew all of the locals yet. She looked to be some sort of wannabe fashion designer. She was in her early twenties. She clearly thought she was doing her bit to save the planet because she appeared to have made a raincoat from a mixture of what looked like crisp packets, sweet wrappers and other items of rubbish.

'I thought it would be a good idea to try this raincoat out while no one was around, but then I got caught in *this* downpour.'

'And how's that working out for you?'

'It's keeping the elements at bay like a top of the range colander.'

'So, it's a wastecoat then.'

'Ha, I guess you're right there. Could I have a coffee please?'

'I'll put the kettle on.' Ben moved round to the kitchen, 'I'm Chance. I'm new here and still trying to learn people's names.'

'Hi. I'm Wendy.'

'Right, I should be able to remember that if I think Windy Wendy.'

'Oh thanks.'

'Sorry, I thought a connection with the weather might stick better than saying something like Trendy Wendy.'

'Would you like a shovel for that hole?'

'Ha. I'll just shut up and make your coffee.'

'That might be best.'

The customers kept coming regardless of the weather and the door mat was turning into a puddle.

A bedraggled looking Bruce turned up. Someone had been kind enough to give him a lift down the last section of Arrow now looking rather like a wide stream.

'No papers today?'

'*Yes.* They are in their usual bins.'

'Oh I thought with the lids on there were none.'

Squelching his boots on the doormat he said, 'This mat is absolutely soaking.'

'Well it would be. I've been hosing it down to help keep people's footwear clean,' Ben joked.

But it was lost on Bruce. 'Well, you want to watch it doesn't get behind your chiller and fuse the shop out.'

'Good point, Herman. I'll get the mop.'

'It's not Herman. It's Bruce.'

'Sorry.' As Ben got to the door with the mop and bucket he and Bruce saw a cyclist caught by a gust, blown across the forecourt to collide with the coal cage. He separated from his bike and came to rest on his backside by the post box. Ben went to the rescue, leaving Bruce to watch on.

'This wind is really frightening,' the cyclist said in a shaky voice.

'If you think this is scary, you don't want to get caught in a *horrorcane*.'

The man laughed, cheering up, as Ben helped him to his feet, checking to see that he wasn't injured.

'Have you got anyone else with you?'

'No,' the man replied with a chuckle of inspiration, 'I *cyclalone*.'

'Ha, nice one. Do you need to come inside for a bit? I can put the kettle back on.'

'Yes. I'll just check the bike over first.'

When he did come in, he asked 'No papers today?'

'*Yes*. They are in their *bins*.'

'Oh I thought with the lids on there were none.'

Ben shook his head. What was up with people?

Later on Harry turned up with a load of things he had bought at the wholesalers. The first thing he asked was 'Were there no papers today?'

'*Yes*. Of course there were papers. They are in their bloody bins.'

'Keep your hair on. I thought with the lids closed there were none.'

'And so it seems does everyone else, but if you leave the bins open all anyone will get is Paper Mache.'

'Fair point. Now do you want to give me a hand in with the goods in the back of my car?'

Once everything was in the store, Harry moved the car away from the entrance, and Ben started going through the invoice, checking against it as he scanned everything onto stock.

With that done, Ben put the cigarettes into their roller-shuttered cupboard behind the counter. Harry worked next to him putting the bottles of spirits away on the shelving beside the cupboard.

Gloria came in. 'So this is where you've been hiding.'

Trying to think what she was inferring, Ben said, 'Yes, I've been a little preoccupied of late to make it down to the pub, sorry.'

'Well then I'll take twenty Marlboro Gold.'

'Sorry Gloria, the boss is right behind me. You'll have to pay today.'

The explosion of laughter in the confined space was followed by the smashing of glass as Harry jumped, dropping a large bottle of single malt.

'Shit!' Harry cursed.

'Never mind, it'll save with the washing up,' Gloria offered.

Ben and Harry could both see that what might work down the pub did not relate to the store.

'Is that what you say when you smash a bottle of whiskey down the Quarryman?' inquired Harry with undisguised irritation as he went for the mop and bucket.

'Oh no. If it's me, I just say *you slippery fucker you!*' she exploded once more before settling up with Ben.

As she left she turned and popped right back in.

'No papers today?'

'No!' snapped Harry.

Ben added 'We got a call from them this morning to say that with the conditions on the roads they were looking for a barge.'

Gloria exploded again and there was a tinkling sound from the spirits shelving. Harry went to investigate as she made herself scarce but he couldn't see anything amiss. 'Don't crack jokes when Gloria is around!'

In the afternoon it quietened down a little, as it often did, and Ben set about restocking the fridges and shelves with things from the broom cupboard.

Jill popped in.

'Hi Chance. I was just passing and I thought I'd bring you that book I said you might like to read.' Handing him a rain soaked plastic bag.

'Oh, thanks Jill.' Ben didn't really read books. He preferred to watch stuff instead. However, there was no watching anything here but the customers and the stock in the store. It wasn't even permitted to have a radio on without a licence apparently. So the book might be good for when there were quiet moments. He took the paperback from her. 'You off to work?'

'Yes. Interviewing someone for an article.'

'Right.'

'Well I best be off. Catch up with you later.'

'Sure.'

When Ben did get a moment to look at Breakfast's in Bed, he was struck by two things. The main character, by some bizarre coincidence, was called Dawn Summers, and there at the end of chapter one was the passage from his dream.

DDT would have remained on the cab roof if the brakes had not locked the six tyres and sent him sliding into the water.

His head hissed with whispers in what otherwise felt like emptiness, as if his short term memory had just been forced out through his ears. He presumed he had fallen, but from where and what had he been doing? He knew he needed to gather his thoughts quickly. He felt the urge to mumble.

'Bobbing uselessly, my mind filled with those damned whispers, each giving differing advice for my present situation, the cab door opened with the driver getting out and I immediately noted the very attractive figure'.

'Here!' Dawn yelled with an outstretched arm from the front grill, bending close to the water.

DDT reached out feeling pathetic in his attempts to grasp the offered hand, before he remembered he could swim, at which point he also realised he could stand up.

Closer now, his heroine looked through his helmet visor. 'You okay?'

'Sure.'

11

Ben had worked out from previous evenings observations that some people leaving the night clubs took a short cut through Wrap Park. So though he had started the evening by checking out the industrial estates, low on late-weekend activity, he had then headed for the park. Now he was dug-in with his OP under the cover of a couple of dense holly bushes with a wide field of view across the two highest footfall pathways.

He was prepared for a long and possibly uneventful wait, with his camera, night vision goggles, heat vision scope and a sports-bottle of water. As if the little flies were not torment enough, the bed of dried holly leaves were managing to poke through parts of his thick camo trousers and jacket. This coupled with it being a really humid night, he felt like he was being skewered *and* basted.

A couple came along the path near the OP. They didn't look like they were on their way to or from a club.

'So when then?'

'Soon.'

'I'm getting tired of waiting.'

'I know honey…I promise it will be worth the wait.'

'It better be. I'm up for it now.'

'I want things to be right.'

'Are you worried about…being clumsy?'

'No, of course not…I'm just waiting for something to…come.'

'Come?'

'I wanted it to be a surprise.'

'You do know I don't mind what you look like?'

'Maybe not but others might.'

The mind boggles, thought Ben as they passed him by.

'We could at least get on her list.'

'She might need a deposit, so best to wait till after payday.'

'When's that?'

'Next week.'

'We could at least check what she needs.'

'Okay, okay.'

It was like street theatre. Ben strained his ears to catch a further clue.

'I'm just going into it casual. I think that's what she'll want.'

The sound of clacking and scraping from loose fitting heels cut in, as two women passed the couple, heading Ben's way. The sound of their shoes and chatter obscured much of the receding couple's conversation, though Ben thought he caught mention of *giving ball room.*

'No Pauline, I told you it's sorted.'

'I'll sort *you* if you don't let me settle up for this one.'

'It's fine, honestly.'

'Not with me it isn't, Kay.'

'It was just a meal.'

'*And* two bottles of wine.'

'So?'

'*Expensive* wine.'

'So? I can afford it. You can't…right now.'

'I don't want to be in debt.'

'I'm not saying you are.'

'But I feel I owe you big time. I'm losing count of how many times you've covered for me. Look, I'm going to give you something towards it.'

'No.'

'Yes!'

'Put that away!'

'I insist, Kay!'

There came the sound of a scuffle in front of Ben. The heels alone sounded like rutting animals. The clearly inebriated women came to pushing and slaps then there was the sound of spilled loose change, rolling across the path, towards where Ben lay.

This was going to get embarrassing. He could see it coming like a train wreck.

'Well *hello* ladies I'm just out for a spot of photographing up women's skirts.'

Or...

'Don't mind me ladies, I got my shots earlier in the day, when the kids were playing. I'm just waiting for it to go quiet, so I can get off home to view them on the computer.'

Ben bit his tongue, keeping very still, imagining making the headlines in the Curston Gazette, the operation compromised before it had really begun, and Aussie denying any knowledge of him to the police. She would enjoy that, he catastrophized. The bitch.

Luckily the coins only rolled as far as the grass edge. Ben almost sighed as he felt his tense muscles relaxing.

Then a note fluttered down all too close to his face.

It was a twenty!

Pauline was stumbling onto the grass after it.

Ben wasn't wearing any cam-cream. He lowered his face into the holly leaves. He felt the thorns piercing his chin, nose, lips, cheek and then eyelids. He held his breath.

'Got it.' Pauline fell backwards as she tried to stand up. 'Owch! I've twisted my ankle, Kay.'

'It's you own fault.'

'*You* made me spill my purse.'

'What's that?'

'What?'

'There. Under the holly bush.'

'Where?'

'There!'

Ben's lungs were fit to burst and his face felt like he'd fallen victim to an unlicensed acupuncturist.

'Oh yeah. It looks like a fiver.' Pauline made to return for it.

'No you don't. I'll get it.'

Ben could hear Kay brushing against the holly, possibly even lifting the branches. He dare not look. He just played dead.

Maybe that was it, he thought. These women would probably have heard about the two dead bodies and just think he was another one then run off to tell someone. Dream on McGregor, he berated himself. They would just phone the police then wait till they turned up, so that they could get a good look at a dead body. The night's entertainment sorted.

'There you go.'

'What do you mean there *I* go? That's *yours*. *And* this twenty.'

Ben thanked his lucky stars as the women moved away and he lifted his leaf encrusted face with a controlled exhale.

When it appeared safe to do so, he slowly moved a hand to his face to remove the leaves, starting with the holly which had penetrated his eyelids.

Time ticked by with no more alarming events, though as darkness fell the park remained busy. However, he started to get the feeling there was someone else out there, like maybe *he* was being watched.

He knew from what Aussie had said, unless she had just been winding him up, that he had a tracer implanted in him. But surely Aussie wouldn't be here in the park too. She had seemed the type to be much too concerned about her appearance to stoop to hiding in bushes, if she could avoid it. Or was that just an act?

If Aussie was out there this should have been a coordinated op, in which case they would both be wearing ear buds and throat mics, with a control vehicle parked nearby.

Slowly he reached into his bag and drew out the heat vision scope.

A group of people just leaving the park lit up like a scene from a Predator movie. Ben turned his attentions to the other bushes. There were small glows, which Ben took to be roosting birds but there were no prone human forms.

Then he thought to scan the trees, to look higher up.

Moments later he spotted something. It was an odd dull glow, like it was either side of the trunk, some twenty feet up. It was not moving, but deserved further investigation. Ben had a hunch there was someone behind the trunk. However, that would suggest that they were not observing the park but something beyond. That could only mean the terrace of houses, whose walled gardens backed onto the park.

After continuing to watch for some time, the hidden figure remaining motionless, Ben decided to make a move.

Slowly shifting position when the coast was clear, he crept out the back of the bushes, placing his camera in the bag but keeping the scope out. Picking the holly off his clothes and dropping it aside, he listened for anyone approaching. He unzipped the sides of his camo trousers then pulled them down round his ankles. Stepping out of them, he pulled them inside out, turning them from jungle camo to commando black before putting them back on. Inverting his jacket to black and placing the scope in a side pocket it only remained to put his pack on and he was ready.

Keeping behind the cover of the bushes, Ben moved slowly around the edge of the park. Every step was made with sensitivity. If he felt resistance under a heel he stopped and tried a different place to put his foot. He couldn't afford to snap a twig. He was also sensitive to snagging branches with his arms. It was almost dark enough to need his night vision but for now he stuck with the scope he held in his hand.

He stopped to check once more. From his new position he could confirm there was a person up the tree, astride two branches, arms down. It was also clear that the person was fully suited up, as there were no exposed zones for the hands and face. In fact, where the eyes should be there was an even lower radiance, indicative of goggles being worn. This prompted Ben to put away the scope, take out his balaclava and goggles and put them on. The scene before him appeared to light up green. The figure was dark against the trunk but still visible.

Ben moved closer.

This could be it he thought, if this *was* the vigilante and not some peeping tom. The guy would have to come out of the tree at some point and Ben would be waiting.

Ben's orders were to bring the guy in for questioning, not kill him, so that might make things a little more challenging. However, the *powers that be* hadn't said *without a mark on him*, so necessary force could be used.

Ben froze as something seemed to spook the figure. The guy's head had snapped round to look down in Ben's direction. There hadn't been a sound from Ben or anyone. Head still turned, the guy remained motionless. It wasn't clear whether he could see Ben.

A minute passed and neither moved. Ben wondered how long they should keep up the pretence before getting down to business. Rather than have to climb up after the guy, Ben would prefer to bring him down as quickly and cleanly as possible, immobilize him then call it in.

In a burst of speed that caught Ben off guard, the figure suddenly ran along one of the thick boughs. Then, just as Ben began to start after him, as the bough began to bend and spring, the guy jumped. He landed on the wall of a back garden and sped along it to the right.

Two can play at that game, thought Ben, as he reached the wall and propelled himself up. Racing after his target, they were as sure-footed as each other. It reminded Ben of obstacle courses he'd had to cross with a much heavier pack on his back.

Ben was convinced by the agility of this guy that he just had to be the one he had seen vanish into the culvert on the industrial estate.

The vigilante would soon run out of wall then be down to street level, where Ben was confident he could outrun him. But as if the vigilante could read Ben's mind, he jumped left, landed on a shed roof, jumped again, landed on a high side wall and headed towards the back of a house.

Ben was hot on his heels following with his own parkour skills. He jumped to the shed roof. However, being heavier it split and sagged. He jumped for the wall, but only just made it, stopping himself from going right over the top by coming down to hands and knees. He used this position to spring up and head along the side wall.

By this time the vigilante had already leaped a large gap from the wall onto a flat roofed kitchen extension. Ben couldn't help but admire the guy. He was like a ninja.

Ben jumped the gap next, realising too late that he wasn't going to make it. He put his hands forward to catch the edge of the roof but this only served to swing his legs in hard. He boots smashed through the large kitchen window. He had only ever done such things with an abseil rope. Unsupported, he lost his grip on the roof slipped backwards in a shower of glass and smacked his head on the paving below.

Getting to his feet there was no time to lose. He was glad no one was in the kitchen. Nevertheless a light came on upstairs. He made it round the extension in time to see the side gate swing shut as well as the upstairs curtains being pulled open.

Speeding down the side of the house, through the gate, into the front garden, he caught a glimpse of the figure heading right.

Ben vaulted the low wall of the neighbours, then their front wall onto the street, where he intended to pick up some real speed. Only then did he note the wetness in his trousers. It wasn't sweat, or urine. He was bleeding but had no time to check how badly. He ran on.

Turning right at the junction with the main road, even with his injured legs he was able to gain on the target, because his legs were longer than most people's. There would be no stopping him now.

Turning right once again and up a poorly lit alley, Ben realised that the vigilante was running back towards Wrap Park. Neither of them showed signs of slowing. Ben was still gaining on the vigilante.

Referring to his memorised map of Curston as the vigilante turned left on a park path, he had a hunch the guy was running towards a dead end. The castle ruins were just up ahead with their high walls, and sure enough that was where the guy made for. They clearly couldn't be a local, Ben smiled.

Then he began to chuckle as the vigilante found himself facing castle walls on three sides. However, the chuckle died away as the vigilante, without pausing, scrambled up the far wall. Where did they think they were going?

Reaching the bottom of the wall, Ben paused. He thought it might be more sensible, considering the state of his legs, to see what direction the guy was going and simply head them off. Standing and watching, he marvelled at the guy's skill and speed.

Ben found himself thinking the guy was like someone from the Marvel Comic Universe. 'It's Venom,' he muttered. 'It's ven…'

Ben felt suddenly rather dizzy, craning back to follow the nameless vigilante's progress.

'It'sven…' then he was falling. Not the vigilante but Ben.

Ben came round by the castle wall in the light of summer's early dawn. He looked at his G-Shock which said it was just after half four. How long had he been out? He looked around. There was no one about. Not that he expected *Sven* the vigilante to be watching.

He got shakily to his feet, blinking. His head was sore too. He pulled down his bloodied tattered trousers. He discovered a few nasty cuts. Luckily they were no longer bleeding but healing. The thought did cross his mind that he might have become a zombie.

He needed to get back to his car, get home and rehydrate.

12

Ben had been unable to grab even a power-nap. On the bright side, he thought, that meant he wasn't subjected to any sleep-reading.

He had driven home sitting on a shopping bag to keep his bloodstained trousers off the seat. Once home he had drawn the blinds and curtains, in case there were any early-rising farmers about, then stripped off. The trousers, which would have to be thrown, were washed first along with the socks and footwear. As this load clunked around the drum of the washing machine he focused on rehydrating and getting protein inside him.

When he went to the pull-out larder he was initially looking for tinned steak. However, his eyes were drawn instead to the tinned salmon and the sardines in brine. He didn't know whether it was a side effect of having been gene-spliced with a starfish but he devoured a tin of each fish, cold. That should have been enough but the craving was still there. He went on to eat both remaining cans of each, making a mental note to revise his shopping list.

Sated, he went for a shower. Noting that he was still dizzy with low blood pressure as he headed upstairs, he made use of the bannister. The starfish side of him might be good for accelerating healing of damaged tissues but it did not magically replace lost blood. It might accelerate blood cell production but he had to be careful. The treatment also did nothing to ease the pain of injury, only the length of the suffering. As he stepped into the shower and felt the water bite, he sucked air through his clenched teeth.

Letting the showerhead rinse the event off, he first inspected the bump on his head. Hidden by his scalp he could feel it there but it probably felt more noticeable than it was. His legs were another story though. There was no telling how deep the kitchen window had cut because the wounds had been knitting back together at an incredible rate.

He reasoned that if an artery had been cut, and his new ability had struggled to repair the blood vessel whilst sealing the surrounding tissues, there would surely be tell-tale swelling. There was none. All there were was a series of ragged bloodless cuts around the backs of his legs in the process of drawing themselves closed.

By the time he got himself dried, shaved and dressed, there was barely time for a cup of tea before he had to head out to open the store up for seven.

Even though he only had to work until twelve-thirty, the weakness due to blood loss almost reminded Ben of endurance exercises on continuation-training. Though in truth that was far tougher, even if he was younger back then.

He sorted the Sunday papers, filled in the temperatures log for the chillers and totted up the fuel readings. Next he counted the previous day's takings, after which the immediate demands on his time were behind him. He just needed to check the shelves were stocked after the previous evening's last minute shoppers. Some people seemed to enjoy turning up for a sixty second dash before closing, often leaving big gaps in the lager and wine chiller.

Putting the kettle on for a coffee Ben thought it might have been an appropriate time to get Jill's paperback out of the filing cabinet and read a bit more, except there was something more important to do before the next customer arrived.

Taking his mobile he moved through to contacts and pressed *Auntie*. Each agent had their own code name for *The Office*. For Ben this was a simple play on words relating, in his mind, to Man from Uncle, a dire TV series from before his time, which they made a half-arsed film in honour of.

When the call was received at the other end he gave his call code. This call code had to change every time he reported in. There was a list of ten code strings, to be used in rotation. He only had to remember which he had used last time. If he got it wrong it just meant that, with suspicion raised at the office, a different set of responses and other routines would be put in place. The calls were always recorded, either way.

Thanking his repaired cognitive faculties the code he recited confirmed his identity and he was asked what he wanted. He was not expected to provide the person's name or a code name, he simply declared 'My handler.'

'One moment please.'

Once the office acknowledged a field agent, their team details were on screen so they could be patched directly though as required. Unless a team member had requested a call block, not wishing to be disturbed or worse compromised. Other team members could just as likely be active in the field.

The call was finally picked up. 'Yyess?' Aussie sounded sleepy.

Ben couldn't help but imagine her lying there in a leather nightie, or would it be PVC, whatever those S&M types wore to bed. He never really got his head around that scene. Pain was something to be endured when pushing your body through its limits to achieve a positive goal. Unless of course it was the mental pain of loss or failure to be put behind you, he thought.

'It's Chance.'

'Oh…Something to report?'

'I made contact with our guy last night.'

'Why didn't you call it in?'

'I've been busy cleaning up the mess.'

'You killed him?!'

'Hold on, here's a customer…That's a pound…Thanks…No we don't…Of course I didn't.'

'Are you talking to me or a customer?'

'You.'

'Right. So you didn't kill him?'

'No. He got away.'

'Unbelievable. I thought you guys claimed you could walk on water.'

'No. That's SBS bullshit.'

'Hopeless.'

'But I've got us a name.'

'A name? That's great news!'

'Sven.'

'Sven who?'

'Just Sven.'

'That's no good. Do you know how many Svens there must be?'

'Seventy-five.'

'Seventy-five?'

'Thanks...and you.'

'What?'

'Sorry that was another customer after a paper.'

'I don't need their flaming retail history McGregor, I'm asking you how many Svens you think there are.'

'Not many?'

'We need a second name to work with.'

'Okay then...Gali.'

'Sven Gali? Svengali?! You idiot McGregor, he gave you a fake name! Don't you know anything?!'

'No he didn't. I haven't had chance to speak to him yet.'

'So who told you, exactly?'

'No one. I'm just suggesting we call him Sven, instead of saying the vigilante this, the vigilante that, the vigilante...'

'Yes, yes. I see. I guess that makes sense. But why Sven? Does he appear northern European?'

'No, no. Never mind. The important thing is he is very skilled and agile. I think we might want to check out parkour clubs.'

'Really?'

'Okay, I think *I* need to check out parkour clubs.'

'But he could have trained in the US for all we know. No, I think that's a waste of your time, unless you can get a photo of him.'

'At a club?'

'Anywhere!'

'Yeah well I'm working on that.'

'I want you getting me good results on our missions. I don't intend to be a handler all my life. *I've* got a career path.'

'Someone's come in…Morning Jill.'

'Is that *her* again?'

'No.'

It was.

'It better n…'

Ben hung up.

'Morning, Chance.' She brought a Sunday Times to the counter. 'Are you okay?'

'Yeah, fine.'

'You look rather…pale. I think you need looking after.'

'Do I…?'

'When did you last eat?'

'Well I…' he couldn't tell her.

'Get yourself along to the Quarryman for a Sunday lunch. It's half-twelve your shift finishes, isn't it?'

'I might just do that…Would you be free to join me?'

'Sadly no. I've got a deadline to meet. Just came for a paper.'

'Okay.'

'Well that's not strictly true.'

'No?'

'I felt I needed to see you, so that I could then focus on the job at hand.'

'Sorry, I don't follow.'

'Oh I'm sure you do…maybe not…what I'm trying to say is do you fancy coming to the cinema tomorrow night, in Curston?'

'I…'

'You finish around seven, right?'

'Yes.'

'Well then, that's plenty of time. Here's my address and phone number,' she handed him a slip of paper, 'and I believe it's your turn to drive.'

'Sure.'

There was that fantastic smile of hers again.

As Ben watched her go he began to wonder if Aussie was right. Things seemed to be developing, and he had to focus on this op. But he particularly liked the way Jill wasn't averse to doing the asking out.

After the shift ended Ben took Jill's advice and went for the Sunday Carvery at the Quarryman's Arms. It certainly hit the spot, and gave him a thirst. He had a Guinness with his meal but once he was finished in the restaurant he went straight to the bar and ordered a second from Peter.

Turning around to a chorus of friendly greetings from his customers, to whom he raised his glass, he spotted Mikey.

'Hey. You know how I told you about my Scottish break?'

Ben nodded, before taking another sup.

'I was telling some guy about it and he starts telling me all about his recent trip to Russia. Well I stand there shaking my head as he goes into far too much detail for my liking. He'd flown into Moscow and taken a week long river cruise, all the way down to the Caspian Sea. He'd taken walks along the river bank, fished in the river, sailed on the river, even swam in the river. Eventually I says to him, you know what mate, you've turned into a Volga man.'

'Urr…' Ben groaned at the pun, noticing that a couple of others within earshot were just frowning. Their geography or general knowledge probably wasn't up to the task, he thought.

'On the subject of rivers,' Mikey continued, 'some of the guys have been doing alright mind, with the trout and the salmon down the river at Curston. I thought how difficult could it be, right? But just the other day I got into difficulty, as to my surprise the pair of waders I had on pulled me under.'

'Really?'

'Yeah…The man from the RSPCA, who rescued me and then phoned the police, put my accident down to sheer stupidity and the fact that the two oystercatchers I had strapped to me were still alive.

'Ugh…'

'Not to be deterred by my near drowning, or the confiscation of my rod and tackle, I decided to make my own. I used bamboo cane and a reel of cotton with a bent needle. However, I soon found I was being heckled from the bank. What on earth d'you think you're doing with these, they said, holding up one of the zip-fasteners I was using for lures. I says, Isn't it obvious. I'm fly fishing.'

Those who had been frowning at the last two attempts at humour laughed now.

Ben decided he should take a turn. 'I took a call in the shop the other day about Harry's cars on the forecourt. It was a guy wanting a car that was good on hills. I said, I don't deal with the autos, and the boss isn't here at the moment, but it sounds like you need one of our six wheel cars. He says I'm on my way. Three hours later he turns up. He looks around the forecourt, then comes and asks have I gone and sold that six-wheeler? I explained we've sold no cars today. They are all there, with four wheels on the ground, one spare, and one for steering.'

The crowd got that one too, luckily.

Before Mikey could go next, Ben took another gulp of Guinness, and launched into another anecdote. It felt like he was on a roll. 'A man came to the pumps at the shop with a green can but started filling it with diesel. Thinking it was for a lawn mower I dashed outside. That's not the unleaded! I called. He says, I know that lad. I'm doing a re-enactment of the Exxon Valdez with an Airfix kit in my wife's fish pond.'

No one laughed. The stand-up died on his feet.

'That sounds like my uncle Max,' says Peter, gathering up empty glasses.

Suddenly there was a commotion and an elderly woman who Ben didn't recognise collapsed from her bar stool and lay still on the damp carpet.

Ben immediately went to her aid, asking if anyone knew her name. It was Mary. Using her name in a reassuring tone he tried to get a response from her as he checked that she was breathing and still had a pulse then putting her into the recovery position.

She wasn't regaining consciousness though. 'I think you'll need to phone for a paramedic.'

'To hell with that, Chance,' said Mikey. 'It'll be quicker if I drive her to Curston in my van.'

'No it won't, Mikey. You've been drinking.'

'Oh yeah.'

'I haven't.'

The crowd turned to see a lad holding a coke in one hand and car keys in the other.

'Thanks mate.' Ben lifted Mary up in his arms, and instantly wished he hadn't. The dizziness returned as he stood back up. Nevertheless, by sheer will power he followed the lad out of the pub without dropping the woman, despite being met outside by a choking cloud of cigarette smoke.

As Ben loaded the dishevelled and dribbling, Mary into the lad's car, he heard Cedric call out from the bench by the door.

'Oyvaddur.'

13

A customer Ben hadn't seen before handed him a ten pound note and a Red Bull. When Ben handed him back a five pound note and some coins the man said, 'You're 'avin a laugh incha? I gave you a fifty, init.'

Looking down at the still open till, Ben could see no fifty pound note. 'For security purposes I've put the rest of your change inside the fiver.'

The man's face lit up. 'Like it mate…Init.'

Ben nodded, wondering what the man was on.

As the bizarre man went out he left the door open which wouldn't help the air conditioning keep the heat down, so Ben went to close it. As he reached the door he noticed a wad of fifty pound notes on the doormat. Bending down to pick up the wad, the ground seemed to go from under him.

Ben woke up on his bedroom floor. He'd fallen out of bed and all became clear. At least once again he had not been sleep-reading.

Later that morning while Rosie worked up a sweat in the kitchen, Ben was counting up the previous days takings behind the counter when Doris, one of the regulars, came to stand looking at the cake cabinet next to the till.

'I wish I could bake like Rosie.'

'Me too, Doris.' Ben paused in his counting. 'I don't know what my problem is mind. Nothing seems to turn out like the recipe. Just the other day I tried to make a tagliatelle bake. You couldn't even taste the telly.'

The woman frowned. 'And what would a telly taste like?'

'These days, plastic I guess.'

'Well I'll take the coffee and walnut cake then please.'

Ben inhaled to crack his favourite joke but was beaten to it.

'I know, yes, I'll have to pay for it.'

Shortly after Doris had gone, Ben checked the takings against the till report then bagged it back up to return it to the safe.

'He'are.' Like a braying donkey Rosie stood at the counter holding out a cup of coffee for Ben.

'Thanks Rosie.'

'I'm up for some air.' Sounding like a pearl diver she nodded towards the door.

'Okay.' Ben put the takings away then returned for his coffee and headed outside to join her, sitting on the wall, awaiting the next customer.

Ben had learned to try and lead the conversations he had with Rosie, or else she had the tendency towards overshare.

'What do you do with your spare time then Rosie? Gardening?'

'I've got an allotment.'

'Right. What do you grow?'

'Greens mainly. Though they play havoc with my double incontinence.'

'Double?' He asked before he could stop himself.

'Oh yes, had it for years. I failed my first food hygiene exam because of it.'

Ben found himself looking at his coffee in a new light.

'Here comes Toytown.'

Ben looked up from his mug to see an elderly woman with a bag on wheels headed for the shop. 'Toytown?!'

'That's what people call her...Edith Tointon has lived here all her life, even when her husband of two years suddenly upped and moved abroad.'

Ben decided to head to the till but Edith turned out to be what Ben had come to class as a ditherer. She was the sort of shopper who never thought to use a shopping list. She would place three items in her basket then go back round to replace two, in a persistent loop of indecision. After almost an hour Edith came round to Ben and heaved the overladen basket onto the counter.

'Another nice day Edith.'

'Not as nice as when I was a child.'

'Oh?'

'It's a little known fact.'

'Is that right?'

'Back in the days before Sevensands was a quarrying village, it had been a secret naval base.'

'Ha. A naval base?'

'Oh yes. Ships used to sail up to Curston, past the castle in the dead of night and take the canal through the marshes, deep into the woods where they could hide their sails.'

'From who?'

'The French of course.'

'Right.' Ben's history had never been great. He wondered if she meant the Normans. 'That'll be eighteen twenty-nine.'

It was Edith's turn to frown. 'Oh no…It would have been way before then.'

'What? No, your shopping comes to eighteen pounds twenty-nine.' Ben looked at the clock while Edith searched her bag for a purse. Only eight hours to go before he could close up and go to the cinema with Jill.

Ben couldn't believe it was the same Jill. What a difference just a bit of eye-liner and lippy seemed to have made. Or was it something else, he wondered, as he stood in her porch.

'Wow. You look…great, Jill.'

'Never mind me. I hear you are quite the hero. Come on inside.'

'Oh, I thought you were ready,' Ben stepped into the still new-looking house.

'Not quite. I'll only be a minute then you can tell me how you saved old Mary.'

'No, you got it wrong,' Ben called up the stairs in her wake. 'It was some lad who took her to the hospital.'

Ben could hear a wardrobe door sliding open and the scratchy-clink of hangars. 'I heard that if it wasn't for you taking charge of the situation, Chance, she could have died of the aneurism!'

'Aneurism?!'

'Brain haemorrhage.'

'I didn't know. I've been at work all day.'

'I'm surprised no one told you then.'

'Maybe they thought I already knew.'

'Maybe.'

There was nothing *maybe* about *this* Jill, thought Ben as he saw her come to the top of the stairs in her short sleeved LBD. It showed off her modest cleavage to perfection. Ben was speechless as she seemed to catwalk it down to him in her heels. He couldn't believe it was the same woman. He tried to recall if he had seen any other woman make such a transformation. She had gone from Plain Jill to Thrill Jill.

'So how did you know what to do, Chance?'

No response.

'First aid training, obviously,' answering for him. 'Chance?'

'You look incredible…Do I need to go get changed? I came straight from work.'

'No time,' pointing at the door. 'Cinema, James.'

'Huh, right.'

Once they were on the Arrow and heading for Curston Jill tried again. 'Where did you do your first aid course?'

'Oh it was a few years ago now, at university. Staff training. I probably should go on a refresher course.'

'I'd be hopeless at that. I can't stand the sight of blood.'

'Really?'

'Really…I go weak and the knees and want to throw up.'

'Wish I'd known earlier.'

'Why?'

'I've already bought tickets for The Bloodletter.'

'You better not have, Chance Dare.'

Ben just smiled.

'Because *I've* already got tonight's tickets. *I* asked *you* out remember?'

'So what are we going to see?'

'The Cupid's Kitten.'

'The what?'

Jill turned away to look out the passenger window, to hide her smirk.

When they came out after the film they were walking close to one another, hands colliding occasionally but not yet joining.

'I never had you down as a Sci-fi fan, Jill.'

'Have you not been reading Breakfast's in Bed? It's a yet to be discovered classic.'

'A *yet to be discovered classic*? Is that even a thing?...I'm only a few chapters in...It's odd...Tonight's film was good though. I like twists and surprises.'

'Me too.'

As they headed back towards the car park they could hear some commotion coming from the seven-eleven on the opposite side of the road.

'Stay here Jill.' Ben went to check.

Inside a Pakistani shop assistant was clearly being threatened by a Caucasian with a knife.

The assistant was pleading, 'I can't. I could lose my job.'

'Just do it!'

'Is there a problem sir?' Ben expected his entry into the shop to calm the situation.

'Beat it big man.'

The assistant just looked on, scared.

'I'd put that knife away if I were you sir.' Ben took a couple of slow steps into the shop, noting its layout, where the CCTV cameras were, and that there were no other customers.

'Or what?' The knife was brought round in Ben's direction.

'Or someone could get cut. And that won't do you any good, sir.'

'Are you a cop?'

'It doesn't matter what I am, sir. I think you should hand me the blade and go.'

'Hand you the blade? Ha. I'll do better than hand it to you.' He took a step towards Ben.

'If it's money you want, you can have what's in my handbag.'

Ben glanced over his shoulder to see Jill standing there.

'I told you I'd sort this.' He reached into his pocket for his car keys. 'Go back to the car. I'll be with you shortly.' He tossed her the keys.

She caught them deftly but stood her ground. 'I'm not going anywhere. You don't need to play hero again. I'll call the police.'

'You two are really pushing my buttons.' The man with the knife stepped forward more menacingly.

Suddenly Ben realised this was not a good situation for him. Yes if he got cut he would heal but that in itself might present a problem, especially with Jill as witness. If she saw him cut and then without even a scar the next day it would raise a number of questions he was not prepared to answer. He half stepped back.

Taking this as a sign of weakness the man with the blade came in fast. Ben sidestepped, grabbed the man's knife hand by the wrist and used his force and motion to pull him around, Ben spinning on his heal. Bringing the knife up and taking the man under the armpit he lifted him off the ground, throwing him over his back and slamming him onto the shop floor, in front of the counter.

The man lay there with the air completely knocked out of him, the knife now in Ben's hand.

'Maybe *now* is the time to call the police,' Jill suggested.

'Please, no. I don't want any trouble.' The shop assistant discouraged the idea anxiously.

'Well then...' Ben patted the prone man down, turning him over for another pat down, locating his wallet and opening it. Rather than check for ID Ben removed the notes.

'What are you doing?'

'Always rob a robber. This should make up for his attempted robbery.'

'He wasn't robbing me.'

'Come on mate, we could see what was going down here.' Ben offered him the notes.

'What *was* he doing here then?' asked Jill, now inside the shop, looking at the condition of the still motionless man.

'I'd rather not talk about it. I don't want any trouble.' The assistant insisted, not taking the notes.

'Okay then, we'll get out of your hair.' Ben pocketed the wallet and notes in one side of his jacket and the knife in the other then dragged the man out of the shop. Pausing to look up and down the street to confirm it was clear, he hefted him up onto his shoulder.

'Are you taking him to the hospital?' asked Jill. It was clear the whole evening was quickly turning pear-shaped.

'Oh he'll be fine.'

'*Fine*? I wouldn't want to be on the receiving end of what you just did there. Where did you learn to do such a thing?'

'Oh I urr did a bit of judo when I was a kid. Never thought that it might come in handy one day.' Ben spotted a bench over by the market square and dumped the man there, like some drunk, checking there was still a pulse before abandoning him.

The trip back in the car had been quiet. Ben had some regrets over getting involved at the seven-eleven. It had achieved nothing for his developing relationship, though it may provide a useful lead when checking out the person's ID with the office.

Initially he was certain the man had not behaved like a vigilante. That changed when he wondered if the Pakistani had been considered a terrorist threat.

Ben started to wonder if he had just been really stupid. Should he drive back and pick the man up? He would surely have come round and left by now. He tried to justify his own vigilante style actions to himself. Tonight's man seemed a little taller than the one he had practiced his parkour with but that still left some questions wanting answers.

Dropping Jill off at her home she simply said good night and went inside.

Bad boy Chance didn't deserve a nightcap.

14

As soon as Ben was home, he photographed the knife and contents of the wallet he had lifted, including one twenty pound note. He didn't want to arouse suspicions having pocketed the rest of the notes. Besides, the store was always getting short on fivers because ATMs never gave them out. Then he bagged the knife and wallet.

Next, he secure-emailed the images to the office in an encrypted folder, and only then did he report in to Aussie verbally on a secure line.

'You did what?!'

'I immobilised him, and put him on a bench in Curston market square.'

'I heard you the first time…Did anyone see this?'

'The shop assistant, of course…Oh and Jill.'

'What were you doing with that excuse for a woman again?!'

'We went to the pictures to see…'

'I don't give a fuck about what you saw. I thought you were out doing surveillance.'

'No.'

'Obviously…So…Any security cameras?'

'There will be the seven-eleven, but I doubt they are bothered. The lad was just glad to see the back of this urr…' Ben glanced at the driver's license again, 'John Collier.'

'So what about any cameras covering the square?'

'Possibly. I couldn't very well try and avoid the cameras with Jill there. It would have looked suspicious.'

'More suspicious than you *mugging* someone? You should have just phoned the police and walked away, Ben.'

'You know how hard pushed they are with all the cuts. I just thought...'

'No you didn't think. I'll tell you what *I* think though. *I* think you were looking to impress that useless slapper.'

'Rubbish. I heard trouble and I went to check it out.'

'Check it out being a euphemism for make things worse. Right I'll get the techies to sort the camera records. Just don't do it again. Focus on the job!'

'Are you going to check out the contents of the wallet? The shop assistant suggested it was not a robbery, so what was it? And maybe there was a link between Collier and those two found stabbed in the park. Maybe some uniforms need to go pick him up for questioning.'

'Don't tell me how to do my job.

'I'm just saying.'

'I know. And I'm saying don't'

It took Ben ages to feel calm enough for bed, after that call. He had texted Jill to say sorry for how the evening turned out, but she hadn't replied. She was almost certainly asleep he guessed looking at the time.

He tried watching some catch-up TV, but just wasn't engaging with it.

His frustration continued to build, which wasn't helping. He had to do something about it. He decided to have a workout in his living room then take a shower.

An hour and a half later he lay on his bed cooling off. He had no shift at the shop the next day, but tried not to make plans as he lay there. Ben tried to empty his mind, and listen to the rhythm of his breathing.

He wasn't sure whether he had drifted off or picked up a book to read, but became aware of his eyes scanning lines.

The heavy cell door clanked open. Two warders strode in and were none too gentle snapping the cuffs on, hands forwards.

He ducked slightly and turned sideways as he stepped out onto the landing. Then as the threesome headed along the third floor to the stairs, Ben's neighbouring inmates made themselves scarce.

'Psycho!' echoed around.

'Ooo he's in trouble now.'

The wing seemed to erupt with gorilla grunts, which failed to intimidate Ben, serving instead to bring a half smile to an otherwise bored expression.

Ben woke just before eight-thirty. The first thing he did was check his phone for messages. There was nothing from Aussie, but more of a concern there was nothing from Jill.

After breakfast he grabbed his back-pack, emptying its contents onto his bed before going shopping. It made sense to shop in the village. There was no staff discount but it was a shorter journey than Curston, plus they stocked a good range of items. Besides, every little helped keep the place going.

When he arrived, around half-nine, he saw one of his regulars standing in front of the paper bins, reading the headlines from the range of newspapers before picking the one he always bought. The man saw Ben coming, looked at his watch and looked back at Ben. 'What time do you call this, Chance?'

'Today is my Saturday.'

'You need to get yourself a copy of this year's calendar then.'

'I work the weekend, so today and tomorrow are my days off. Eddie does these.'

'More information than I require.'

'Yet you read the papers.'

'Actually I'm only interested in the crosswords.'

'Really? I can feel some cross words coming on, myself.' Ben went inside.

Celia was there, blocking access to the counter with her pram and complaining. Eddie was not behind the counter but desperately searching for something in the store cupboard for the old lady who was now pressed up against the counter by Celia's pram.

When Celia saw Ben trying to shop she turned on him. 'The service in this fuckin place is fuckin diabolical. Never, mind the fucking tins there, Chance. I've got a fuckin life to lead!'

'Sorry miss Trap I...'

'What did you fuckin call me?!'

'Sorry, I'm still trying to learn people's names. I meant Trench.'

'It's Trent! And don't you fuckin forget it. Now get serving.'

'I just came in for some shopping. It's my day off.'

'Fuckin day off! I wish I could have a fuckin day off from this sprog!'

The regular with his paper could see the queue at the counter was going to take some time, so cut in and reached past the pram to put the correct money on the side of the till for Eddie, when he returned. 'Money's on the till!'

'Found it!' called Eddie, having extracted himself from the cupboard with a bottle of Lee Perrins.

'You'll find it up your arse if you don't get a move on you little shit,' Celia snapped.

'Do you mind moving your pram then so I can get in then?'

'Fuck me! Do I have to do every fuckin thing round here?!' Celia shifted the Pram back.

'Thank you, dear,' the claustrophobic old lady who had been trapped behind the pram sounded quite relieved.

'Who fuckin asked you for your fuckin two pennies worth?'

'Sorry.'

'So you should be, with a fuckin face like that. God knows what fuckin critters you're harbouring under those fuckin rhino jowls.'

'I beg your pardon?'

'Beg all you like, granny. You've got all day to fuckin potter about. I've got my fuckin hands full.'

Eddie made it in behind the counter, scanned the bottle and announced the price.

The old lady started to search through her purse for the correct change.

'Fuckin give that to me, we want to be home by fuckin Christmas.'

'I...'

Celia snatched the purse.

'I'd give that back if I were you, Celia.' Ben now stood behind her, his pack full of shopping to put through the till, since there was no spare basket.

'Or fuckin what?'

'Or you could be done for *mugging*.'

'*Mugging*?! Says the fuckin *shoplifter* with his fuckin bag brimming!'

'*You* have the basket.'

'I'm a fuckin paying customer, and don't you fuckin forget it. I keep this fuckin place afloat, the amount of fuckin times I'm fuckin here.'

'Maybe you should try shopping elsewhere.'

'What are you fuckin saying?'

'I'm saying that I think this store and its customers could do without you effing and blinding.'

'I ain't fucking blinding anyone!' Celia shoved her basket on top of the selection of chocolates, thrust the purse back at its owner then struggled to turn her pram around, instead of simply backing it out. The pram knocked a few things off the shelves as it swept past. 'You can all fuckin shove it up your fuckin arses!'

Celia's baby never stirred once. Ben hoped it was because it had learned to sleep through its mother's ranting, rather than anything more serious.

The old lady shook her head, 'Celia was a horror to teach even in the infants. The spit of her parents.'

'Sorry about all that, Mrs Foster.' Eddie apologised.

'Not to worry, Eddie.' Mrs Foster turned to leave. 'Chance might have seen her off.'

'We can hope.' Ben placed his pack on the counter for Eddie. 'Do you want to put that through, while I sort this lot out?' He first put the fallen things back on their shelves then took the basket which had been left on top of the chocolates to return its contents.

On the way back from the shop with his dozen tins of fish and assorted other items, Ben's mobile rang. He hoped it might be Jill as he fished it out of his pocket but it was Veronica.

'Aussie. I'm just on my way back to the house. I can call you back from there.'

'No need. I just called to say two more bodies have been found in Curston. In a terrace house near Wrap Park. Which is somewhat ironic.

'Why?'

'They were both cocooned on cling-film.'

'For disposal?'

'No. It looks like torture. They were found seated, facing one another across a table, wrapped to dining chairs.'

'Right.'

'According to the neighbours they were a gay couple who kept to themselves.'

'So possibly a hate crime then?'

'Do you really think I'd be calling you with a hate crime McGregor?'

'Well...'

'When the plastic was removed they were both found to have burn marks from being Tasered.'

'Okay.'

'There was an empty open safe at the back of a kitchen cupboard, and on the dining table were packs of what they are calling Liquid Crystal, on the streets.'

'Right.'

'*And* the younger of the two men was the one *you* almost killed last night.'

'Wasn't his evening, was it? So what road was their house on?'

'Thirwell Street.'

Ben checked his memorised map and it was very likely the house he had spotted Sven observing from the tree in the park.

Hearing nothing from Jill by late afternoon, Ben texted to ask if she was okay, then went to the pub.

Cedric was outside on his bench sitting below the large hanging basket, smoking as usual.

Ben got a Guinness from Gloria and managed to return outside without any explosion of laughter. He decided to sit next to her granddad and see if the old man could say anything other than his favourite word.

'Nice afternoon, Cedric.'

The old man just grinned and took another drag on his cigarette. The smoke seemed to change direction and head for Ben.

'Has the bus been through yet?'

Cedric just shook his head. Did that mean he could understand what was being said to him, Ben wondered.

'Have you been watching the tennis?'

'Aye. The women's singles were good this year.'

So Cedric *could* speak other words after all. However, Ben wished he'd picked a different topic of conversation since he had not been watching the tennis.

'You know that one who won this year, in the finals?'

'Yes?'

'She came second last year, when I was at Wimbledon watching her.'

'Oh.'

'She doesn't take losing well. Vulnerable state of mind she were in.'

Ben just nodded.

'Oyvaddur.'

Ben felt irritated that he hadn't seen where this was going. He checked his phone to forget about it but seeing there was still nothing from Jill it only made him more irritated. He was just about to tackle Cedric about his constant suggestions when the bus pulled up across the road with a hiss of brakes.

Only a schoolgirl got off the bus. She looked about twelve.

As the bus pulled away and she walked towards the row of houses by the village green, Cedric blurted 'Oyvaddur.'

Before Ben had really thought about it, he had brought his clenched left fist down hard on the old man's sunburned head. The cigarette flew out of Cedric's mouth with the impact, before he slumped forwards. Ben grabbed Cedric's shoulder to stop him tumbling right off the bench and pulled him back into it. He was unconscious but still alive.

What had he done now? There'd be more ear-bashing from Aussie if he didn't cover this mess up. This needed some quick thinking before anyone saw what happened.

Ben unhooked the large hanging basket, which was a bit tricky to get off its hook. He made it look like it had come down on Cedric's head and ended up in his lap. Satisfied with the appearance of an *accident* Ben went inside.

'Gloria! Your granddad appears to have been knocked out by a hanging basket coming loose.'

'Not again.' She seemed in no rush to go investigate, continuing to pull a pint for a customer. 'Lucky coincidence that. Someone was with him last time that happened too.'

15

It occurred to Ben that the nights would soon begin to draw in and the darkness might enable more vigilante activity and sightings, if things weren't all wrapped up by then.

The Liquid Crystal lead showed promise because Sven, if true to character, would not be leaving the Curston area until the whole cancerous operation was routed out, from investors to chemists to runners.

Even if those criminals got scared and ran, Sven would likely track them to the next place. There was no evidence that Sven had been operating abroad yet, but there was nothing to suggest he wouldn't.

Nevertheless, Sven could have acquired access to international security data. He certainly had access to military equipment for his illegal activities.

Once again it occurred to Ben that he was in no rush to capture Sven. He had nothing against the guy's intentions. In fact, he began to wonder whether it might even have been Sven who had once saved Adam and him from Frank Chesney. They had been drugged and bound up. It was Frank who had removed the little finger from Ben's left hand. They would certainly have both died if their paths had not crossed with Sven or whoever it had been.

Ben couldn't be seen to be neglecting his duty however. If Sven just happened to finish his *clean-up* in the region before Ben managed to bring him in, that would be fine by him. It would give him more time to spend in quirky Sevensands before he was moved on to the next mission on the list of pending operations.

There was the situation with Jill though, if he couldn't patch things up with her it could take the shine off remaining in the village.

Later, photographing a fuel station and a man at a cashpoint, Ben turned and looked up across the road onto the roofs. He had that feeling he was being watched again, though he could see nothing up there. However, it would only take the turn of his head to have the person duck out of sight. Or was he just getting paranoid?

He headed down Curston's high street stopping to look in the windows. He was using reflections to check behind him without turning his head, which was an old counter-surveillance trick, though it worked better in daylight.

Finally he saw something as he looked in a charity shop window. Sven was standing in front of a chimney. Ben appeared to take interest in a headless mannequin illuminated by the LED street lighting.

Dropping to a crouch he brought his camera up. He struggled to get the autofocus off the mannequin to focus on Sven's reflection. He turned the lens to manual and tried again. Sven was still there. He took his shot then adjusted the exposure and took another couple of shots.

He wondered if he could get Sven to follow him along the high street to where the buildings dropped in height, which would improve the angle of shot he could take. He stood up and headed further along.

Coming to a video store window he checked the reflection once again and confirmed that Sven was keeping up with him.

Pleased with his initial success of capturing his first photos of Sven, Ben started to question what Sven was doing tailing him. Sven knew he was the person who gave chase the other evening but what value was there in tailing him?

If Sven was as good a hacker as he was now believed to be, it was highly likely that he had found out who Ben was already, and why he was there. However, Sven was surely only in the Curston area to take out a large number of criminals, not to play cat and mouse with Ben.

Was Sven not a lone wolf after all? Was he a contract killer, paid by another crime boss maybe? How were his activities funded? Was he under orders to track Ben now? What would be learned from tracking a tracker? Was Ben going to get tailed back to Sevensands? Was that going to put the people there at risk? Was that going to put Jill in danger? Or was Sven dealing with his own questions up there and wondering whether to make contact?

Ben saw a bench up ahead and decided to sit there for a while, to force Sven to make the first move. If he lost him he would no doubt catch up with him another time. It seemed worth a try.

Sitting on the bench he could not check for a reflection in a window because he was facing out into the street. He could not look up without making things obvious, so he took out his mobile and checked for messages.

Nothing from Jill. Nothing from anyone.

He spent a little while with an app that was supposed to be able to teach him Spanish but after some weeks of effort it was failing miserably. It had been taking him through levels of translation exercises that left him believing that Spanish people spoke like Yoda. He might get the gist of what was meant but it was all back to front and lacked logic in its construction. However, Ben would be the first to admit that over the centuries English had been turned into a train wreck with its own inconsistencies.

Sven did not come down out of the shadows to make contact, so Ben got off the bench and moved further along the road to check another reflection. Sven was still up there. Ben decided to take a different tack. He turned to look up at Sven.

They stood there looking at each other as they had done the other evening, neither moving until Ben made to lift the camera then Sven was off. He hadn't ducked out of view but instead ran along the roof tops. Ben took a burst of shots then followed.

Running down the pavement Ben just needed to get to where Sven would have to come down and then lay in wait for him. Then they might have that *chat*, he thought.

Coming to the end of the row of shops where a road turned up off the high street, Ben ran round the back and spotted a fire-escape. The bottom ladder was retracted, as was the case with the next fire-escape along. In sight of both of them Ben hid behind a couple of large wheelie bins and waited.

Sven appeared above the nearest fire-escape but just stood there looking over the edge for Ben. Spotting him by the bins he waved.

'Cheeky bastard,' Ben had had enough of this. He put his camera away, put the pack securely on his back then burst out from between the wheelie bins. Leaping up under the fire-escape his height enabled him to grab the ladder. He half expected it to come crashing down on him like some *you've been framed* moment but it must have been secured above.

He swung with a single arm chin-up and used his other arm to pull himself up onto the first level of the fire-escape. Once up he bounded round and up the levels to the top.

Sven was waiting back down the way he had come. He was clearly playing with Ben but Ben was definitely up for that little chat now. He raced after Sven.

Sven reached a ladder which connected to the neighbouring roof, some eight feet higher. His legs were a blur. When Sven got to the top he paused for a cheeky look back.

Ben took the rungs two at a time but there was no letting up, as soon as he was up Sven was off. 'Hold it Sven!'

Sven kept going.

Ben chased Sven along the rear edge of the shop roofs, noting that the fire-escapes did not come as high as the roof tops here, and the row of shops was coming to an end. Sven appeared to be cornering himself again, just as he had at the castle.

'What are you doing?!'

Sven made no reply.

'Just stop and talk to me!'

Ben couldn't believe it, Sven just jumped off the roof. It had to be suicide.

Sven vanished into the upper branches of an oak tree like an ape. Ben skidded to a halt at the edge and watched on. He could tell from the movement of the leaves that Sven was not falling but deftly swinging and jumping his way from branches to boughs to the bottom.

Finally Sven stepped out from under the tree, looked up and waved like a taunting mime artist.

'Cocky bastard.' The challenge was on. Ben took a run up, and without further thought than preparing to grab the first branch he came into contact with, he took the leap.

The first branch hit Ben in the face, stunning him. He fought to stay in control of the situation, reaching out for a passing branch but falling backwards from the blow to the face. The next branch struck him on the back of the head hard, spinning him forward. He felt a rib go as his chest impacted with a bigger branch.

On a downward path spinning one way then another, he heard some of the equipment in the pack smashing. He remembered the parachute tree-jumps they had had to practice doing in The Regiment. It struck Ben that this was not a just game of cat and mouse with Sven. He had just made it pure Tom and Jerry.

Ben hit the ground hard. It knocked the wind out of him. He tried to maintain consciousness.

Where had he landed? What condition was he in now? Where was Sven?

Ben had landed face up in a ditch. Blinking his eyes to clear them his ears were hissing like rushing water. He couldn't afford to be confused. He had to get Sven, but Sven came to him. Prodding him, patting him down, and pulling the pack out from under him.

Ben's limbs seemed unresponsive, were they broken or just stunned? Then a dreadful thought occurred to him.

Another downside of this starfish gene-splice which was being trialled on him, was that if he broke bones and was left for any length of time, he could end up with deformities. Unlike that Marvel Comic Deadpool character, Ben's bones would not miraculously reset as they were before. Instead they would simply knit together in whatever position they were at rest in. He couldn't afford to fall unconscious or he might end up like some living breathing swastika.

He blacked out.

16

Ben woke up in bed but not his own bed. His bed didn't come with hand cuffs and an IV drip.

'Hospital?'

He tried to remember what happened last night.

He had been trying to capture Sven. He'd seen him on the roof and better than that had actually photographed him. Then he had laid in wait by some wheelie bins for Sven to come down, and now this. What had happened? Surely he hadn't dozed off and got run over by a refuse truck?

He examined both arms. They looked fine, though the movement alerted him to the fact that his head and neck were sore. He looked down at his legs, covered in a sheet, lifting each leg in turn. They felt fine too, but he could tell by his efforts he definitely had a broken rib or two.

Outside the door of his room he could see the back of a police officer.

'Hey!'

The officer turned then reported into his radio, watching Ben through the window. When he was ready he came in.

'What happened to me officer?'

'We were hoping you would tell *us*. We had a report of someone snooping around on the roofs of commercial premises. On investigation we found you in a ditch.'

'Right. Well *I* was after that person on the roof.'

'Were you now?'

'Yes. I had photographed him and wanted to know what he thought he was doing.'

'No one was found on or off the roof other than you, with your damaged camera.'

'Bollocks!'

'It's true.'

'No, I mean I'm cross about the camera. Would you pass me my phone so I can make a call please?' Ben craned his sore neck to try and look at the bedside locker.

'Sorry sir, but there was no phone, no wallet, or any form of identification found on you. You looked like you had been pretty thoroughly beaten up.'

'So why am I handcuffed?'

'Just a precaution. There have been a number of *incidents* around Curston of late.'

'Yeah, I know…I really could do with making that call. Could I use your radio?'

'Sorry, I can't do that.'

Ben couldn't ask the police officer to contact the office for him. 'I really need to make the call if I'm going to get your questions answered for you. No doubt someone is coming to see me after you reported that I had regained consciousness. Maybe you can ask them to bring a phone for me.'

'I'll see what I can do.'

Veronica stood at the end of his bed wearing that glossy pink plastic smile of hers.

'You've probably guessed I'm not happy,' she warned, peeping under the sheet at his injuries.

'What, you think I am?'

'The camera equipment will need replacing.' She moved up the side of the bed squeezing Ben's sore ankle before moving higher up.

Ben winced. 'Did you at least get the memory card?'

'It had been removed, possibly before the camera was dropped in the stream.' She squeezed his aching knee.

Ben hoped she wasn't intending to go any higher.

'What were you doing there, letting yourself get beaten up *so badly*?'

'The whole thing must have been a setup.' Ben still couldn't remember past the bins. However he was convinced he was right. He didn't think Sven had support but couldn't work out how he had apparently got the drop on him so easily. 'Crafty bastard.'

'While you spent the night lying around in this *pamper lounge*, an industrial unit was set ablaze. Four people burned to death inside, padlocked in, it would seem. Initial forensics has found traces of Liquid Crystal trapped within melted plastic. The unit is now believed to have been a drug distribution depot masquerading as an online catalogue firm.'

'So you think Sven took care of me so that he could take care of them?'

Veronica sighed, her hand now hovering over Ben's left thigh, her metallic pink fingernails looking quite threatening. 'I'm wondering about putting someone else onto this, McGregor.'

'No!'

'Well you're really not making a good job of things, are you? I've only got your word for it that you've even *seen* this Sven. All *I've* seen is that you got beaten up, possibly as a result of trying to impress your girl after that cinema date, as if you're are on some romantic break.'

'No. It's not like that, Aussie. If the camera didn't get busted you'd see.'

'Possibly.'

Ben growled his frustration. 'I'll kill him.'

'That's what's worrying me. We need this vigilante brought in, *alive*, and after this little *incident* I really wouldn't be surprised if you did bring him in dead.'

'Would…just a little bit dented…be okay?'

Veronica had had enough and started to leave.

'Hey, Aussie, the cuffs. Can you take them off now?'

'I think you need to recuperate.'

'No. I'm ready to go.'

'Oh I bet you're just itching to get back to that Silly Jilly.'

Ben bit his lip as Veronica came across to give the handcuffs a mock inspection. Then she leaned in closer, her long hair trailing across Ben's arm and chest as she further invaded his body space, bringing her rosy lips seductively close to his, locking eyes, 'I'm sorry…don't seem to have the key but don't worry sweetie, I'll…sort you out.'

There was a stirring beneath the sheet. Veronica gave a low throaty laugh and turned away.

Ben stared after her. What was her problem?

Jill's gate was almost musical as it squealed open. Ben heard the gravel path accentuate his limp as he made his way to her front door.

Hearing him coming she opened the door before he could reach for the bell button.

'Hi Jill.'

'Hi.'

'I thought I should drop by because you haven't returned any of my texts since the other night.'

'Sorry, Chance but can you blame me? I didn't know what to say to you after that stunt you pulled at the seven-eleven. I never thought you were such a violent man.'

'Such a...?'

'And now look at you, you're hurt aren't you.'

'Well...'

'Did that guy come after you with a bunch of his mates?'

'It wasn't...'

'That's *exactly* why I didn't want you getting involved.'

'I fell! Okay?'

'Fell? Off what, a ladder?'

That seemed to bring a flashback of something and Ben stalled.

'Look, come inside. I've only just had the kettle on...Chance?'

'Urr…Okay…Thanks.' He limped inside and followed Jill to the kitchen trying to gather his thoughts. 'I was out for a walk trying to get my head straight, about you not replying and all, and slipped on a slab of rock in the woods. I came down hard on my side, giving myself cracked ribs for my troubles.'

'Cracked ribs, just from falling to the ground?'

'Don't you believe me?'

'Well they do say the bigger they are the harder they fall. Here,' Jill handed him a mug of black tea then opened the fridge for the milk. 'Do you take sugar?'

'One thanks.'

Jill made herself a mug then sat in front of Ben at the breakfast bar. 'Look Chance, the thing is I don't do relationships anymore. Putting the other night aside for a moment, you seem like a stand up sort of guy but I'm so busy with my work that I don't have the time to offer much more than friendship.'

'I'm fine with being friends, especially friends with benefits.'

'You're incorrigible,' she smiled warmly. 'But with those ribs I don't think you'll be claiming any benefits for some time.'

17

Ben felt like he was in zero gravity and being hit from all sides by two-by-fours. He was falling, his arms and legs thrust out and he jerked himself awake.

Lying there in the early hours, collecting his thoughts, he started to recall his leap from the roof to the tree. Who the hell had he thought he was, Bear Grylls?

Was Aussie was right after all, he began to wonder. What if he wasn't up to this? Maybe the reason he rather liked his cover, as Mr Chance Dare store assistant, was because now in his forties he was finally over the hill and due for putting out to pasture.

He checked the time on his replacement mobile. Sven no doubt had his other one along with his wallet. While the wallet was pure Chance Dare, if or when the phone was hacked into it would be more compromising.

Ben wasn't going to worry over his losses. Things could have been worse, much worse. Besides, Sven would probably know that Section 13 were looking to discuss his future, rather than completely remove him from the equation. They would probably want to turn him, to work for them. Ben thought it would be ironic if he was told he had to work with the cocky bastard.

Ben remembered Sven's piss-taking wave, which had goaded him to jump.

At the store Ben looked up from counting the previous day's takings to see Toytown coming in, expecting another hour long, round the aisles, dither session.

However, this time she came straight to the counter. 'I remembered something the other day, Chance.'

'Did you now?' Ben returned to the counting, only half-listening, half-hoping she would get on with her shopping.

'There was a man who used to come door to door, selling salt.'

'Oh.'

'None of this *packaged* stuff.'

'Uh huh.'

'Used to sell it by the sack, he did.'

'Right.'

'In those days if the ships didn't bring in enough barrels of seawater to boil off, they used to make do with cattle urine. Bye heck it used to make your eyes smart, especially when you put it on your fish and chips.'

'Lovely.'

'That wasn't the only thing that made your eyes smart and your lungs heave in them days though.'

'No?'

'There was a young lad. He would be getting on a bit now mind, if it wasn't for the accident.'

'Oh dear.'

'He used to burn tyres to heat his bedroom, and one night he was that tired from his quarry work that he forgot to pull out the flue.'

'Died of the flu did he? I guess a lot of people did in them days.'

135

'Aye.' She turned away to start her grand tour but then turned back. 'Have you got any of those doggy bags?'

'Yes they are over in the pet food aisle.'

'Oh *are* they, right. I'll be eating out later.'

Later on, Ben was adding goods to the weekly warehouse order via the till. He could hear Rosie oversharing with another customer by the paper bins, as she took her breather from the steamy kitchen.

'The wedding was nice enough considering the tramp my Will was marrying. Her family seemed to have put on a nice buffet but it didn't agree with me. I was sick as a dog right after their prawn mayo sandwiches. Funny thing, my husband came down with the very same thing the next day, after his lunch. I do hate seeing food go to waste.'

'Well, they do say, one man's rubbish is another man's treasure.' The customer said in parting as he came into the shop with his paper. He picked up a loaf and half a dozen eggs then came to the counter. 'Morning, Chance.'

Ben couldn't quite remember the customer's name, though he was certainly familiar enough to have been asked at some point. April showers were coming to mind but Ben wasn't stupid enough to call the guy April. 'Morning. Sorry, I've forgotten your name again.'

'Peter Patterdale.'

'Of course.' He tried imagining Peter Rabbit patting Dale Winton as a possible better memory trigger then started ringing the shopping through the till.

'Could I also have a bottle of the Gordon's Gin please?'

Ben turned and reached for the largest bottle, being the most popular size.

'Oh no, the smallest one will be just fine.'

'Okay.'

'It's for the dog.'

'The dog?'

'Yes I'm going to give her some before the post arrives. I'm expecting an important letter from the HMRC which I don't want shredded like the rest.'

'Why don't you simply get her into the back of the house and close the door on her?'

'Oh I couldn't be so cruel.'

'Cruel?'

'I'd much rather get her drunk. I'm not really sure I'd go along with crushing her ribs.'

As Ben entered the Quarryman's Arms there was a peel of laughter but no accompanying explosion. So he could tell Gloria wasn't around.

'Isn't that right, Chance?' called Mikey.

'Pint of Guinness please, Peter.' Ben turned to face the group gathered round Mikey. 'What's that then?'

'I was telling them a guy came up to you the other day with a plastic bag full of tentacles and plonked it on the counter. He says *Don't say I never give you nothing*, and you says *What is it?* He replies *Here's that sick squid I owe you*...Didn't he?'

'Yeah, no word of a lie,' Ben just went along with it and the group laughed again.

'Did you hear about old Cedric, Chance?'

'No?'

'It's not his week. First he gets knocked out because the hanging basket falls on his head, now Gloria has had to go pick him up from the police station. Makes you wonder if he's going to make it a hat-trick before this week's out.'

'Was he lost, or arrested?'

'Assault charge apparently...Told Gloria it was a sign of how this country's losing its way, with right wing zero-tolerance attitudes. He said he had only gotten into the swimming pool, while the women's synchronised swimming session was on, so that he could practice a nice bit of breast stroke.'

The men laughed while the women tutted.

'I've had a spot of bother with my garden, with me being so busy with work,' Mikey continued. 'It's getting so overgrown that the wife is worried about rats. So I thought to get a gardener in. After a few days I've noticed he's been avoiding the bit at the bottom. So I says to him *I need you to sort out the bottom end mate.* Then he gets all weird about it, claiming the animals need some plants to call their own. Says he is prepared to deal with most sorts of plants but he has his limits. He certainly never does anything with *animal's orchids.*'

The group groaned.

'This guy I know was telling me about his Smart TV. Said it was learning what programmes he shouldn't be watching. I asked, how's that possible? He says he might have been watching too much sport, for example.

The screen tells him to press the red button on his remote, so he does and it switches off the TV.'

That got a mixed response.

'This bloke I got talking to the other week was telling me about his troubles with internet dating. He said he believes he's making good choices but you can't tell till the date. The first one, a real looker, early on in the date tells him up front that she has lost all of her toes in an industrial accident. He couldn't be doing with that.

'The next on his list, an attractive woman who enjoys long distance walking, ends up explaining that she did a walk to the South Pole for charity. But get this, for her efforts she's lost all her toes to frostbite. That was the last he saw of her.

'He tells his mates about this dreadful coincidence, but they say the oddest thing is that he lets *that* bother him. It's then suggested that he go see a doctor about it.

'He starts to think his mates could be right, so he goes to the docs, explains about his failed dates and asks whether the doc thinks he has a problem.

'The doctor says yes, you're lack toes intolerant.'

Those who were drawn into the story gave a big groan.

The door opened and Jill came in.

'Hi Jill,' Chance greeted her. 'What can I get you?'

'It's okay, I can buy my own.'

Ben wondered if he had done something else wrong.

'Do you want another pint?'

Ben looked at his glass, less than a third full. 'Okay, cheers.'

With drinks sorted they retired away to the snug.

'How's things been at the shop?'

'Oh the usual. Bizarre conversations with customers.'

'Like what?'

'There's a woman comes in, seems to be coming in more regularly at the moment. Maybe she sees me as a captive audience for one of her local history lessons, me being stuck behind the counter.'

'Well a bit of local history could be quite interesting.'

'Sure, but I don't think what she's telling me can be right.'

'What, so you're an expert on the area now?'

'Well no but I find it difficult to believe that *way back, when times were hard* people used salt made from urine.'

'Mmm, that does sound a bit suspect.'

'Also, today there was this guy who seemed to think I was suggesting he stop his dog from shredding the mail by crushing it.'

'Maybe it was how you said it.'

'D'you think?'

'What did you say?'

'All I said was, when the mail's due, take the dog into the garage and secure it in a vice.'

'You didn't!'

'No, I didn't.'

Jill sighed.

'So how's your work going?'

'I have a deadline coming up.'

'What's the article about?'

'I can't tell you that.'

'Oh okay. I'd be interested in reading some of your previous articles though.'

'I'm sure you would, but that's not possible either. I write for different papers, magazines, and zines under other names. I can't tell people any of my pseudonyms.'

'Oh.'

Jill could tell she had just made Chance feel like he couldn't be trusted. 'Look, after I sort this next contract out, what do you say we get away, just for a few days?'

'I'd like that but I'd have to check with my handler.'

'Your *handler*?'

'My boss, Harry.'

'But you said *handler*.'

'I meant boss.'

'Who accidentally says *handler* when they mean *boss*?'

'Okay boss *and* handler,' Ben had to think quickly now. 'I'll level with you, as well as my job at the store, I'm involved with a group of people who mentor vulnerable young adults.'

'Oh Chance, that's wonderful. Why haven't you mentioned this before?'

'As I'm sure you will appreciate, each case is confidential.'

18

Ben turned over and felt something in his hands and sluggishly looked down, trying to open his eyes and keep them open. He was too sleepy for this nonsense. He was holding a paperback. He seemed to be reading more in his dreams lately than he did when awake. What was that all about? He focused on the words, and had a weird sense of mind-reading echo.

Ben turned over and felt something in his hands and sluggishly looked down, trying to open his eyes and keep them open. He was too sleepy for this nonsense. He was holding a paperback. He seemed to be reading more in his dreams lately than he did when awake. What was that all about? He focused on the words, and had a weird sense of mind-reading echo.

This was going to be a game-changer, Ben decided as he opened the second of the packages delivered to the house that afternoon. He was pleased he had thought to discuss his idea with the techies. This should put him back in Aussie's good books.

It was a drone and not an off-the-shelf one either. This had a few security service extras, just like his car. In addition to the fifty megapixel camera, there was a heat sensor camera. He was going to track Sven from a height, then at an appropriate time and place swoop down on him. That was when he'd give the mime artist something to cry out about with the built-in Taser system.

Excitedly Ben discarded the instruction manual pieced the kit together, took it all out into the front jungle, placing in on the roof of his car, and found that the batteries were not charged.

Like a kid in something of a huff, he brought the kit back inside and set it charging, next to the replacement camera. Only then did he pick up the manual and start reading it. He soon counted himself lucky that he had not already begun using it. He read that if the user did not input their new GPS point of operation as *Home*, in the event of a problem the system could attempt to fly back to its previously designated home point. In the case of this drone that was probably London. Another potential ear-bashing from Aussie nicely avoided.

Ben went and made his evening meal then checked the drone's progress. This charging was clearly going to take all night. After all it was a big battery, needing to be fully charged for the Taser as well as the rotors. There was also a spare battery he ought to sort too while he was at it.

He decided not to wait around. For the night ahead he would have to try Plan B, which would involve a bit of creativity. This plan had been inspired by a lecture at the photography club about using baiting stations to get better shots of wild animals.

Sightings of Sven had all been pretty much down to luck so far it seemed. Curston covered quite an area, and even though Ben had been searching the most likely spots for vigilante activity, Sven could just as easily be observing elsewhere. However, out of sight did not mean out of ear-shot.

Ben chose an alley near the Hot Spotted night club that led down towards the sports centre, behind some terraced houses.

'You, y'wee bastard!' Ben boomed in aggressive Glaswegian.

'Who me?' he switched to a petrified Brummie squeaking rather nasally.

'Yes you…Give us y'fuckin wallet!'

'Alright, alright, take it easy…I've only got me bum-bag.'

'That'll do y'fuckin nancy boy! Hand it over!'

'Can I at least keep me bus pass or I'll not make it home.'

'Listen pal! I can tell you're not too brilliant. S'let me make it easy f'you, if y'dinny give us the fuckin bag, y'might not be makin it through the *night*! D'y'ken what I mean now y'southern faggot?!'

'Please don't!'

There followed a growl of frustration then the sound of heavy body blows as Ben punched into his palm repeatedly, adding winded noises, before crashing into some wheelie bins and knocking one over.

'What's going on out there?!' a resident called.

Ben ran on the spot, making his feet sound like a receding thief, then lay down near the rubbish, bursting a fake blood bag under his head.

Ben waited, and waited. Eventually a gate was unlocked.

'Dot?!' a croaky old man called.

'Have they gone Ted?'

'There's a body out here?' The man drew closer.

Ben kept still with his eyes closed.

'Shall I call for an ambulance Ted?'

'Don't be stupid Dot! If he isn't dead, I'd be quicker getting my old Triumph out of the shed.'

Ben waited out, wondering whether the man referred to a car or a motorbike.

'How bad is he, Ted?' The woman had now come into the alley.

'He could just be drunk.'

'But what about all the shouting?'

'Maybe he's an actor.'

'An actor?'

'Yes Dot, you know street theatre.'

'I'll get the purse and we can try throwing money at him and see if he gets up.'

'That's the brightest idea you've had all day.'

There was no sign of Sven coming, so Ben made noises of coming round and slowly got to his feet.

'Are you okay lad?'

'Yes, yes, I'll be fine.' Ben continued his bad Brummie accent as he started to stagger away.

'But you're bleeding from your head,' Dot warned, 'You might have a confession.'

'A contusion.' Ted corrected.

'No really. I'll be fine.'

'How about a strong cup of tea?' Dot offered.

'No, no.'

'She means with brandy?'

'Oh…Urr…Thanks but no…I must be off.'

'I told you he was a drunk.'

'Good job you didn't get the purse. His act was appalling.'

Learn from your mistakes, Ben thought. Playing the victim clearly wasn't the thing to do, so he made his way down to the park. After hiding in the shadows for a while he put on his next show.

In his poshest voice Ben bellowed, 'The grind is going rind and rind! That scoundrel's taken my wallet! Stop! Thief!'

Ben ran out of the shadows as fast as he could, making heavy foot falls to attract attention, heading straight for a couple on the path. He could easily have run around them but he was after maximum commotion.

In snarling Glaswegian again, sounding like his father, he warned, 'Get out me fuckin way, y'filthy shite-arses!'

Barging past and receiving dirty looks he came to a junction in the path. Straight on would be no good. It exited the park through a gate in the railings, so he turned left.

Ahead of him was a man with a small dog.

'Get y'self home, y'daft twat! This's no place f'doggin!'

Surprisingly the man let his terrier off its lead and before Ben knew it the fluffy bundle of teeth was snapping at his ankles. Ben put on extra speed, turning one way then the other but couldn't lose the dog. He felt it bite a trouser leg only to get thrown off then come straight back to the attack.

Ben decided his only chance was to leave the park so that the dog would return to its master. However, as he shot through the nearest gate and onto paving, the dog was still there growling in its frenzied desire for blood and pain. Where was Sven when you needed him? Ben wondered.

Crossing a road and running up hill, beyond the receding calls from the dog's owner, Ben and the terrier entered a housing estate. There Ben learned from another mistake. It was no use trying to lose a small dog by weaving in and out of parked cars, because it could simply run right under them, as two successful bites to his calves proved.

He was sorely tempted to stamp on the dog now, but he'd rather not. Otherwise he really would be living up to the miserable scenario of someone who approved of crushing a dog.

In the estate, he had a light-bulb moment, remembering a scene from the Doc Martin TV series. He entered someone's garden and as the dog came right in after him Ben side-stepped straight back out and closed the gate after him. The dog's snarling jowls tried to force their way through the bars in the gate desperate for another taste of Ben's flesh.

'You dumb fucker,' Ben panted. 'Not so smart after all.' Ben turned and walked away.

The sound of claws landing on pavement and scrambling to pick up speed caused him to look back however. The terrier had cleared the garden wall like a Crufts show dog, and before Ben could shift his mass out of the way, jaws sank firmly into his right buttock.

'SHIT!!'

It only intensified the pain trying to pull the snarling dog loose, so Ben decided there was only one thing for it. He gripped it tightly round the throat and waited for the jaws to relax. He was surprised how long that took but eventually the snarling went quiet and the dog slipped into unconsciousness. Even then it required some twisting to get all the teeth out.

He knew the dog wouldn't take long to recover so needed somewhere secure to leave it. More secure than a garden, obviously. He began trying car doors as he limped on, with the intention of shutting the terrier inside an unlocked one.

He didn't fancy his chances of finding one left open these days with all the electronic locking systems.

Locked...locked...locked...open, ALARMED!

The alarm made such a racket as the door was opened that it shocked the dog back to life.

It wriggled free of Ben's grip and they were off again.

Biting back the pain in the arse Ben powered on up the road. The terrier was still trying to recover its wits, so Ben was in with a chance. However, just as he turned the corner onto another road, the terrier began barking with rage. The terrier wasn't the only dog in the vicinity either. The alarm had woken the whole neighbourhood.

The terrier came skidding round the corner after Ben, soon joined by two other barking dogs. One Alsatian and what at a glance over Ben's shoulder looked very much like a Pitbull.

Ahead was a school. He ran through the school gate and closed it after him sliding the latch across. The angry dogs crashed into it, all wanting blood.

'Can we just call it a night lads? I've had enough of this now.'

They moved off. Ben sighed but then considered that this was their neighbourhood, for two of them at least. They probably knew of another way onto the premises.

He ran for the nearest building. It was going to be locked at this time of night but he just needed to get onto the roof via a drainpipe and wait for the canines to get bored, or the police to arrive. At this point he didn't care if Aussie had to play the *get out of jail free* card again.

He heard the barking getting closer. The lads had found their way in. Limping as fast as he could down a paved path at the side of the building Ben spotted a drainpipe. Hoping it would take his weight, he started to make his way up to the guttering two stories above.

This would have been so much easier to accomplish without a series of dog bites. Nevertheless he managed to get up and pull himself clear onto the school block's flat roof. He wanted to just lie there, but decided it best to move to the other side and consider where to go next.

He wanted to head home but first he needed to be sure the dogs had had enough time to get bored and give up.

He lay down on his less painful left side. It wasn't much less painful. He still had his aching ribs on that side, which none of the evening's activities had helped with.

He closed his eyes, listening to the barking slow and soften. Then he slipped into a power-nap.

He woke chilled but alert. He didn't react. He didn't move. He just listened. Years of training had stayed with him. He knew he was no longer alone on the roof. He sought to assess the situation. Was it the dogs?

It wasn't police. He was sure of that. The footsteps were not heavy enough. These were barely a whisper. Also police would likely have been talking as they approached, or at least their radios would have been buzzing. No, this *had* to be Sven. This evening's fuck-up might not be in vain after all, Ben hoped.

Sven was almost on top of him, when Ben grabbed an ankle, locking on with a big hand.

Sven executed a spin, as if launching into a reverse kick and twisted loose of Ben's grip. Ready for this, or some other counter, Ben sprung both legs forwards, rotating on his prone left hip, crashing the top of his shins into Sven's ankles to bring him down. Ben didn't waste this motion. He carried it through to bring himself to his feet. Only to discover that Sven had taken Ben's leg sweep and turned it into a back flip to spring off their hands and stand facing him.

Ben thought, so this was where the Hollywood showdown big fight scene would be, on a school roof, except he really couldn't be bothered getting into a fight now.

'Sven man, just *stop*. We need to talk.'

Sven said nothing.

'I think we've got off on the wrong foot. I just want to say, if it was you, a while back, who saved Adam Underwood and I from that psycho Frank Chesney, that was much appreciated, thanks. I don't even care that you massacred his whole audience. They had it coming to them in my book, especially since I was given to understand the *event* normal involved kids.'

Still nothing'

Ben tried levelling with Sven. 'Look, I've had a shit night but I'm bringing you in…Five just want a chat.'

Still Sven said nothing, just watched and waited for Ben's next move.

Ben looked Sven over from where he stood. This had to be the closest he had got to the guy so far, whilst fully conscious. He appeared to be wearing dive-suit style body armour. Ben reasoned that it must be pretty light weight, hi-tech material, to allow Sven the agility he clearly had, and that would not have come cheap.

Sven wore dark goggles on his balaclava, and Ben wouldn't be surprised if they were wi-fi enabled, feeding him with data. Nothing Sven wore looked standard issue. Not even his gloves or boots. If the kit was custom made, this had to be someone who loved their DC and MCU comics and films. This showdown scene would have been laughable if Ben hadn't seen all the case material. Interestingly Sven didn't appear to be carrying a weapon. That said, he couldn't see Sven's back.

'Okay Sven, is there an easier way down from here than a drain pipe?'

Sven didn't even shrug.

Ben turned away, heading towards the drainpipe he had climbed up, hoping this non-threatening gesture would encourage Sven to follow.

It didn't.

Ben turned, starting to feel exasperated again. 'Look, I get this *moody silence* is your *thing*,' he emphasised with air quotes, 'but we really need to move past this.'

Still no response.

'Oh…Maybe I'm being stupid here. Maybe you *can't* talk. *Of course…*' Ben tried to recall the sign language he had been taught in the negotiation skills class, and signed 'Are you coming?'

Sven returned the international hand sign 'wanker'.

Ben wondered for a moment if he had mistakenly signed 'cumming'.

Whatever. He had had enough. He strode up to Sven and attempted to take him by the wrist. Ben would throw Sven off the roof to get him down if he had to. With that kit on, he shouldn't be too dented.

What followed began like some surreal dance. Ben found that the harder he pulled or pushed the less control he seemed to have. Sven moved beside him like a fluid machine, eerily soundless as if no effort were required. By the time Ben considered it might be Aikido or Tai Chi he was on his back, then he was flipped onto his front with his arm twisted up and back, and his wrist put in a painful lock. Definitely Aikido. He winced.

'Okay, okay!...Let me try something else...What do *you* want?'

Sven's only answer was to release the hand and step back.

Ben got back up, massaging his sprained wrist. He had tried to be nice about it, now it seemed rougher action was required. He stepped forwards slowly, feigning the beginning of another request.

'Can we just...' he lashed out with a lightening roundhouse punch which was supposed to make contact just below Sven's left ear and render him unconscious, except his head was no longer there.

Ben received a kick in the stomach for his troubles, knocking the wind out of him followed by a punch to the face. Ben heard his nose crack. The pain flooded into his head like white hot steel. He could taste the iron in it, but forced himself to focus through the cloud of pain. He was used to what came with fighting rough.

Ben went into a spinning back kick, looking to knock the wind out of Sven with his extra reach, which should give him time to get his own wind back. It was not possible to fight efficiently if oxygen couldn't get to the muscles.

Another problem that prevented a person fighting properly was finding that their opponent was so fast they could step into the back kick, block up against the knee and drive an elbow into the genitals.

This pain was worse than the blow to the nose. Ben felt a dreadful cold nausea, his body going into shock. He had to fight it off. There was no air coming to him. Sven looked untouched. Silently dancing circles round him. Most people made some noise when fighting. Was Sven even breathing? Was Sven actually Dawn? No, he was sure she would have spoken cryptically by now.

Ben refused to believe Sven wasn't human, that he didn't have a weakness. He just needed to find out what it was, before it was too late.

Air rushed back into Ben's lungs with an involuntary gasp.

Ben reflected that each time he had thought Sven was cornered it had just proved to be Ben falling for a set-up. Ben looked around. Was there something *he* could use to his advantage? Of course, the emergency button on his phone.

He slowly reached into his pocket.

'Don't worry Sven, I'm not going for a gun. I just want to…'

In a blur Sven lunged forward and kicked the phone clean out of Ben's hand and over the edge.

'What the bloody fucking fuck is your problem?!' Ben flew at Sven punching and kicking without pulling his blows, the whole *bring him in alive* brief forgotten and the life he possibly owed him.

Sven blocked every blow with ease, delivering close quarter attacks with knees and elbows, which left Ben with dead-arms and dead-legs and bruises to add to his collection of bites.

Finally, Ben couldn't control his limbs anymore. He collapsed. This he knew was when the killing blow would come, when he, the aggressor, was totally humiliated. Ben thought of Meg, Robbie and Beth.

Sven just watched.

Ben tried to reason what was going through Sven's mind. If he was not going to kill Ben, what was being achieved here?

A hazy sort of dawning occurred to Ben.

'Oh I get it. I'm supposed to be your *messenger*! I'm to go back to Five, beaten with my tail between my legs, to tell them to leave you alone. That's why you've been setting me up instead of taking me out. *I'm the fall guy.*'

Sven turned, and almost soundlessly, ran to the edge of the roof and jumped.

'But I'm no quitter Sven!' Ben growled, struggling to his feet to go after the vigilante.

At the end of the roof Ben discovered Sven had jumped onto a fire-escape. He saw Sven running up through the school grounds towards the estate at the back.

Ben took the same route down. His body ached with the damage done to it, but he pushed on through the pain barrier. There would be no giving up while he had control of his body.

Off the fire-escape he half strode half-jogged across the school grounds spotting a gate ahead, connected to an alley. He caught a glimpse of Sven turning left at the end of the alley as he reached the start.

Pushing his every fibre to go faster, he was almost gagging on the pain. He made it to the end of the alley in time to see Sven enter the front gate of a house further up the road on the other side.

Crossing over he bounded after him, knowing he needed a plan for what to try next *if* he could catch Sven up. He looked around for inspiration as he closed in, also trying to second guess Sven. He was probably going to go straight down the side of the semi-detached house through the back garden and into a back alley to make his escape. Ben referred to his memorised map as he arrived at the front gate. There was no back alley to these houses.

There was a sudden roar of an engine and something dark was racing towards him. It was all happening too fast. It couldn't be a car. He was on the foot path. Then the answer hit him and he went spinning into the road. It was a bike.

He stopped rolling and turned in time to see Sven vanish down the road. Ben did manage to catch sight of the number plate though and he smiled.

So *this* is where Sven has been living. Ben staggered back to his feet. He felt wrecked. He rubbed his mouth with the back of his hand and saw blood on it, probably from his nose. He would need to straighten that out pretty quickly.

He went back to the house and up to the front window. Looking at his reflection rather than the dark interior of the front room, he realigned his nose bone and cartilage with an audible click and received another face-full of white hot metal.

Then he tried the door. It was locked and there seemed no point in knocking. He went round the back but decided this was a job for someone else, in the morning.

He headed slowly back to the school to look for his phone. If it was still working he would report in with a rather more upbeat version of the night's events.

19

Ben showered then checked himself out in the mirror. The curved rows of puncture marks had already closed up. However, the bruising looked bad. He massaged his aching muscles before making a mental note to try sleeping on his front despite his ribs.

He fell asleep quickly and stayed that way till he was brought out of it by his alarm. He couldn't remember what day it was at first.

'Friday,' he announced after some thought. He brought a hand to his bruised and achy face and tested his nose. It was the right shape and angle but it was a good thing his shift was the mid-afternoon into evening one, as it would give his wounds more time to heal. He felt like he had been hit from every direction over the last couple of days.

However, the drone batteries would now be charged and that meant this evening was going to be payback time.

Ben had not been long in the store when a tall thin man in a shooting jacket dropped by. He spoke with an accent that suggested great wealth.

'My dear man, I do hope you can help. It's been quite tiresome but I have been absolutely everywhere locally and your shop is my last chance.'

'I'll do my very best sir.'

He smiled hopefully, peering behind Ben at the spirits shelving. 'I've been to Tesco, Waitrose, M&S, Nisa, and the Co-op. I just want a 70cl bottle of Jura single malt scotch whisky.'

Ben reached behind him 'You're in luck. We have one.'

Taking a closer look the man remarked 'Oh how tiresome. Do you have it in a different shaped bottle?'

'No.'

'Pity.' With that he was about to leave but turned back with another thought. 'You wouldn't happen to sell something called Liquid Crystal would you?'

Ben began to wonder whether this guy was for real, or some sort of wind-up. 'Liquid Crystal?'

'Yes I heard from a friend of a friend that it is my daughter's wedding, near here, tomorrow morning, and that if I absolutely insisted on going along uninvited I should get hold of something called Liquid Crystal.'

'Oh let me see. I'll have to check in the cupboard if we have a bottle.' Ben turned to open a cupboard behind the counter, playing along.

'Good god man, I can't be having it at room temperature. Whatever next? Don't you have a fridge?'

'Well yes but that's full of chocolate, on account of the heat,' he lied.

'Yes, yes, of course. Well another time then.' The man left Ben shaking his head and wondering if there was something in the water in this area, and whether he might already be too far gone himself.

A young woman Ben recognised as Claire came in and straight to the counter. She always wanted Marlboro cigarettes but switched between the types she asked for.

Before she could say anything Ben asked in a flirty manner, 'Are we touching or going for gold today?'

'Twenty Touch please, Chance. You seem in a good mood.'

'Yeah?...Maybe it's something in the water.'

'Oh I do hope so,' she chuckled.

After Claire had left he noticed a woman crossing the forecourt. She had an odd way of walking, like she was trying to cross her legs, or had some form of hip-dysplasia. She was clutching her mobile and muttering constantly.

Entering the store she inquired, 'Mind if I use your loo? I'm fit to explode.'

'Yes, just there,' Ben pointed to the door just outside, labelled *Toilet*.

'Thanks,' she staggered out and round.

No sooner had the woman disappeared into the toilet than those in the shop could hear the very things the woman might have hoped to conceal.

'What the fuck do you bloody arse-wipe morons think you are fuckin doing?!! Texting me yet again, while I'm out for a walk, to tell me that I have to wait another fucking couple of months for my fuckin hip operation!! I bet it's because you've got some fuckin queue-jumping rich twat slipping you a back-hander or fuckin three!! I have half a mind to come down there and kick the living shit out of you fuckers!!'

Ben wondered whether that was Celia's mother. He stepped round to the kitchen and enquired of Rosie, who simply nodded.

Later on Harry dropped by to check the shop's turnover, carelessly chucking his car keys down.

'I'm glad you came in Harry. I wanted a word about holiday.'

'Oh mmm holiday.'

'I was just wondering about having a few days off.'

'Well I don't think you have worked here long enough to have earned any holiday, Chance.'

'Okay well it doesn't have to be paid leave. It would just be for a few days, like I said.'

'Oh I don't know. You see that's when *I* was planning on being away.'

'I haven't said when I want off yet!'

'Well it's just that it's a difficult time of year for staff to have holidays, at the moment.'

'At the moment?'

'Yes, yes, you know, between Christmas and urr…Christmas.'

'No worries.' Ben tried to hold his cool. There was more than one way to skin a cat, he thought. 'I'll sort it another way.'

'Good…Now I've got to get to the bank, though I seem to have mislaid my car keys.' He started looking among the invoices left in different piles behind the counter. Not remembering what he had done with them he thought it worth checking the filing cabinet. With no luck he grew more irritated.

An old lady approached the counter. Ben watched her peering at the sweets closely, clearly quite short sighted, with her glasses on the top of her head. 'Are *these* Yorkies?!'

'No you blind bat!' Snapped Harry 'That's bars of chocolate.'

'There's no need to speak to me like that young man. I shall be writing to my local MP, with a nice cup of tea.'

'You'd be better off using a pen,' Harry returned to his search.

'A cup of tea?' Ben asked in an attempt to defuse the conversation.

'Yes, yes. Keeps me calm when people like you lot wind me up and get me all upperty!'

'Well it'll take more than a cup of tea to calm *me* down.' Harry threw back at her. 'I need to get to the bank and I can't find my car keys.'

'Well if these disorganised sweets are anything to go by it's no wonder you can't find anything.'

When the woman had gone Harry mumbled 'Upperty Cuppa tea cow.'

Ben turned then pointed at a box of sweets stacked under the table behind the counter.

Harry looked at where Ben was pointing. 'What the hell...What are the keys doing there, Chance? I never put them there!'

After Ben had put the unsold papers out for collection and locked up the store he went to the Quarryman's Arms. Mikey and the usual suspects were in. Ben went to the bar and ordered a tonic water ice and lemon.

'And what are you havin?' asked Gloria.

'That *is* mine.'

'Oh I thought it was Jill's.'

'She might be along later. I'm going to be driving.'

'Takin her anywhere nice?'

'Urr no.'

She exploded with laughter. 'So you're taking her somewhere horrid?'

'No. I'll be out doing photography tonight.' He made no mention of the drone.

'Won't it be a bit dark then?' she handed him his drink. 'One eighty.'

'Exactly.' Ben searched through the change he had in his pocket.

'Yes. Exactly one pound eighty.'

Ben single-handedly passed her the coins without saying a word in case she laughed again.

'Isn't that right?!' Mikey called across.

Ben turned to see Mikey was looking at him, along with those listening.

'What's that then?'

'I told them I was in the shop looking at the ingredients and cooking instructions on the back of a frozen pizza, and I came across to you and said "I have a question," and before I could ask it you said "Pizza boy's name".'

The small crowd laughed, but Ben wasn't really in the mood for Mikey. 'So what was the question?'

'What?'

'What were you going to ask me about the pizza?'

'Oh urr, I can't remember now,' he turned back to the others as Ben headed out the door.

It was a nice evening, and even nicer that Cedric wasn't on the bench outside the door. So Ben decided to sit there. He wasn't there long before Jill came along. Ben greeted her with 'Tonic water ice and lemon?'

'Sure, but I'll get it,' she went inside.

When Gloria exploded he found himself wondering what Jill might have said, then she was out and sitting next to him.

'So how was your day, Chance?'

'Oh, run of the mill. Yours?'

'Well I finished the article I was working on, you'll be pleased to hear.'

'Great.'

'So I was wondering whether you asked Harry about taking some time off?'

'Well I did…'

'And…?'

'He said I wasn't due any yet, because of not working there long enough.'

'But you suggested you could take unpaid holiday, didn't you?'

'Sure but he suggested it was never a good time for the staff to take holiday.'

'What an arse.'

'I know right. It would have been good to get away, just the two of us. I'll have to work on him.'

'Yeah, you do that. Grind him down.'

'Ha,' it sounded to Ben like Jill was suggesting violence.

At the sound of heels on cobbles they both looked up to see Veronica looking smartly dressed, as usual.

Ben almost asked her what she was doing there but kept his cool.

Veronica stopped in front of them with a large bag slung over her shoulder. 'I've been trying to ring you.'

Ben patted his trouser pocket. 'I left my mobile at home.'

'We've got to go, or we'll be late to the hotel.'

'What?' Ben looked from Veronica to Jill and back again, wondering what Aussie was playing at.

'Don't say you forgot?'

'Forgot what?'

'You made me a promise,' she said milking the act with a pout.

'When?'

'The other week…Come on, I've got the whole weekend sorted.'

Ben was speechless. He couldn't go off with Aussie when he had just told Jill he couldn't get time off to be with her. What could he say that would excuse such a thing? Jill wouldn't want anything to do with him after this. He tried to think fast.

'I wondered why you weren't holding a Guinness?' Jill sounded hurt.

'What? No. I was going to be driving.'

'Yes. Driving me,' insisted Veronica. 'Come on sweetie, let's go. Please! I got here as soon as I could.'

Ben was gritting his teeth with the awkwardness. Aussie was certainly working her ticket, for maximum damage. He slammed his drink down on the table to the side of the bench in exasperation and stood up.

'Bye,' Veronica gave a very catty little wave to Jill.

'I'll call you.' Ben offered Jill.

'With what?'

'I'll get the phone.'

'Oh don't bother.'

'Thanks for that Aussie,' he said catching her up.

'Anytime,' she clicked the remote on his car, parked at the side of the pub.

'Where's your car?'

'On your drive.'

'But how...?'

'I have spare keys for your car and house, remember, as your handler. Now drive,' she threw him his keys, which she had picked up from the house.

'I need to go back to the house for my phone and some fresh clothes.'

'I've packed all you need. It's in the boot.'

'The phone?'

'Still in the house I guess,' she shrugged.

Ben growled as he opened the driver's door, seeing Veronica get into the back. 'Why are you sitting back there? Afraid I might *hit* you?'

'Not at all. I have a ton of work to do on the way down.'

'Where are we going?'

'Birmingham.'

'Birmingham?!' Ben pulled so hard on the seat belt it locked before he could click it home. This just frustrated him further and he growled again.

Veronica smoothly clipped her belt home then reached into the bag for her laptop. 'Yes this op is on hold for the moment.'

'No! You can't do that. I'm so close to getting Sven. This evening I was...'

'Forget it. You did good though getting that number plate.'

'But...?' Ben finally connected the belt and started the car.

'It turns out to be one of ours.'

'A Section 13 plate?'

'No, but still a *Five* plate. So we are having to check all black ops going on with other sections before we know what we are to do next with Sven.'

'What the *hell*?' Ben turned the corner and seeing Jill was still there he gave an apologetic wave but she didn't wave back.

20

Ben was silent most of the way to the M6. Veronica refused to have the radio on so the only sound above the engine was her nails tapping the keypad.

Ben had spent some time trying to think of a credible reason for this trip which Jill might believe.

He considered saying that Aussie was in fact his Mentoring Handler. Also, that the trip was a rapid response to one of his mentees, a known flight risk, running away. Plus there were concerns over a possible suicide attempt. He had to help find the lad and talk him round to coming back to his carers and of course schooling.

That didn't sound half bad, he thought. It just didn't fit with Aussie's act, which had suggested, this was more like a fun weekend away for two. Unless he could convince Jill that that was just Aussie trying to cover up what was a confidential mercy mission. It might work. Then again it might not. Jill didn't come across to him as anyone's fool.

'Aussie?'

'Hang on. Let me finish this.'

Ben waited a bit. 'Done?'

'No.'

'Stuck on a *word* maybe?'

'No. I'm trying to get this report finished.'

'Can I borrow your phone?'

'No you're driving.'

'I was going to pull into a layby.'

'You haven't got time.'

'Oh come on, it won't take *that* long.'

'Yes it will. You are going to try and explain to that fuckwit why you are off with me rather than her. As if there wouldn't be an obvious reason, to anyone with eyes in their head. Then because she's a fuckwit it's going to go badly. It'll turn into an argument which will become a protracted one because you are so bull-headed that you won't leave it be. I'm doing you a favour Ben.'

'Doesn't feel that way to me. Feels more like you screwed things up on purpose. What was with all that sulky act, suggesting we had a weekend away planned?'

'Cover.'

'You've certainly covered me in shit. I doubt Jill will talk to me again.'

'I know right...Which is why you don't need a phone...You can thank me later.'

This wasn't helping Ben's frustration, so he decided to try changing the subject. 'Did anyone check out the address I reported in, before that plate number put a hold on things?'

'Yes. It belongs to a Robert Pearce.'

'Is that Sven's real name?'

'Only if Sven is a thirty stone couch potato in his spare time.'

'What?'

'Turns out Mr Pearce is one of those many Facebook idiots who posts up his holiday details in real-time. Letting everyone and their dog see when their property is unoccupied. Sven will have found or been given this information for a safe parking space for his bike.'

'So the bike is the only real clue.' He began to think if only the techies had supplied charged batteries for the drone so he could have used it immediately and brought Sven in by now.

However, he'd probably have had to carry the can for compromising someone else's op then. Inter-departmental communication at *Five* was crap at times. 'So what are we going to be doing down in Birmingham?'

'Will you just let me finish this damn report? I'll brief you when I'm done, as long as you promise to shut up and let me complete the next two in peace.'

'Okay, okay.'

Veronica passed him a lead.

'What's this?'

'The laptop battery is getting low. I need you to plug the cable into the USB socket.' Her tone was very condescending.

'Tell me Aussie. Are you like this with everyone?'

'Only those I consider to be my *tools*.'

He glanced at her over his shoulder and wondered if a damn good spanking wouldn't soften that nasty girl image she seemed to work so hard at.

Heading south on the M6 Ben began to slow, to pull onto the slip road for the Lancaster services.

'What are you doing?'

'I need a pee.'

'No you don't. Keep going. The only P you're after is P for Pay Phone.'

Ben grumbled under his breath.

'Forget about her. I really don't see what you see in her. You do realise you are punching way below your weight.'

'Am I now? We seem to have a connection.'

'Connection, ha.'

'Yeah. She intrigues me. She's a journalist you know.'

'What the *fuck* are you doing looking to hook up with a journalist of *all* people?'

'It's not *because* she's a journalist. She's a good person.'

'Oh well, *there you go then*, she's *definitely* not right for you in that case.'

'What's that supposed to mean?'

'Look, tomorrow morning you'll be meeting Gina Oakley. She'll keep you occupied.'

'If I wanted a dating agency I'd have gone online.'

'Don't be a prick Ben. Oakley is ex-Five. A private detective working for Devereux-Norton Associates. We are considering bringing her into Section 13.'

'I think I've heard of her...Isn't she the one they call the Super-Jinx...created that massive crater they have down in the Chilterns?'

'One and the same.'

'Why *the hell* are we getting involved with *her*?!'

'I've just got this concluding paragraph to finish then I'll explain.'

Ben exhaled loudly. Maybe Oakley was Aussie's idea of payback, he thought. Ben tried to remember what else he had heard about

Oakley. There was something about an uncanny intuition, as if she had some other-worldly tap into situational information not available to others.

Veronica closed the laptop and placed her hands on top. 'So, Oakley has come across what she believes to be one of these Serious Organised Vigilante black van abduction teams she's crossed paths with before. They appear to be operating out of an industrial unit in Birmingham.'

'Where do *we* fit into this?'

'I've been asked to stand in while her handler is away.'

'Hold on. You said she was *ex-Five*.'

'Officially, yes, because she is something of a jinx. Nevertheless, she occasionally connects on ops that *Five* would rather consider deniable.'

'I see. So I'm there to ensure things don't go wrong.'

'No. You're just along for the ride.'

'*Along for the ride*?!'

'You need to up your game, Ben, if you're going to keep on my *good* side. Consider this next couple of days as a bit of re-skilling.'

'And I guess we are just bringing these guys in for questioning.'

'We have suspicions that they may be an all-female team. But yes bringing them in alive, plus the person or persons they have abducted.'

Oh well, Ben thought, since he was not allowed to chase down Sven for the moment, this could be a bit of fun. 'You did explain to Harry didn't you?'

'Harry?'

'My boss. He'll need to know I won't be opening up in the morning.'

'No worries. It's all sorted.'

'Really? He seemed pretty adamant that I couldn't have any time off.'

'I've told you, I've sorted things...There's been a bit of a *fire*.'

'*What?!*'

'Ben I'm, what is it that you say, *pissing you*,' she laughed, and opened the laptop back up. Conversation over.

Ben fumed. He wondered if he could prank her back. Like the pranks he used to pull with his Admissions lads. Wipe that plastic smile off her face.

He looked in the rear-view mirror and could see she was concentrating on her next report. Then he noticed a single head-light some way behind them; a bike head-light.

After checking in at the hotel and getting into the lift Ben was looking forward to putting things straight with Jill using the phone in the room. He hoped his cover story worked and it didn't turn into the argument that Aussie had predicted it would.

'Look Ben,' Veronica's tone softened, 'I know I've scuppered things between you and Jill, so let me make it up to you and buy you a beer or two in the bar.'

Well, he guessed, that was the least she could do. 'Okay I'll be there in ten.'

'Don't ring her.'

'What?'

'Just leave it be. That's an order.'

Ben said nothing. The lift doors opened on their floor and they went to their separate rooms.

Ben wasted no time unpacking. He picked up the phone from the bedside table and called Jill's mobile. It rang and rang and went to voicemail. She probably knew it was him and was ignoring his call.

'Hi Jill. I'm sorry. I just wanted to explain. Now that I know what's going on. I'll call again later.' He couldn't very well say he wouldn't be staying by the phone because he was going to be downstairs drinking with Aussie.

Ben sat at the bar for some time waiting, and had made a head start with a couple of lagers before Veronica came down. She had changed out of her suit into a sequin dress for some reason.

'Nice dress.' Ben couldn't help his honesty.

'Glad you like it...What are you drinking?'

'Peroni thanks.'

Veronica turned to the barman. 'Another two Peroni, please.'

'A pint and a half?'

'*A half*? What do you take me for you flaming drongo. I'm an *Aussie*. So that'll be two pints.'

She took the stool in front of Ben her knees coming into contact with his. She looked at his remaining third of a pint. 'Feeling more relaxed now?'

'A little.'

'Good. We're *off duty* now.'

'Right.'

Veronica adjusted her dress and the side split revealed a thigh which she pretended not to notice, as she side-flicked her head, tossing her long hair over a shoulder.

The drinks arrived and she thanked the barman giving him her room number with a look that made it clear that was only for the tab.

'So how long have you been working for *Five*, Aussie?'

'Two years.'

'Two?'

'I hadn't intended to get into this line of work. I started out trying to get into film and TV. I did my acting degree in Brisbane, and I guess I was full of myself. After all, I thought, with my looks and charm who wouldn't want me in front of a camera right? But I was getting nowhere. I came to the UK believing my chances would improve across here, but surprisingly not.

'I did some temping for a while serving food and drinks at events for the rich and famous. Then one day at one of the events there was a terrorist bombing.

'I wasn't hurt because I was in the kitchen at the time getting the next order. However, a lot of people were badly injured, and some were killed, including a close friend of mine. I decided I wanted to do something about it and went online the next day after giving my statement to the police, and found you could apply for jobs at MI5.

'After the interview and vetting process I was sent for training. It felt good to actually be wanted for something so I studied hard.'

'Well if it's any consolation Aussie, I'd have watched you.'

'Thanks but that's all behind me now...Let's not talk about work,' she placed a hand on his knee.

Ben finished his second pint and picked up the fresh one Veronica had bought him.

Veronica moved her hand up his leg as if to steady herself as she leaned in closer. 'It is incredible to think you've only just had a broken nose among other injuries and there isn't even any bruising left now.'

'I thought we weren't going to talk about work.'

'No, I'm not. It's just I've never slept with anyone who is physically perfect before.'

'What?'

'I'm just putting that out there,' she batted her eyelashes before taking another mouthful of Peroni.

Looking down at the still moving hand on his leg Ben ventured, 'Isn't this sexual harassment?'

'What, and asking if I was going to watch while you got undressed in that cell wasn't?'

'Touché...I thought you had forgotten about that.'

'Oh no. I wouldn't forget *that*.'

Ben could see where this was headed. Aussie was looking to get him into bed to make sure there was no way back to Jill. But then was he such a man of principles?

The lads would say he was going soft if they heard he was giving up his chance with Veronica. Was he actually *in* a relationship with Jill? Weren't they just *friend-zoned*? Yet sleeping with Aussie would feel like cheating on Jill.

Even if he didn't sleep with Aussie, would Jill believe him, after he had said he couldn't get any time off? No, no, he thought, he'd have to be a prick to do that to Jill, even if she hadn't answered his call. Who was he kidding, he *was* a prick. Even Aussie said he was.

As if she could read the thoughts running through his mind, Veronica leaned in further and kissed Ben softly on the lips. He didn't pull away.

21

What was in front of Ben now? Whatever it was, it made disturbing reading.

Ben made himself stop and think for a moment.

'This is a trap!'

Veronica nodded.

'Just keep calm. Control your breathing. I'm going to get you out.'

He couldn't risk trying the door handle till he knew more about the device. He bent down to start checking over his car, and spotted the bomb straight away. It was under the chassis directly below the driver's seat.

Ben wouldn't be able to get his head under the car to check the device's status, even if he took his helmet off. He reached into his belt pouch and brought out a mirror. Stretching an arm under the car he confirmed the device was in a casing with no wires leading out of it. So it wasn't connected to the ignition or door handle. But it likely had a mercury trip switch so it couldn't be removed. It clearly had a timer too, and they now had less than two minutes on its display.

Ben had a dreadful sense of déjà vu. Not just the sleep-reading, but something that had once happened to his mate Adam's girlfriend, and that had not turned out well.

No time to lose Ben got up grabbed the door handle and pulled but it was locked. He turned his HK MP7 round and hammered at the window with the butt. However, this was a customised vehicle with bullet-proof glass.

Veronica, panting through her gag, stared at Ben with terrified eyes.

'What the hell Ben!' Veronica shook him awake.

'Ugh, oh. Sorry. Bad dream.'

'PTSD?'

'Possibly. Possibly something else.'

'Something *else*?'

Ben wondered about confiding in Aussie about the dreams he had been having since the treatment. 'Yeah, it's nothing.'

After Ben finished his full English and Veronica her continental she took a turn in the driving seat, taking them to the address Gina Oakley had provided them.

Sitting in the passenger seat Ben kept watch on his wing mirror. He thought he had seen a black motorbike following them, half a dozen cars back but then it was gone. Maybe that weird dream had made him paranoid.

'You seem a bit quiet this morning, Ben.'

'I have my moments.' He had tried ringing Jill from the phone in Veronica's room when she was busy in the shower but it had gone to voicemail again. Jill was definitely ignoring him, he conceded, and who could blame her?

'Thinking about last night?' Veronica enquired. 'I know *I am*, and looking forward to the second act.'

'Aren't we on duty now?'

'Sure sweetie, but until we rendezvous with Gina, I thought we could indulge in some *polite conversation*.' She moved a hand from the gear stick to his knee.

Maybe *polite conversation* was some Aussie euphemism. What was her game, he wondered. Was it just an act? Ben had to be honest, he found Aussie very sexy, though more than a little nuts.

Veronica pulled into Gina's road but Ben wasn't looking ahead for the house number. That was Veronica's department. He was keeping a trained eye on the wing mirror. Sure enough as they pulled up outside Gina's house Ben glimpsed a black motorbike pass the end of the road, doing less than twenty miles per hour, its rider looking their way.

Why would Sven have followed them here? Ben wondered. He knew it didn't make sense. If it was a *Five* op that Sven was assigned to, then surely he would have to stay up north. There was only one sensible conclusion to draw, Ben decided, they had picked up a new tail. As soon as he had solid proof he would inform Aussie.

'Are you coming?'

Ben turned realising that Veronica was already out of the car.

Together they went up the empty drive to the front door and Veronica rang the bell then took a step back and squeezed Ben's ass.

What was she doing? He wondered. Trying to throw him off guard and make him look the fool as Gina opened the door?

A man answered it.

'Hi. I'm Veronica Coultard and this is Ben McGregor, we're here to see Gina.'

'Oh hi, I'm Will Norton. My wife is running a bit late but should be back anytime soon. She said to expect you. Do come in.'

They were ushered into the lounge.

'Gina went out paintballing again with Ethan.'

'Your son?' asked Veronica.

'No. Gina's mentee.'

'Right.'

'Between you and me, I think she should be taking him to yoga classes or getting him into, I don't know, allotment gardening. Or something else calming, rather than hiking and running with heavy packs on his back and paintballing. He's a rather...urr...*aggressive* young lad.'

'Maybe she's trying to channel the aggression to develop his control,' Ben offered.

'He wants to make selection for the SAS when he's old enough.'

'Does he? He should keep training then.'

'That's what she says.' Then Will frowned. 'It's just he's a bit *disturbed*, that's all I'm saying.'

'We all have our *demons*, Will.' Veronica suggested then looked at Ben.

Ben returned a quizzical look.

Will looked from one to the other, sensing something was going on between his two guests. 'A cup of tea or coffee maybe?'

'Coffee please,' Ben replied.

'We'll both have a tea thanks.'

'*Oh-kay*.' Will turned away for the kitchen.

'What was *that* all about?'

'Sorry Ben, but I don't want you getting hyper when you've got a busy day ahead.'

'*Hyper*? I've only had one coffee for breakfast.'

'I know but I just…'

'Just what?'

Will returned looking from one to the other. 'Do you take milk and sugar?'

'We'll have milk but no sugar.'

'Right.' Will gave Veronica the nod and turned away, sensing a growing awkwardness.

'Just what?' Ben repeated.

'I just need to see you…doing whatever I say.'

'In that case I think we have a problem, Aussie. You're a control freak.'

Veronica tried to lighten the mood. 'That's Control Freak Boss to you.'

There came the sound of a key in the front door then it opened and Gina swept in. She looked like she had been dragged through a hedge backwards. Exposed areas were mud and paint spattered, suggesting the paintballing overalls and goggles had been in a worse state. Ben was struck by how orange her curly hair was. Then he remembered hearing that she had, or used to have, a nickname of some drink that wasn't around any longer, what was it? Orangina.

'Sorry I'm late folks. I had to have some serious words with Ethan today. Paintballing really is only about using strategy and stealth to take out the opponents with the paintballs. The rules don't allow for booby traps, martial arts, and sling-shot rocks. He should know that by now. He's already got us banned from two venues. He just gets a bit carried away. Like some of his opponents, ha…I shouldn't joke.'

Ben looked uncertain as to whether Gina was just playing with words, that some opponents had to be carried off the field, or that the whole anecdote was just a wind-up.

'No worries.' Veronica waved it aside.

'Anyway, can I get you both a drink?'

'Will's got that all in hand.'

'He's good like that. Look, I'm just going to grab a quick shower and change then we can be on our way.'

Gina sat up front while Ben drove and Veronica dealt with emails from the back seat. Between directions from Gina, Ben asked her about her experiences with *Five* and since. It sounded to Ben like she was yet another agent who should have been treated better than she was.

After that conversation topic had run its course Ben pressed on something more personal. 'I've heard it said that you have some sort of super-intuition.'

'I wouldn't go as far as to consider it a *superpower*, and *having* also suggests being in control of it. It feels more like creative guess-work that so far has proven correct. A bit like how some authors say they hear or see their stories as if someone else is telling or showing them what to write.'

'I see. So does it come to you as sights *and* sounds?' Ben was debating whether to say something about his sleep-reading. Gina may have some insight into that but for some reason Ben wasn't comfortable about sharing that little gem while Aussie was in the car, in case she insisted he go for further mental health assessment.

'It always seems to come as visual knowledge, like seeing through a fog to the recent past or near future.'

Ben nodded. He could relate to the fog that he had to struggle to read through. But why did he have to read rather than see images. 'Have you always been like that?'

'As far back as I can remember but I don't get them frequently, and certainly not on demand.'

'So there wasn't something that happened when you were a child that kicked it all off?'

'What like touching a meteor, or being shat on by a wise old owl?'

'Ha.'

'Not that I recall…Why the interest?'

Ben looked over his shoulder. Veronica seemed focused on her emails, unless she was making notes of their conversation. He shrugged. 'Oh, just curious.'

There was another long pause then Gina said, 'So you're curious about the super-intuition, but not about the super-jinx, interesting.'

'Well I didn't think you would want to talk about something so *negative*.'

'To be honest it's more of an issue for other people. Shit happens, usually to others in my proximity, and often in my favour.'

'Like that ship sinking and the crater in the Chilterns?'

'Well I accidentally got peoples backs up for those incidents, I admit. I've been told I'm a loose cannon. But when there's no other option what can you do? I had to stop a terrorist leaving the country on his ship. And that crater, well that was just down to not fully understanding the security system I was dealing with, because my super-intuition wasn't helping.'

'Meta-interference.'

'What?'

'Oh just a phase I picked up from someone. I believe it means that it wasn't going to turn out any other way.'

'Right.'

'So, in short, you're telling me to watch my back working with you?'

'Well let's say you certainly don't want to get on my wrong side.'

With Gina's final directions it brought them to an abandoned industrial estate that looked like it was about to be demolished. While Ben could have driven there guided by the sat-nav it wasn't Standard Operating Procedure to use it during an op in case it was hacked into and they were tracked.

Ben had the distinct feeling they were being tracked anyway. If he had a spare moment with Aussie and Gina out of the way he needed to check the car with the scanner stowed under the back seat.

Turning a corner Ben was surprised to see police cordon tape across the road but not as surprised as he was by the sound of an explosion. He drove straight through the tape.

'I was going to suggest you park up outside the area.' Gina apologised for not being quicker with her directions.

One industrial unit had smoke coming out of it.

Ben screeched to a halt, reached under his seat, activated his weapons case, took out his Glock, then was out of the door and running before Aussie could finish saying 'What the...' as she tried to stop her computer shooting of her lap.

Ben could hear gunfire and shouting coming from inside the unit. As he got closer, shifting the safety off his weapon, he could make out what was being shouted.

'Clear!'

'Clear!'

Ben returned the safety, as Gina and Aussie exited the car calling after him.

Four men in black came out of the smoke. The lead man looked at his watch before looking up and spotting Ben.

'Big Ben!' he called as he removed his gas mask.

'Disney! Good to see you, mate.'

The two men hugged.

'Real sorry to hear Tic didn't beat the clock-tower. How's Shins doing?'

'He's doing okay...He's with the Training Wing now.'

'Ha. Teaching the art of killing Cassowaries with your bare hands?'

'Ha, yeah he'll never live that one down. So how are you keeping these days?'

'Well after the shit hit the fan with all that stuff which Adam Underwood dragged me into, *Five* suggested they'd help me out if I helped them. So presently I'm a store assistant.'

'A store assistant?'

'Cover for a Section 13 op.'

'Right. The *thing* that's going pear-shaped.'

'I wouldn't say it was going pear-shaped. Rather there appears to have been some internal miscommunication.'

'Well I was told you needed to up your game by tagging along with us for some practice.' Disney pointed behind him. 'We've blown two units waiting for you bunch of tortoises to arrive. Got four left. Spare suits and weapons are round the corner there, in the Land Rovers, for you and Gina.'

'Isn't Aussie…I mean Veronica suiting up?'

'Yeah right.' Disney snickered, shaking his head. 'Miss Congeniality?'

'Sounds like you know about her.'

'Oh yeah…Come on get kitted up. I'll brief the six of us in ten, over there.'

Ben turned to see Gina standing behind him. 'I didn't hear you coming?'

'Yeah. And some people don't get the chance to tell me that.'

'So you're no stranger to this?' Ben asked as they headed round to the vehicles.

'After basic training I was on a number of missions with the SBS and a couple with the SAS.'

187

'Any preference?'

'Sure. The SBS.'

'Oh?'

'Because I look better in a wetsuit than one of these,' she said as she took the kit the quartermaster handed her.

22

Ben wasn't sure he'd seen Aussie go quite that shade of cross before, or was that her disappointment? She had clearly been expecting him to come back to her hotel room with her for Saturday night live entertainment, but he simply told her there was a *no sex before an op* rule.

She had stormed off to her room, probably to check whether that was really a thing. Incredulous that Ben could refuse a second night with her.

Ben took his chance and went down to the car. He lifted the back seat and took out the bug scanner. He got a reading as soon as he turned it on. The whole car gave the same reading. He switched to his left hand. The scanner calmed down. He swept the car inside and out. It was clean. Then he scanned his right hand. That was where the tracker was.

He felt the flesh between his thumb and index finger, the obvious place, but could feel nothing. He wondered if it might be implanted in a bone. He lifted his hand to his mouth. 'I don't know if you fuckers are listening to me as well as tracking me, but you now have a problem. I think Sven is tracking me with this.'

Ben returned to his room and tried calling Jill again, only to go to answer machine once more.

'Look Jill I'd rather have spoken to you but the fact is I've been asked to help track down one of my vulnerable young adults who's run away. Aussie is the handler that I mentioned. I don't know when I'll be back but hopefully soon. Oh and in case you are wondering about the things Aussie said when she came to get me. She said that was her idea of covering up. She doesn't know I've told you about the mentoring. I told her she has made things awkward between us and she says she's sorry. Okay, I'll call round when I get back.' Ben hung up.

Rather than feel better for getting that off his chest Ben felt worse for having lied and it didn't help to say that it went with the job. He did not get much sleep.

The next morning Ben rang Gina's doorbell while Veronica waited with the engine running. Gina was ready and came straight out.

'Ben.'

'Yeah?'

'I know we've planned this op the best we can considering the minimal information but take extra care today okay.'

'Sure.'

'I know you've been out of the Regiment for a while now and yesterday's practice will have been a bit of a warm-up, but things have changed. These SOV's are a tricky lot, using the latest technologies.'

'So we could find ourselves walking into a trap?'

'Anything's possible.' Gina opened the passenger door and got in behind Veronica.

'Thanks for the heads-up.' Ben sat in the front passenger seat and Veronica pulled away before he had the door closed. She was holding a grudge, he decided, as he clicked his belt home, prepared for more quiet treatment.

Gina lent forward so she could be heard above the over-revved engine. 'How are you this morning Veronica?'

'Quietly confident.'

Ben wished he felt the same. No one had called the op off after he had spoken to his hand but then why would Sven interfere with this op if he was a *Five* asset?

The target industrial site was very similar to the one they had practiced on yesterday. There were OPs set up to the front and rear of the identified unit. Disney, Ben and Gina lay on a flat roof, some way back from the edge overlooking the front of the unit. It had a large roller shutter vehicle door and a smaller shuttered entrance doorway. Both were electronically locked rather than padlocked, which made a prior check of interior layout and contents problematic.

Disney's three troopers, Mac, Cathay and Rubber manned the rear OP situated in bushes behind an eight foot metal-spiked fence. The rear of the unit had only one door, a fire escape, probably steel reinforced. The unit had no windows or skylights.

Informed by intelligence from Gina, Disney had held a *Chinese Parliament* with the whole team to develop their plan and discuss best OP positions and tactics, using images previously taken from a drone. The main site did not have much in the way of security cameras. However, the target unit did have a camera at the front and rear, guarding the doorways and their approach. When they did go in it would have to be with the Regiment's usual *Speed, Aggression and Surprise*.

That said, they had to remind themselves that this was a live extraction of abductors and abductee. Shots were not to be fired unless fired upon, and in that situation the aim would only be to disarm and immobilise. No double tapping.

The best way to achieve this was not to go in hot as soon as the black van appeared, when personnel were still likely to be wearing body armour and carrying weapons.

The unit was expected, from Gina's intelligence, to contain one or two sound-proofed prefab modules, used as film studios where the snuff movies, for sale via the Dark Net, were being filmed.

So the plan was to let the van enter the premises and the shutters close back down, then wait out for people to remove and stow their kit. They might remain in a state of readiness for the first ten minutes of return but then begin to relax. So the decision was to blast the front and rear doors simultaneously at thirteen minutes.

Ben inquired of Gina in a hushed voice. 'You didn't mention how you came across this abduction team, if that's what we have here. After all they have been very difficult to track down, like urban myths with little evidence of who they are.'

'We caught them on drone by chance…'

'We?'

'Well Ethan, actually, and…'

'Your mentee?'

'Yeah.'

'What were you doing involving a minor?'

'He's sixteen now.'

'Still…'

'And he has history…'

'That goes without saying as a mentee…'

'History with *these* people. He was abducted when he was fourteen.'

'I heard they only took adults with anti-social interests.'

'I'm not sure that's a strict rule. Anyway, they were observed taking someone from a park near here and Ethan and I tracked them.'

'So they operate any time of day, not just under cover of darkness.'

'Mostly at night but typically when least expected.'

Disney used his throat mic to give a sit-rep shared by the ear-buds. His report was followed by one from Mac. Both sit-reps were acknowledged by Veronica as their controller, sitting in Ben's car, tucked away out of sight. It was the closest of the three vehicles, looking most civilian.

The hours ticked by, slowly. Some of Ben and Disney's OPs had lasted weeks, never mind days. At least here they were not crawling with buzzing and biting insects.

Evening had arrived and with it the rumbles of tummies. Disney slowly and quietly offered round protein bars.

'I'd rather suffer the emptiness thanks Disney,' Gina softly declined.

'I'd rather eat a Boost, but go on then,' Ben reached out.

The bars had already had their wrappers removed then been rewrapped in cling-film to reduce noise, looking unpalatably like *hard routine* faecal waste parcels.

'Thanks a lot Disney.'

'So this op you've been pulled off of, Big Ben…'

'Put on hold.'

'Right…What's the problem?'

'You know I can't talk about it.'

'Not the details, sure.'

'I was sent to extract a vigilante from up north, only it would now seem that he could be terminating people for *Five*. And from first-hand experience, tracking and fighting this guy he seems to be SF trained.'

'You think he's *one of ours*?'

'Could be. But that would suggest that whoever is handling him believes the drug-running network he is bringing down is involved in funding terrorism.'

'Yeah, *Five* don't often tread on the National Crime Agency's toes over serious crime unless it *does* involve terrorism.'

'Maybe this Sven, as I refer to him, has made me a little paranoid but I think he has been…'

'Hold on. We have company.'

The three of them looked down the lane to where the vehicle sound was coming from just as a black van turned a corner and headed their way. The roller shutters of the target unit began to lift by remote even before the van had arrived.

'X-rays van has arrived, Control. It is now entering the unit...' Disney reported the vehicle's registration.

'Acknowledged. Over.'

The shutter was descending back down even as the van was passing under it, wasting no time. Yet there was no sense of speeding, no screeching of brakes. The whole thing was a smooth operation, suggesting it had possibly become routine.

'Unit now locked down, Control. Over.'

'Acknowledged. Wait out thirteen. Over.'

With all eyes-on and ears straining to hear anything happening inside, they heard nothing. No banter, no angry bravado, or cries for help.

The thirteen minutes felt more like half an hour.

'Blue team and red team you are clear to prepare entry. Over.'

Blue team rose from the roof with their Heckler & Koch MP7s, and in a fluid motion swung down over the edge and dropped to the ground.

Red team approached the rear security fence, threw a Kevlar mat onto the spikes and were over the eight foot fence with their weapons in seconds.

It only took seconds to reach the front and rear doors, apply the C4, remote detonator, step aside and report in.

'Blue team and red team you are green for go. Over.'

The two blasts came sounding like one, followed by two flash-bang stun grenades then the six masked figures were entering through the smoke to confront the scene inside, checking for trip wires or beams.

The van was spotted immediately, parked up round the back of a single porta-cabin. There was no one about though. Not a soul coming to check out the commotion, possibly because they were putting kit back on inside the porta-cabin.

Wasting no time Ben ran at the door to the porta-cabin yanked at the handle. It was locked. He shot out the lock. It was dark inside till he lobbed in a flash-bang. Entering the strobe-lit studio full of torture equipment, Ben followed by Disney and Gina found it empty.

'Check the van, and behind the cabin!' Ben yelled as he switched on his torch now that the stun grenade's strobe had died. He pressed on into the cabin checking anything that might conceal a person. There was nobody there. 'Clear!'

Ben came out to see the others standing behind the van, its doors open, looking at one another in disbelief.

'What *are* these people?' Ben called across to Gina, 'Fucking *Magicians*?!'

Gina pulled away her mask. 'Might as well be. I told you they were tricky.'

Suddenly she had a look in her eye, stripped off a glove and ran round to the front of the van. She placed a hand on the bonnet then went into a blur of motion with her torch looking over the concrete floor for something.

'What are you doing, Gina?'

Standing behind the van sweeping the floor with her torch beam, her only answer was 'Control. We need you to bring the car into the unit immediately. Over.'

There was no response.

'The unit must be blocking the signal, Ben. Go get the car.'

'What's going on, Gina?'

'That van is a clone decoy. It's cold. They've gone *underneath* the unit. There must be a pressure sensor over there to lift the floor up, or lower it.'

'Right.' Now he understood. 'Control, I'm coming across. Over.' He tried to contact Veronica again as he sprinted out the front door.

The vehicle shutter was being opened back up again as he ran up the lane and round the corner to the car. He knew something was wrong as soon as he saw it, and more importantly saw Veronica just sitting there.

Reaching the driver-side door there was a lot to take in.

Veronica couldn't move. Ben glanced into the back and forward into the foot-wells. The keys were gone from the ignition. Veronica's hands were bound to the steering wheel with cable-ties. Her ankles were similarly bound to the brake pedal. Her neck was held firmly to the stem of the headrest and she was gagged with the cloth used to wipe the windows.

Most disturbing of all was the plastic bag over her head. However, Ben could see it was still billowing with her breathing, secured round her throat by yet another cable-tie.

This had only just been done. His first thought was to open the door, but he looked over his shoulder, was he being watched? He looked back and noticed two small holes in the bag in front of Veronica's nostrils. The bag wasn't intended to kill her. *He was.*

Ben made himself stop and think for a moment.

'This is a trap!'

Veronica nodded.

'Just keep calm. Control your breathing. I'm going to get you out.'

He couldn't risk trying the door handle till he knew more about the device. He bent down to start checking over his car, and spotted the bomb straight away. It was under the chassis directly below the driver's seat.

Ben wouldn't be able to get his head under the car to check the device's status, even if he took his helmet off. He reached into his belt pouch and brought out a mirror. Stretching an arm under the car he confirmed the device was in a casing with no wires leading out of it. So it wasn't connected to the ignition or door handle. But it likely had a mercury trip switch so it couldn't be removed. It clearly had a timer too, and they now had less than two minutes on its display.

Ben had a dreadful sense of déjà vu. Not just the sleep-reading, but something that had once happened to his mate Adam's girlfriend, and that had not turned out well.

No time to lose Ben got up grabbed the door handle and pulled but it was locked. He turned his HK MP7 round and hammered at the window with the butt. However, this was a customised vehicle with bullet-proof glass.

Veronica, panting through her gag, stared at Ben with terrified eyes.

He pulled up his jacket and reached into his trouser pocket. He had the spare keys. He showed Veronica to help her relax then pressed the remote unlock.

There was no explosion as he opened the door but there was no time to waste even if the timer still had a minute or so left, they needed to get well clear. He took wire clippers from his belt and cut through the first of the plastic ties at Veronica's throbbing throat, then lifted the bag free.

As he pulled the gag loose Veronica shouted, 'Sven is…!'

23

It was all a confusion of light with distressed sounds and smells, a nightmarish mass of screaming struggling hell. There was furniture, food, drink, clothing and jewellery.

In that mass there was a Glock 5 and Heckler & Koch MP7, a Kawasaki Ninja and more, all being forced together in some pressurised dream sequence.

Ben's arms were so heavy, his vision was blurred, in fact he wasn't sure he was looking out of both eyes, and the ringing in his ears went on and on and on. But over that he could hear voices coming and going as if down a tube and under water. He couldn't seem to say or do anything though.

'Ben! Ben! Can you hear me?!'

'Medic!'

'You're going to be okay, mate.'

'Immediate air-evac required.'

Darkness returned, only to boil off with the deep thrumming approach of rotor blades.

'Massive trauma.'

'Stemming blood loss.'

'Possible multiple fractures.'

The downdraft from the AugustaWestland 109C. helicopter seemed to set the exposed areas of Ben's body on fire. The sensation only seemed to ease when he was loaded inside the aircraft's belly. He sensed Disney climbing in with him.

'I'm here mate.'

'Disney?' Ben finally forced what sounded like a whisper.

Disney leaned in closer to hear through Ben's mask which they had to keep in place because of the wire clippers.

'Where the *fuck* is the book?

Disney wasn't sure he'd heard right. 'Say again.'

'The book I'm supposed to be reading?'

'What book mate?'

The next few minutes, or was it days, was a confusing mishmash of consciousness or dream states, each becoming less surreal than the last until finally something made enough sense to be reality, possibly.

Ben was in bed, in a room he recognised as almost a home from home. He was back in the experimental regeneration clinic. He looked down the bed. He still seemed to be looking with only his left eye. His face felt bandaged. He tried moving his legs. They ached, but they moved. The only problem was he appeared to have no feet. He tried to pull the sheet back for a better view but his aching arms could only brush at the sheet with his bandages hands.

'*What the Fuck*?!' He tried to remember what had happened.

Ben kept waking with a craving for fish, especially tinned salmon with those crunchy bits of bone. He guessed his body was after calcium for bone development as well as protein. He didn't know what was in the drip he was connected to or in the food the nurses kept plying him with but it wasn't salmon. Maybe it was something better. Or maybe they were still learning what to do and he needed to tell them.

Some memory of Sunday was coming back to him.

There had been an explosion. But that timer couldn't have timed out. He knew things seemed to slow down when a person was in a life threatening situation but that would have slowed the timer too.

What did Aussie say to him...'Sven is...' What was Sven? ...Behind him? No, he'd have been caught in the blast too. People would have told him, wouldn't they? But then they had made no mention of Aussie yet, even when he'd asked after her. Maybe she was still critical and they couldn't say either way.

The bomb under the car and Aussie all bound up. That was Sven's doing, had to be. Ben was certain of it. Aussie had seen Sven, even recognised the agent. Yes that's probably how he got so close to her without her raising the alarm.

He had set the bomb off remotely, to be sure of getting them both. But why would someone from *Five* do such a thing? That would suggest *Five* had a kill order out on them. It made no sense. If there was a kill order on him he would have been finished off already, not back in the clinic. No there had to be more to it. He was determined to find out. Then he was going to make Sven pay.

Ben fell asleep contemplating switching the drone's Taser for something less stunning, more permanent.

Ben woke to a voice he recognised. He opened his eye to welcome the visitor but then he saw it was Cynthia and groaned.

'Quite the Captain Scarlet aren't we McGregor,' she was holding the sheet up at the bottom of the bed. 'Fascinating…What were your feet before the bomb blew them off? Twelves?'

'Yes.'

'Well I'd say you'd already take a nine.' She moved up the side of the bed and sat on the edge. 'Lucky you still had your mask on when you went to rescue Agent Coultard. If you hadn't, your wire clippers would have penetrated your brain. Not just your eye. You might still have been okay but there are likely to be limits to what you can be recovered from. Anyway, I hear a couple more days and you shouldn't need any of the dressings back on.'

'Then what? A month of rehab?'

'I do hope not. I need you back to work ASAP.'

'Nobody will tell me about Aussie. How is she?'

'Most unfortunate. You really must stop getting your handlers killed McGregor. It gets all rather costly, not to mention a bit of a staffing nightmare.'

'So the blast killed her?'

'Somewhat. Not being part Mysteron like you. I'd like to say she wouldn't have felt a thing but since you shared her last moments with her there's no sense in trying to lie, is there.'

'But the blast armour...under the car...It should have given some protection.'

'Indeed, McGregor. However, *you* opened the door, and while the blast hurled you away she, being tied in, burned to death before anyone could get her out.'

'*FUCK!!*...It was Sven.'

'Yes, the vigilante. Something of a Wile E Coyote that one. Except much more successful. Took you and Agent Coultard out of play *and* created a diversion that let the X-rays all escape with their captive to goodness knows where.'

'So who is running Sven? Surely they need to be held to account.'

'There's the thing. That *Five* plate was cloned. The original had been in operation around Dover for the past few weeks on a totally unrelated op. Sven could have cloned anyone's number plate but chose that one.'

'So we are dealing with a person who has access to MI5 data and systems, and they don't mind us knowing?'

'And a whole lot more probably. That's why they need to be brought in immediately so we can deal with the holes in our security...And hopefully gain access to certain other agencies holes.'

'Right. Look, I'm convinced that Sven was able to track me through the tracer you had placed in my hand.'

'You found that did you? We needed to keep tabs on such a valuable asset you understand. In case something went wrong and we lost contact with you.'

'Well it needs to be removed if I'm going to stand a chance of catching this guy.'

'Yes. I'll see that is taken care of.'

There was a long pause with Cynthia just looking at him. 'So, I'm wondering who is expendable enough to be made your next handler, or dangerous enough to be your partner.'

'What do you mean?'

'I'm considering having Agent Oakley help you bring Sven in.'

'You can't be serious. She said shit happens around her and she's not kidding. It's true. She's a super-jinx.'

'What makes you think you aren't *both* jinxed?'

'Two wrongs don't make a right.'

'What are you saying? You're not up to the job?'

'No, I'm...'

'I could just ask Gina to sort Sven while you grow up a few shoe sizes.'

'No. I want to bring Sven in myself.'

'Oh I don't know. Oakley *is* a very smart lady. You know, she was right about the industrial unit. The floor did lift up. While you were airlifted here she returned to the unit with the three remaining troopers. They found a small bunker and underground parking with an escape tunnel. Before the X-rays left, they clearly had time to set the computers and communications systems to self-destruct. I doubt forensics will get much out of what was left behind.'

'Could I ask a favour, Cynthia?'

'You could try, but I am already rather *pushed*.'

'I need to use a mobile, but as you can see my hands are not yet fit for purpose.'

'You people and your social media. Life does go on without Facebook you know.'

'It's not that. I need to let my boss know I've been involved in a car accident.'

'I *already* know.'

'My *boss at the store*, for my cover.'

'Right. Okay.'

'Oh, and a friend.'

'Now you've gone too far.' Cynthia got up and headed for the door.

'No. Wait. It won't take long.'

Cynthia turned back as she reached the door with a sigh. 'I'll have a nurse sent in for you to instruct.'

'Thanks.'

The nurse who Cynthia sent was a male nurse. That shouldn't have mattered, just that the Asian woman was easier on the eye. Ben explained he wanted to send two texts rather than call so that it appeared to be notification from another person. The texts needed to be different but not contradict one another.

The text to Harry explained that Chance had been involved in a Road Traffic Collision but should be back to work soon.

The text to Jill explained that Chance had found his mentee hooked up with some joyriders in Birmingham. Before the lad was safely apprehended the chase resulted in

Chance being badly hurt in a Road Traffic Collision but should be home soon.

The nurse asked whether he should also add that Chance was missing Jill. Ben agreed that was a good idea.

While they waited to see if there would be any response, Ben asked the nurse if it would be possible to get hold of a book called Breakfast's in Bed. He might as well finish reading the novel while he was laid up. It would give him a good reason to go round and see Jill to return her book when he got home.

After twenty minutes or so with no return texts the nurse had to leave with his phone but promised to let Ben know if something came through.

Ben didn't expect any replies. Jill didn't trust him and Harry would also be mad at him for taking off.

The very next day all the bandages and dressings were removed and stayed off. Except for one dressing on his right hand where the tracer had just been removed. There would be some physio and tests to run before he could be discharged but now at least Ben could turn the pages on the book he had been provided with and had both eyes functioning again.

Previously he had only got a third the way into the book, reading during quite moments at the store. Now that he had the time to really get into it he found it both funny and disturbing. Disturbing mainly because the Dawn Summers character seemed an exact match for the Dawn Summers he and Adam had known.

Jill was right about one thing with the book, the twist at the end had Ben start reading it again from the beginning. He had the time.

Ben was discharged two days later. There had been no responses to those texts.

The transport Ben had been provided with was not what he was expecting. He thought he might just be given a lift home by his new handler but no new handler or partner had been appointed, yet. Instead he was handed body armour and a helmet then taken out to the parking lot by one of *Five's* techies.

He had been kitted out with an electric racing bike. He was given the details by the techie before he was left to get into his body armour and return to Northumberland.

The bike's torque enabled it to do zero to sixty in two seconds; something to be wary of. It had a top speed of two hundred miles an hour and a battery range of four hundred miles, on open road. The engine sound could be switched off for stealth purposes on this customised version. There was a thumb print secured locker under the seat containing a Glock and spare ammunition, and the helmet had a heads-up display with night and heat vision facilities, provided he kept its camera lenses clean. And finally, so that no one could hot wire the bike easily it had a thumb-print ignition.

24

Friday afternoon Ben was back in the store. *Five* had been round in the morning for the keys to remove Veronica's Mercedes from his drive.

He had also called round to see Jill but she wasn't in. He would call back later, with her book.

'Oh you are back dear.' Ben looked up from the till to see Edith had come in, no doubt to give him a less than credible history lesson.

'Yes. I've been away.'

'Been anywhere nice? My uncle once brought back a giraffe from China.'

'But giraffes come from Africa.'

'The Emperor was closing his zoo because too many of the visitors wanted to try eating his collection. My uncle took pity on the giraffe and had it sailed back to England. It was a long and difficult voyage.

'Then, when he did get it back here, the neighbours began complaining that the giraffe was looking into their bedrooms, invading their privacy. They couldn't afford curtains in them days, or ciderdowns. Sex was the only way to keep warm, and the giraffe was putting them right off. They were losing sleep too. A solution had to be found.'

'So, was the giraffe taken to a local zoo?'

'No but it did feed the village for a month.'

As Edith was leaving, having bought only a paper, Cedric was on his way in.

'They've let you out then.' Ben greeted.

Cedric nodded to Edith's back, 'Oyvaddur.'

Later on in the afternoon Harry dropped by.

'Nice of you to grace us with your presence.'

'Sorry about that. I got called away without warning.'

'*You people* don't have *any idea* what I've had to endure to cover your shifts on top of *all* my other responsibilities.'

'Well I've recovered now.'

'Oh yes *the crash*. Well if you don't mind me saying it doesn't look like you were hurt badly, so maybe you can return the favour and cover some extra shifts here over the next couple of weeks.'

'I...'

'Good.' He turned grabbed some milk and a loaf and left like an overt shoplifter.

Mikey came in next and picked up four bottles of Weston's cider. 'I've decided to finish early today and put my feet up in front of the telly.' He placed a twenty on the counter.

'Oh.' Ben rang it through.

'Well, the job's ahead of schedule.'

'Great.' Ben handed Mikey his change.

'This cider is definitely my favourite now. I had a mate who used to do home brew. Did a batch of cider once and told me how he had tried some new type of clearing agent. However, I could see there were still bits floating in it, so I says 'I'm not sure the treatment's worked. What are these here, some process cider-flecks?'

'Wiping my feet. One, two, three.'

210

Ben and Mikey looked round to see Winston.

'I best be off then, Chance.' Mikey headed for the door shoving the change into his pocket. 'Bye Winston.'

'Bye Joker.'

Ben was looking forward to closing up and getting out with the drone and settling his score with Sven.

Closer to closing time, Ben's peripheral vision was drawn to the person in fluorescent pink jogging kit coming along the road. He looked up to see Jill slowing further, looking across the forecourt at him. She altered direction and headed into the shop.

This is it, he thought. He didn't wave. He thought that might be pushing his luck. This was where she told him exactly what she thought of him. Good job no one else was in the shop to catch what happened next.

Jill came right up to the counter and leaned across it, looking up into his eyes.

'Look Jill I really am…'

Her hands pulled him down and she shut him up with a kiss on the lips.

'I didn't expect that…I thought you were going to tear me a new one.'

'Are you kidding? You are such a hero.'

'I don't know about that.'

'Saving that lad from joyriding or worse, getting injured in the process…'

'But you didn't return my calls or text.'

'Well, phones make me anxious. I prefer to deal with things in person, Chance.'

'Right. Well you had me worried.'

'Ha. *I* had *you* worried. Oh you silly man.'

'So, are we good?'

'Of course. Look, come round for dinner tonight.'

'I can't...' He couldn't say what he had planned or even cover by saying he was going out to do photography, not right after the accident. He wanted so much to get that bastard Sven but even to say he was too tired would have been somewhere between lame and inexcusable. '...Okay, I'll come. What time?'

'Say eight.'

'Eight.'

'There, that was easy wasn't it.'

Ben sat across the table from Jill. She had cooked pan fried sea bass with marsh samphire.

'Compliments to the chef.' Ben clinked his glass of white wine with hers.

'Thanks.'

'Light years ahead of the hospital food.'

'I should hope so. Do you want to talk about it?'

'It was pretty tasteless.'

'No dafty, the accident.'

'Oh...Not really.'

'Confidential I guess.'

'No, it's not that. Things got out of hand. Aussie, my handler, died in the car.'

'I'm sorry, Chance.' Jill reached across the table and touched his hand. 'Were you close?'

'I was right next to her.'

'No, I mean had you been in a *relationship*?'

Ben's mind flashed back to the two of them in bed. She was a wild thing but so controlling. 'No, of course not.'

'You feel tense.' She stroked his hand. 'I give a good massage. I think after dinner has settled I should help you relax.'

'Oh you don't have to do that.' Ben was trying to remember if there were any scars Jill would be expecting to see.

'Don't be silly. I'd love to. It's the least I could do for my hero.'

They laughed and joked as they made small talk over the meal.

Jill served vanilla panna cotta for afters, and opened a second bottle of white. However, despite the ease of the conversation they didn't get more than halfway down the second bottle before they retired upstairs.

Ben thought Jill might have forgotten about the massage but when she unbuttoned his shirt and felt his pecks she soon remembered. 'You're still tense, Chance. Are you okay?'

'I don't feel tense.'

'Take it from me, *you are*. Sit on the bed. Get those trousers off.'

Ben hoped he wasn't getting involved with another control freak. He had enough on his plate. He removed his trousers and chucked them onto a chair by Jill's dressing table. Then he lay back on her bed.

'Face down to begin with. I'm starting with the back then I'll turn my attention to your front. I guarantee this will relax you.'

Ben heard zippers and sliding material. He started to turn.

'Just lie still. Try and clear your mind.'

213

He felt her bare thighs as she straddled him.

'What style of massage did you say it was you do?'

'This? It's sensual massage.'

His mind went to Aussie and how it had been with her. Pretty amazing. Then his mind fast forwarded to the car and the blast, then any stirrings he had went. He had to put that behind him. He was here with Jill now. Things were finally moving forward.

Jill's hands moved their way down each arm to give her attentions to the wrists, hands and each digit, which it would seem required to be sucked. That done, she moved to the spine and the muscles to either side. She was clearly in no rush and Ben wasn't complaining. Her hands were gifted there was no doubt about that.

Jill backed off the bed in order to work her way down each leg. He felt stirrings beginning. He tried to empty his mind rather than make that *don't think of something* mistake.

When Jill got to his feet she slowed. 'I've never seen feet like this before.'

'What? What's wrong with them?'

'Well, nothing's wrong, exactly. It's just the skin is so soft. They are like...giant baby feet.'

Ben tensed up again. He had to think quick and had to relax. 'I guess that's what comes of years working behind a desk.'

'Is it?...Well I think they're lovely.'

Ben expected to be told to turn over as soon as she was finished with his feet but her hands moved back up his calves and thighs together to caress between the legs first.

'Okay, Chance. You can turn over now, for the dessert.'

Watching him turn she smiled at her handiwork and could see he wanted her there and then, but that would have to come later, she wasn't finished with the treatment yet. By the time she was, Veronica would be a pale memory.

25

Ben had clearly misjudged *plain Jill come thrill Jill.* She had beaten Aussie hands down in the bedroom department. He couldn't stop thinking about her. He could barely concentrate on the customers never mind spare a thought for Sven. He had to pull himself together. He was on a mission. Where was his training?

He used the frantic routine of sorting the Saturday papers and getting the store up and running to force his brain to focus. He made a number of stupid mistakes including: putting the coins in the wrong compartments of the till; loads of the same pies in the oven; and pulling four loaves off their shelf, as out-of-date, though he later spotted they still had two days on them.

Eventually, his *sneaking out of Jill's* started to feel like the previous day. He finally thought he was getting his head together when she came into the store.

'Here you are. I was going to make breakfast.'

'Right well, weekends I'm up at the crack of dawn to get this place up and running.'

'I see...Well that's alright then as long as you weren't just um, rushing away.'

'Rushing away?'

'Look, I'm sorry if I embarrassed you last night.'

'Embarrassed me?'

'Yes. About your *baby feet.*'

'My…? No, not at all.'

'Cos if you did feel awkward…I'd be prepared to let you into a secret.'

'A secret?'

'Yes, something about me I haven't shared yet.'

'Intriguing.'

Edith came into the shop and stopped proceedings.

'I'll take a look around,' Jill said, 'and tell you when she's gone.'

'Believe me Jill, I'll *know* when she's gone.'

'Ha.'

Edith's dithering approach to shopping drove Ben up the wall as she seemed to almost play Pac-Man with Jill. Ben served two other customers before Edith finally arrived at the counter.

'Morning, Chance.'

'Morning, Edith.'

She pointed over her shoulder at Jill, still perusing. 'I'm not sure that woman knows what she wants.'

'I think you could be right, Edith.'

'Do you want to be seeing to her first?'

'No I think I'll give her a seeing to after…I mean I'll see to her afterwards.'

'Do you have any specials on today?'

'Pardon?' He found himself thinking about what he was wearing. He had on last night's clothes. A bit dressy for the shop work maybe.

'Offers, Chance?'

'A chance of what?'

'Are you okay?'

Ben looked across at Jill who was clearly watching him struggle. 'I'm fine. Just my

217

concentrations a bit off this morning.' He made an effort to start scanning Edith's shopping through the till.

'Oh concentration is very important my boy. I used to be a member of the WI's parkour team. When Floss lost concentration and broke an ankle doing a back-flip off a bollard, because someone had moved a bin. I had to step up as Team Captain.

'It felt great to be Captain, but with great power comes great responsibility. I got them to the regional finals and I'm sure we would have won, if they hadn't had to completely replace the whole course mid tournament because of my flatulent diarrhoea.'

After Edith left and was out of earshot, Jill burst out laughing. 'Was that for real?'

'I know right. The people in this village are a bit nuts.'

'Are you including *us* in that statement?'

Ben mirrored Jill's smile. 'Possibly...So what was this *revelation*?'

'Revelation? I'm not sure I'd class it as a revelation, as such. It's just...I like dressing up.'

'Ha. Don't all women?'

'No. I mean fancy dress.'

'Oh...You mean in the *bedroom*.'

'*No* not in the bedroom!' she looked at his expression, 'Well maybe. But fancy dress parties. Like the charity event in the village hall next Saturday. I think there's tickets meant to be on sale in here, according to the Arrow.'

'Oh, right. There are tickets for something in a box here.' He turned to the side and opened it up. 'Yep. I'll sort these.'

'No, let me.'

'But you did dinner last night.'

'Well you can do dinner tonight.'

'Tonight?' He had to get out and catch Sven.

'Don't you want to…?'

'No, no…I mean yes yes.'

'I think you are tensing up again.'

'I'm fine.'

'I think you need another massage.'

'I urr think you might be right.'

'Well then, it's a date. I'll come round to yours for eight. Or are you working here late?'

'I…No that's fine. Do you have any problems eating anything?'

'Well I draw the line at Fugu.'

'Fugu?'

'Yes, you know that deadly puffer fish dish.'

'Right. Well I'm not sure that was on the menu. How about a chicken biryani?'

'Oh you cook curries?'

'Not exactly. I was going to cheat and get us a take-away.' He was looking for an excuse to get out with the drone, but could see that was going down like a lead balloon. 'Okay, no, I'll do us pulled pork and roast veg.'

'That sounds lovely. I'll bring a bottle, and something else.' She leaned across the counter and kissed him.

'I'll…see you later then.' He watched her leave empty handed. He had clearly been the only thing on her shopping list.

Around lunchtime Mikey dropped by for a hot pie plus some choc and pop.

'You like walking don't you Chance?'

'I like to take my camera for a walk, sure.'

'Know anything about ticks.'

'You can pick them up from long grass. Best to check yourself over after a walk but if you find one you need to lift it free without squashing it or leaving the mouth parts behind, or you could get an infection.'

'So, quite a bit then.'

'Why? Do you think you have one?'

'A mate of mine recently removed one from his leg. He's keeping it alive.'

'Why?'

'He toys with it, turning the plastic container over and over, keeping the tick moving.'

'So he's trying to punish it?'

'I did ask him about that. D'you know what he said?'

'No.'

'Tick in the box exercise.'

'Ugh.' Ben couldn't believe he'd fallen for another of Mikey's jokes.

Just before eight o'clock there was a knock on Ben's door. He opened it beaming a smile to find a Goth with a shoulder bag standing there.

'Oh sorry, I was expecting someone else.'

'No you weren't,' said Jill kissing him with her black lips.

'Oh...' Ben was confused. Dinner wasn't supposed to be fancy dress, was it? 'Come on in.'

She put the shoulder bag down on the kitchen table, took out a bottle of red with a cheeky grin. 'Screw?'

'Sorry?'

'Corkscrew. This needs to breath.'

Ben knew how it felt. 'Right…Just in the draw here.'

'Thanks…' The pop of the cork came with a new topic of conversation. 'Nice bike you have out there.'

'Do you like it?' he turned away from her for a moment to attend to the contents of the oven.

'Well it looks nice…Quite big isn't it.'

'I guess.'

'Is it diesel?'

'Ha, no. What makes you think that?'

'Just looks different to other bikes I've seen.'

'No, it's electric.'

'You mean like battery powered?'

'Yes. It's a racing bike.'

'You race bikes?'

'No…I just took a shine to it.'

'Really? I thought electric bikes only did thirty to forty miles per hour.'

'This can do zero to sixty in two seconds, with a top speed of two hundred.'

'Two hundred?! Where are you going to get to do that sort of speed?'

'Well…I'm not am I…It's about knowing it can.'

'*Is it?*'

'Sure. Have you never ridden a motorbike?'

'No. They're an accident waiting to happen, if you ask me. Can't stand up on their own without a leg. I prefer four wheels…or tracks even.'

'Tracks? Ha…So what, you're *Tank Girl* tonight?'

'Maybe,' she ran a hand down Ben's arm. 'You're tense again.'

'No I'm not. I'm fine.'

'Fine is usually a lie. Is it something I've done?'

'No, well it's just I hadn't expected you to turn up as a *Goth*.'

'Well I'm not really a Goth. I sometimes have to dress differently for my journalism work. Whatever I think will help me get the story. I'm sorry. I just thought it might be fun for you to see me as someone different.'

'But why? I want to get to know the real you, not a façade.'

'Well okay. If you want to know the *real me* I'll go change.'

'No. I didn't mean to upset you.'

'You haven't, believe me. Where's your bathroom?'

Up the stairs and along the landing.

'Okay I'll be back in ten,' she grabbed her shoulder bag off the table.

'Sounds good,' Ben turned his attention to laying the places for them.

When Jill came down again, she wore a long red dress but no make-up and no black wig. In fact what she did have was a number one crew cut.

'Crikey,' Ben stood there with his spatula dripping sauce on the tiled floor.

'Well you did say you wanted to see the real me.'

'I did…I do…I just thought you had a blonde bob.'

'I wear wigs.'

'Right. Have you had chemo?'

'Good grief no. Hope I never have to. Wigs are just *my thing*. If you don't like this look I can go put the blonde bob on. I brought it with me, just in case.'

'No. Don't. You look lovely. You have a beautiful shaped head.'

26

Ben was looking up from where he lay next to Jill. The book hovered in the air above his face. Open for reading. Although the room seemed dark and most of the text was too dim to see properly, he could clearly read some of it.

It came roaring out of the dark like a train, lifting Ben off his feet and hurling him down the gully, tearing the drone from his grip. He fought in vain to regain his balance in the storm which now included whipping and scratching branches, as well as mud and stones.

Then he was hurled free, weightless for a moment. He caught a flash of his surroundings as he fell from the high bank into a swollen burn along with the sliding land. An angry thunder clap could be heard even below the cold murky water. As he fought to lift his head above the rapids for air, his arms and legs were striking rocks and debris. He tried to grab hold of anything he could to help himself up and out. But the few things he grasped for were torn from his grip on his flume ride down into Curston.

He tried to remember the content of what he had sleep-read. This thing, whatever it was, needed to serve a purpose, not simply torment him.

Battered by the floodwater that he tried to rise above, Ben bobbed up and caught sight of a bridge during a lightening flash then he was under it, entering Curston's old industrial estate heading for the river and deeper trouble. Another flash, as his head surfaced momentarily for more air and he glimpsed the nearly choked culvert just up ahead. His fingers clawed at the stonework to the side, which proved as much use as grabbing for a grinder. It felt like nails were being torn free. Then he was into the dark tunnel which had no breathing space.

Trying desperately to recall, he did remember something. He had to reach out to the left to grab the ladder he was rushing towards.

He needed to know what came next. He tried to reach out to turn the page but his arms were far too heavy. He knew this was his sleep-reading, just a dream, so maybe he could will the pages to turn.

'Turn over. Turn over!'

Jill woke Ben with a gentle shake of his shoulder. It was just after four in the morning.

'You were talking in your sleep.'

'Was I?' That was a concern.

'You seemed to be getting quite frustrated.'

'What was I saying?'

'It sounded like *turn over*. You only said it a couple of times but you sounded distressed.'

'Really?' He feigned having no idea.

'Like you were trying to get someone to turn over.'

'I don't remember dreaming about anyone.'

'Should I have left you?'

'Maybe…It's nothing. Sorry if I disturbed you.'

'So it's not PTSD?'

'PTSD?'

'After the crash?'

'What crash?'

'The car crash.'

Ben cursed himself. He needed to be more careful. 'Oh the *car crash*. Can you get PTSD from a car accident?'

'I don't see why not, if it's traumatic enough. Flash backs and the likes. Sorry I shouldn't have mentioned it.'

'No it's okay. Look, I'm going to head home, so you can get some more sleep.' He found himself wondering if there was time to get out with the drone, even just for a practice.

'Or, we could…' She pulled him closer.

The Sunday papers were not holding Ben's focus and he had to recheck both the Times and the Telegraph to work out why he had some left over supplements while others were short. It turned out he had put Times supplements into the Telegraph, and Telegraph supplements into the Times.

He had to get his head together and nail Sven. Sunday evening was to be *the night*, except now it wouldn't be. When he had tried to excuse himself from another night with Thrill Jill, by explaining he had a photography assignment deadline looming, Jill had insisted on coming along. She said she wanted to see what he got up to.

He tried to put her off by explaining that it involved creeping around in the dark looking for situations of interest, it only seemed to encourage her further. He went back over the conversation in his head.

'What makes a situation of interest?' she'd asked.

'Well it could be the way that pattern or form are lit by evening light or by street and security lighting. Or it might be an event taking place.'

'Like what?'

'I don't know…Two people pulling up in cars to talk to one another, or the shadow cast by someone walking their dog, or the different expressions of people queuing at an ATM.'

'So spying on people?'

'No not spying, and anyway once you have an image of someone you now have to get them to sign a model release form or you can't use your photo of them. Some people don't want their images used and get cross that you took the picture in the first place.' Ben found himself hoping that the mention of paperwork and social awkwardness would do the trick and put her off.

'Is that because they think you are asking them to be their model?'

'I don't know. I guess people are more paranoid these days.'

'Well I wouldn't want my picture taken without being asked first.'

'But then you would be conscious and wouldn't behave the same.'

'True.'

'Have I put you off?'

'Oh no, not at all. Maybe it's something I can do an article on.'

Ben groaned inwardly. 'Well, if you are coming you'll have to wear black clothes to reduce the likelihood of appearing in reflections.'

'So dress like a spy?'

'Urr...'

'Chance?!'

Ben turned to see an early customer waiting for a paper. 'Sorry, I was miles away there.'

'There are no papers outside.'

'No. I'm sorting them.'

'I thought you said you were miles away,' the impatient customer tried to make light of not having papers ready by seven o'clock, even though Ben was not paid to start work until seven.

'The supplements are in the wrong papers.'

'You can't trust anyone to do a simple job these days, can you Chance?'

'No. There's always someone out there looking to ruin your day. Here, you go.' Ben handed the customer the copy which had become somewhat torn during delivery, having been at the bottom of the pile.

Shortly after Ben got the papers sorted, the pies into the oven and the previous day's takings counted, Mikey came in.

'I could just do with a bacon and egg sandwich.'

'Sorry Mikey, Rosie doesn't work weekends. The kitchen's closed.'

'But what's that I can smell?'

'The pies.'

'Oh go on then, what have you got?'

'Cheese and onion, steak and kidney, steak and ale, beef pasty, scotch pie, chicken curry, chicken and mushroom, and sausage rolls.'

'Well the first one then,' Mikey said to wind Chance up.

'Well come back in half an hour then.'

'Are you winding *me* up?'

'They're not ready yet.'

'What sort of restaurant do you call this?'

'A *customer tolerant* one?'

'Okay I'll just have a paper then.'

'You'd get more nutrition out of a pack of rice cakes.'

'Yeah but only just.'

Ben had no spare bike helmet for Jill to ride pillion and from what she had said previously about motorbikes she would not have agreed to ride pillion anyway, so Jill had driven them both into Curston. She parked in the sports centre car park and from there they made their way up the hill to the high street.

With camera in hand and a tripod slung over his back, Ben's aim was to make this activity so tedious with photography jargon and fiddling about with settings that Jill wouldn't want to come again. It seemed to Ben that it would be more tactful to deal with the need for his own space that way.

As they moved along the high street to the west end of Curston, Ben explained about aperture, shutter speed and ISO settings, at great length. Jill just listened. Ben hoped for both their sakes she had just switched off. It would be worrying to find she was soaking it all up. He went on to describe how low-key shots could be created to darken surroundings and draw attention to illuminated areas. Then he explained how by using his tripod and a neutral density filter on the lens he could create extended exposures where moving objects became blurred or even invisible.

They arrived at the cemetery and pushing the big iron gate open Ben went inside. A few minutes later Jill was gripping his hand.

'Don't you find this a bit spooky, Chance?'

'Spooky?'

'Yeah spooky…It's a graveyard.'

'You don't believe in ghosts do you?'

'I didn't think I did but I feel like there's someone or something watching us.'

'It's just us here. But I have an idea of something we can do with the camera now we've mentioned ghosts. I just need to…Yes this would be perfect…Lean up against that gravestone while I…'

'Are you kidding?'

'No. I'm going to show you how I can make you look like a ghost by extended exposure.' Ben took the tripod from his back and started extending the telescopic legs.

'If you'd said you wanted to do that I'd have come dressed as a ghoul.'

'Don't worry, this is just to show you how it's done, not to take a prize-winning shot.'

'Did you see that?' Jill's voice dropped to a whisper.

Ben looked up to see where Jill was pointing, behind him down the side of the crematorium. 'What?'

'A man. He was just *there*. When I looked straight at him he dodged out of sight...Let's go. I'm not comfortable here.'

Ben didn't want to get Jill involved with Sven, if indeed it was Sven looking for another confrontation. However, he did need to put Jill off coming out on these evening forays. 'Hang on. Stay here. I'll go look.'

'No, Chance. I don't want you bashing someone else up. It might be the crematorium warden.'

'Why duck out of sight then? Don't worry I'll be back in a mo.' Ben moved quickly and quietly, round the side of the building then down the back, checking behind gravestones and bushes as he went. When he came round the other side he looked at Jill.

'Did you see him?' she asked.

'No.'

She pointed across the crematorium. 'When you went round he darted across the graveyard into those trees by the wall.'

Ben raced between the gravestones to the trees.

'Chance! Leave it!' Jill hissed.

Ben ignored her. He couldn't see any obvious tracks on the ground, or broken twigs on the bushes. There was nothing.

He swung the camera around to his back then grabbed the top of the wall and lifted himself high enough to look over. There was a lane on the other side but there was no one to be seen in either direction. Ben dropped back down and returned to Jill.

'What's gotten into you, Chance?'

'What do you mean?'

'Well running after that guy like that?'

'I'm just curious I suppose. He was acting suspicious after all.'

'And *we're* not?'

'Well a little, I guess. What did he look like?'

'Shorter than you.'

'Obviously.'

'And dressed in black like us.'

'Right.'

'Could it be another member of your club out doing some photography and we scared him off?'

'You know you could be right.'

Ben returned his attentions to the tripod and soon connected the camera then launched into a boringly detailed description of the pros and cons of landscape and portrait oriented compositions. Finally he took the shot and half way through the ten second exposure got Jill to move away from the gravestone.

Finally he showed her the result on the camera screen. A transparent Jill.

'Creepy.'

'A bit cliché too I guess. I'll just take a couple of shots of this building from different angles and then we'll head off.'

'Home?'

'No, just back along the high street.'

'Oh.'

'If I want to get an unusual shot of a building I might try and shoot from higher up by climbing a tree or by photographing from low down, in this case from a grave. It's best to consider the best angle of the building first then look for an interesting viewpoint to...'

'Did you hear that?'

'No.'

'I thought I heard someone calling a name. Maybe there's more than one person out there.'

'Well we do recommend that photographers wanting to be out and about at night don't go alone. It's best if they can find someone like-minded to go with them, what with all the things you hear in the news.' Ben had said it without thinking and cursed himself inwardly for introducing cause for concern when the aim was for boredom. 'What did it sound like?'

'I'm not sure...McGregor, I think?'

'McGregor?...Urr I don't think we have anyone in the club by that name. Must be someone else.' Now he was convinced it was Sven. Cynthia would not have done anything to compromise him. He needed to get Jill home then get straight back with the drone. 'Well let's head back along the high street. We can go this way.' Ben pointed to a small gate that led to an alley he knew connected to the high street further along.

Halfway along the high street Jill nudged Ben's arm. 'You okay? You've gone all quiet.'

'Have I?'

'You've been chattering non-stop about your photography but since we left the graveyard you haven't said a word.' Jill's head suddenly looked up.

Ben turned to look but saw nothing. 'What's wrong?'

It was the roofing Ben had chased Sven along and then fallen from.

Jill shrugged. 'I could have sworn I saw someone up there looking down at us.'

'Urr well like you said it could be another photographer, looking for an interesting viewpoint.'

'From a roof?'

'Sure. Why not?'

'For one thing it's dangerous and two it's probably illegal.'

'Well that's their lookout.' Ben hooked her arm with his and headed off along the street. He had to get back out there alone ASAP.

'Steady on Chance. You're going too fast. My legs *are* shorter than yours remember.'

'Sorry I wasn't thinking.'

'No. It's like you are thinking about something that you're not telling me.'

'Like what?'

'Are you cross with me?'

'Cross with you? How could I be cross with *you*?'

'I don't know. Your mood seems to have changed. I'm wondering if it's something I said.'

'I urr...I think you could be right about PTSD. My mind has started replaying the crash since we went into the crematorium...'

Jill wrapped her arms around Ben, the best she could. 'I'm here for you, Chance.'

She held his hand as they walked back to the car, but he was silent again, he was trying to use window reflections and his peripheral vision to see if he could spot Sven tailing them.

On the drive home he kept glancing in the wing mirror for any sign of a tail, which at his height required a rather slumped posture.

'You're still pretty tense, Chance. Maybe I should massage you.'

How could he refuse that? But he had to get back out and catch Sven. 'I'll be fine.'

'It must be bad if you're turning down one of my massages. Do you feel you can talk about it now maybe?'

Ben gave a long sigh then made up his story, knowing that whatever he said he'd have to be smart about it and remember the details. 'I was driving with my handler in my car. We were trying to catch up with a stolen car which had been taken by joyriders, one of whom was my mentee.'

'How did you know your mentee was in a stolen car?'

'The police told us it was stolen.'

'So if the police were handling it, why were you involved?'

What was this, a courtroom? 'There were two police units, but it was a big estate, so when it sounded like they could lose the vehicle *and* my mentee, I offered to support them.'

'Wasn't that up to your handler?'

'Well yes, I suggested it to her and she confirmed our support with the police.'

'Right.'

'So anyway, whoever was driving the stolen car was becoming more and more reckless, speeding, mounting the pavement and cutting across grassed corners with trees. Then we thought we had them. They turned down a cul-de-sac, with bollards at the end. But they knew exactly what they were doing. The stolen car mounted the curb onto the footpath. Then it zipped between the end bollard and the wall and into the field beyond. I tried to do the same but screwed things up. It's *all* my fault. I have no training for that sort of thing. I was caught in the moment. And now Aussie is dead!'

'It's not *your* fault. You can't blame yourself.'

'The car bounced as I hit the curb, struck the end bollard, span the car round and over. I spilled out, but Aussie was trapped. The collision must have ruptured the fuel tank because it exploded. Aussie burned to death. I should never have suggested we give chase.'

'I thought your car was a diesel?'

'No. Petrol.'

'Well if anyone is to blame it would be the police. Letting you take part in the operation sounds like it would be against the rules.'

'Anyway, the police caught the lads the other side of the field and called an ambulance.'

'They must have justified it somehow in their report I suppose, or surely they would have charged you with dangerous driving.' Jill pulled up outside Ben's place. 'Can we go to the pictures tomorrow night?'

As long as he caught Sven tonight, Ben thought. 'Okay...but let's not watch that latest Fast and Furious.'

Quickly donning his bike body-armour then putting the drone in his back-pack, he grabbed his helmet and was off, back into Curston. He parked the bike by the fire escape at the rear of the terrace of commercial premises he had climbed onto previously. He wouldn't be going up a height again this time. That was the job of the drone.

He soon had the control unit prepared with home-point set and the drone's rotors were spinning up. He had only played with Robbie's toy drone before and that one had proven to be rather unstable. At least that was how he explained to his son why he had smashed it into a train coming into Newcastle Central station.

The drone lifted off and went straight up. Altitude inhibitor programmes were now required by law, with certain areas of air-space being banned completely. However, this MI5 drone could go wherever it was sent. Nevertheless it did give the pilot altitude alerts and collision warnings, which Ben tried to pay attention to.

Watching the control unit's split screen Ben could see both the night vision camera view and the heat sensor view. When he was up high enough but not so high he would miss Sven's heat signature, Ben began an overlapping spiral search pattern. The patterns covered the town centre first then took in the park and housing estate. Next he flew over the industrial estates.

The controller was able to direct the drone at quite some distance. However, towards the end of the search Ben had to jog around to keep within range. Otherwise it was going to simply quit and return to Ben's designated home-point, by his bike.

Ben spotted a number of people out and about but no one on their own, unless you counted walking a dog as alone. There was no one riding a motor bike either, or up a tree or clambering over rooftops. There was no sign of Sven at all. Eventually, as the battery got low, the drone headed back to where Ben's bike was.

He ran back to join the drone. He could fit the replacement battery that he had brought with him but there didn't seem much point. All he had gained for his evening's efforts was learning that running around Curston in his body-armour, trying to keep up with the drone, was hot work and it made him look like a suspicious numpty. He decided to dress more casually in future.

27

Monday morning, before work, Ben looked through pages of costumes on eBay. He was searching for something people would see as fun for the charity do at the weekend.

There were general theme costumes like pirates and vampires. There were separate accessories like masks and fat suits. You could create your own character, with make-up sets to help do an even better job. Then there were the specific character costumes, like Batman and Spiderman. Considering what had been done to his genes in the name of science and national security Ben seriously considered going as Patrick Star from SpongeBob SquarePants. The idea only lasted sixty seconds as they didn't do the starfish suit in anything close to his size. Ben wanted to make good use of his size, so he finally decided to place an order for the Predator costume.

Ben arrived at work for nine o'clock and took over at the counter from Rosie, who had opened up the store for seven. As she went into the kitchen Mikey arrived and went straight after her.

'Two bacon and egg rolls please, Rosie.'
'Sausage rolls?'
'Bacon and Egg.'
'Two sausage rolls, bacon and egg.'

'No sausage rolls. Just the bacon and the egg.'

'Don't you want a baguette or a ciabatta?'

'A roll. Times two.'

'Papers are round the other side.'

With a shake of his head Mikey looked at his watch and shrugged, he'd be late for work again. He went to the fridges to find his favourite Lychee drink then to Chance at the counter.

He placed a can of Lychee plus a bottle of coke on the counter for his colleague. 'And two bacon and egg rolls, Chance.'

Ben scanned the drinks and rang the rolls in.

After Mikey paid, and while he waited for Rosie to finish cooking the bacon and eggs, he said 'Did you hear about that woman who said she could remember generations back to previous lives? She wanted to change her name by deed-pole to Irene Carnate.'

'Oh very good.'

One of the farmers came in with filthy boots, dropping clods of what Ben hoped was only mud onto the floor. 'Got any tuna, Chance?'

'Should be by the salmon in the middle aisle,' he pointed.

'Right, yes.' He squelched over to the counter where Mikey still stood.

'D'you remember when it had to be Dolphin-Friendly Tuna?' Mikey mused.

'People aren't bothered what tuna is inside, these days,' said Ben.

'Unless it's Piano Tuner.'

'Ugh.' The farmer grimaced with disgust. Then he reached way down inside his stained shirt towards what might have been his underpants groping for loose change. At which point Bruce arrived with a pack fit for a Sherpa, which he had to remove to get through the door.

'Herman!' Mikey called.

'It's Bruce!' he corrected without looking as he struggled inside for his fortnightly supplies.

Inside his struggles only continued as he tried to remember where was best to place the pack before filling it up. Stepping aside to let the farmer out he then dumped the pack in front of the counter, which would mean Ben would have to stretch over it, once again, to reach any of the customers.

'Come on Bruce. Who do you think I am? Reed Richards?'

'Who's he?'

'The guy from the Fantastic Four with the stretchy limbs.'

'Well it's better there than blocking an aisle. I won't be a minute.'

'He's not wrong there, Chance.' Mikey smirked, 'More like half an hour.'

As if the store had not already reached capacity, Edith entered for what looked set to be a round of competitive dithering with Bruce.

After a few minutes, while Ben attempted to clean up the mud, the two of them clashed over access to the tinned foods.

'I haven't got all week, Herman.'

'It's Bruce!'

'There's a bad storm coming.'

'Rubbish. You only need to check the Met Office website to see we have two weeks of hot weather to look forward to.'

'Well it's coming, regardless. Mark my words.'

'You don't know what you're talking about. We have weather satellite data these days for *accurate* forecasts.'

'Aye, that's what they said in seventeen-ten when the big storm came out of nowhere. It drowned quarrymen in the middle of eating their bait, washed half the village out of their netties, and created the marsh down at Strayden which used to be the estate's rose garden before that.'

'No. You're talking utter rubbish.'

'On a wet night, walking along the Arrow past the marsh it's said you can still hear the dead retching up floodwater.'

'Nice,' said Mikey.

'Y'bun is ready,' Rosie called.

'What about the other?'

'Why didn't you say you wanted two?'

Bang on one o'clock, Ben was attempting to eat his sausage, bacon and brown sauce baguette, which Rosie had made for him. A string of lunch-time customers came in as if they had all been waiting for him to try and take a break. What's more his mobile rang with the Ghost in the Shell theme. This meant the call was from *Five* but he couldn't answer any phone when he had customers to serve. Seconds after the ignored call there was a water droplet sound which meant he had been sent a voicemail, which would also have to wait.

Opportunity to check the mobile started to look promising when Ben was down to one customer. However, he remembered this was Nadine the farmer's wife who loved moaning about illnesses, and the weather. She also had a bee in her bonnet about those people who complained about her approach to what she termed *dog-emptying*.

Nadine placed the store's only basket on the counter and launched straight in. 'Phyllis, on the Arrow was having a right rant at me last night, because Horace had been into her garden and left a steaming pile on her forget-me-nots.'

'Remind me again, Horace is your husband right?' Ben feigned ignorance as he started scanning goods.

'Ha no. Nadine would certainly have something to complain about if George had dropped his keks in her garden. No, Horace is my Great Dane. Anyway I told her it's all good for the garden. She said if she had wanted that sort of thing on her flowers she'd have emptied half a dozen cans of Chunky on her beds.'

'Nice.'

'So I said if she hadn't wanted a visit she shouldn't have left her gate open.'

The store phone started ringing. Ben ignored that too.

'Then she says she didn't. Horace had stepped over the wall. So I suggested she invest in something higher. I added that this is what you get if you live in the country and if she didn't like it she should move back into Curston.'

'That'll be fifty-two eighty.'

'That seems a tad steep.'

'Well that does include the Diesel.'

'Oh yes I forgot all about that with you taking so long,' she complained.

They looked out the window to see an Irish Wolfhound sitting in the driver's seat of Nadine's old Land Rover Discovery, licking the window and leaving streaks of what looked like brown sauce behind.

'Looks like Zena's gone and put one in the foot-well again. That's with you wittering on. I'll have to clean that out before I pick up Miriam from the vets.'

'Another dog?'

'No. My Nephew.'

'Nephew?'

'Don't get me started. My sister said it was all the rage twenty years ago.'

Ben wondered what she was talking about but didn't dare extend the conversation.

As soon as Nadine was out of the store Ben took another bite of his rapidly cooling lunch but now the brown sauce was not so appealing. He asked Rosie if she could cover for him at the counter while he returned a call.

She nodded and he went outside, behind the cars for sale. He checked his voicemail first. It simple said *'Report in'*.

When he called control with his code he was told that Cynthia wanted to speak with him and was put through.

'How's it going McGregor?'

'Quite busy with the customers.'

'I'm not interested in the damned shop, McGregor. I'm asking about Sven!'

244

'I'm afraid I haven't made much headway. He's been trying to keep tabs on me it would seem, but I guess it's more challenging for him since I had my tracer removed. I reckon he'll be tracking my phone now though. I've been entertaining the idea of leaving my phone somewhere that looks like an OP and then setting up an ambush. But to be honest I was hoping for more support.'

'Well I haven't managed to sort you another handler yet.'

'I meant more intelligence information. I thought GCHQ might have tracked where Sven lived by now, or where this drugs lab is based so we can second guess Sven's target.'

'Well GCHQ are busy with a load of other more pressing problems right now, and the police are not sharing much regarding the drugs lab. Sven is most likely to locate the lab first and since there have been no reports of another commercial premises being destroyed we can assume that they have not yet been discovered. The lab isn't believed to be in Curston though.'

'What? Even when a number of people associated with it are in the area? It has to be *somewhere* close by. I'll start looking further afield tomorrow.'

'What's wrong with today?'

'I can't blow my cover. My shift doesn't finish until seven then I've agreed to go to the pictures.'

'The pictures?! We're not paying you to go on a jolly, McGregor! This wouldn't be with that *Jill*, Veronica mentioned?'

'Well yes.'

'You were warned not to get involved.'

'It's part of my cover. Fitting into the community.'

'*Is it*? It sounds more like dereliction of duty to me.'

'I'm sorry you feel that way Cynthia.'

'Just bring Sven in. I don't care if you blow your cover doing it. Just bring him in. This week!'

'After what he did to Aussie, believe me, I want him off the streets now as much as you.'

The movie Ben and Jill went to see was supposed to be a horror. It certainly seemed to have Jill's nerves on edge, going by the way she was gripping Ben's hand at times but Ben wasn't engaging with it. He was conscious of the edge of the screen the whole time and the people in the audience jumping and gasping.

The problem Ben had with horror movies was that they typically involved a group of young people who had no idea how to deal with a psycho-killer.

Ben had his own real-life psycho-killer to deal with.

He had thought that Sven was only killing criminals, but that had all changed since the car bomb. Now it was personal.

Since speaking to Cynthia his plan was to check Google for industrial units in other towns and villages in the vicinity, then at night to use the heat sensor camera on the drone to see if he could find the drugs lab. He doubted it was just in someone's loft but he couldn't rule it out.

He had a hunch that what he was looking for was bigger.

He wondered whether the techies could send him a chemical analyser for the drone to give it a nose for sniffing out the lab's exhaust fumes.

Jill screamed, letting go of Ben's hand to put her hands to her mouth, mirroring half the audience. Ben just shook his head at the sudden reveal of the film's hero all bound up and bleeding.

Ben's mind was on Psycho-Sven. Once he had him down and trussed up like a Christmas turkey he'd have to keep him out of sight until a unit from *Five* could come and pick him up. It seemed advisable not to involve the police. The fact that Sven had been able to operate as he had for so long raised the question whether he had certain people in his pocket.

28

Ben struggled to move and had trouble opening his eyes. They felt gritty. He blinked. Then he saw the book. It was out of reach. He squinted to read what words he could make out.

Ben coughed the choking dust from his dry mouth and as he did so he realised he was in an enclosed space. He also noted the tickling trail moving across his forehead that meant he was either sweating or bleeding. Since he was not overly hot it was most likely blood.

He tried to move. There was a lot of weight above him and it shifted. Dust trickled into his left ear and over his neck, but not before he heard the scraping sound of rock or concrete. Trying to control his breathing in the dark he had to think about what had happened to him, to better understand his situation.

He remembered trying to tackle Sven…and then this. But there had to have been more in between. Had there been another explosion? It would seem so.

He tried moving his arms. Only his left arm was possible to move. He worked his hand up towards his face then pushed outwards. He felt a large lump of rubble fall away to provide some dim light and fresh air.

He shifted more rubble away and tried to pull himself towards the hole he had created.

Then he remembered...His legs were broken.

'Chance! Chance!' Jill was shaking him awake again. 'You were having another bad dream.'

Ben groaned. He hoped that was all it was, a bad dream. Trying to look on the bright side he told himself the previous sleep-read had not happened so why should this one. It had to have been just coincidence with those previous dreams.

'PTSD again?'

'Sorry Jill...I think I'm going to go take a shower.'

In his bathroom Ben tried to think of a credible reason for not spending all day with Jill. She knew it was his day off. He would have to tell her he had a mentoring meeting come up at short notice, seeing as he had not already mentioned a meeting was due. Obviously he couldn't come out with that immediately on exiting the shower, he reasoned. He'd have to wait until *she* took a shower, so that he could have had time to receive a text or email.

Minutes later, having dried off and left the bathroom, he caught Jill giving him an apologetic-sad look from his bed, with her phone in hand. 'Sorry, Chance, I know you were probably expecting to spend the day with me but a job has come up.'

'A new contract?'

'I'm afraid so.'

'Oh, well it can't be helped I suppose. Work brings the money in.' Ben tried not to sound even slightly relieved.

'Thank you for being so understanding, Chance. I'll make it up to you...Why don't we go up to the Edinburgh Fringe next week, for a day or two? Catch some shows.'

'Sounds great.' Ben hoped he would have brought in Sven by then, so Edinburgh might help soften the blow when he had to tell Jill he was moving away. It had been good while it lasted but *Five* wasn't going to leave him in Sevensands. Also, he was no good at long distance relationships, especially when he had to lie about his identity.

'I'll sort accommodation and some tickets. You like comedy right?'

'Sure. I like a good laugh. Surprise me.'

As soon as Jill's car had reversed off his drive Ben was booting up his laptop, to search for towns and villages surrounding Curston which might harbour a drugs lab.

Most villages lacked good enough access roads to support an industrial estate and its associated traffic. Sevensands had one as a cast-off from the quarrying days. Though Ben had checked that out some time ago he hadn't got a drone then and wasn't looking for exhaust vents for a Liquid Crystal lab. Strayden and Strawford both had some units to check on, as did Haughton and Camberley further out. He even made a note to check out the Curston Science Park, up on the hillside to the south of Curston, a mile or so out of town.

Ben knew he could not afford to limit himself to obvious sites though. He had to look for anything with a large enough floor space, anything secure enough to conceal drugs production. That meant warehouses and barns, so agricultural sites would all need checking too. That made for quite an extensive check-list.

Finally, with a route plan for the day, kit packed, he donned his bike gear and set off with an open mind.

First on his check-list was Sevensands industrial site and its three farms. There was nothing obvious but then Ben knew it wouldn't be an easy task and would require a bit of luck to spot something actually going on. After all he thought, you only had to watch something like Breaking Bad to know what some serious backing could do to hide a drugs lab, and these people *were* serious.

From Sevensands Ben rode down to Strawford, checking out a couple of farms on the way, by which time he realised this was going to be no quick job. The industrial estate at Strawford, to the rear of the train station, only had four units. Two of those looked unused. It hardly classed as an estate.

Ben had almost finished his inspection there when a police car pulled in and a police woman got out.

'Do you mind me asking what you are doing, sir?' the officer asked. 'I have had reports of suspicious activity and I see you are using a drone.'

'If I was doing anything illegal I'd have made a run for it when you turned up.' Ben continued watching the screen on the controller. Considering the state of policing in the country now, he didn't want to tell her more than he had to. 'I'm a security contractor.'

'Can I see your ID please, sir?'

'I don't have any on me today.'

'I'm going to have to ask you to move on then, sir.'

'No worries. I'm almost done.'

'Now, sir.'

'I'm just bringing the drone in,' Ben didn't sound at all rushed as the drone came across and down to its home-point.

The police officer continued to watch as he packed the drone away, to be sure that he was going.

Ben got on his bike and the police officer got back in her car. He saw that she was reporting in as he put on his helmet, activating his heads-up display to review his route map.

Pulling out of the site and turning right to go over the level crossing he saw via his rear view camera in his helmet display that the police car was now following him instead of going the other way. So clearly this wasn't over.

He decided to leave Strawford up the steep bank to the north of the valley. He held to the thirty speed-limit as he rode through the village with the police car right on his tail. However, as soon as he hit the sixty limit sign he showed the police officer how much acceleration his electric bike had, even uphill, and left the car standing.

The climb was dotted with sharp bends. With his heads-up, Ben was prepared for these turns which would further slow the police car. When out of sight, on the straighter stretches, Ben put more speed on. To further ensure that he lost his tail, Ben turned off down a dirt track, not holding to his planned route. This detour would bring him back out near Sevensands, which was on his way through to Strayden anyway. The track was full of pot-holes but the bikes suspension coped admirably.

A little later, at the Strayden site he was just about to launch his drone again when he turned to see the police officer pull in. 'You've *got* to be pissing me!'

As the police woman got out, Ben looked up into the clear sky and guessed the officer was being supported by satellite tracking, cheaper and stealthier than helicopters these days.

Ben took the initiative, reading her badge number as she approached, 'Look Office urr…six-three-five-seven. I have a lot of ground to cover today, and I really don't need a chaperone. But since I don't have my ID on me, I tell you what I'm going to do. I'll call my control to call your control. Then *you'll* get a call and we can each get on with our day. Okay?'

'If you say so, sir.'

She clearly thought he could be bluffing, so Ben took out his phone and once through to *Five* he gave his next authentication code and his sit-rep referencing the officer's badge number, then hung up.

Both Ben and the police officer stood watching one another, arms folded. Ben knew she was only doing her job but he really could do without it.

What seemed like ages but was barely more than a minute the police officer was called off.

'Sorry Sir,' she sounded fed up.

As she returned to her car Ben called after her. 'You weren't to know luv.'

'See you around.'

'I hope not.' Ben got on with his inspection.

After Strayden and then Haughton, Ben stopped at Curston for some lunch then headed up the south bank of the valley out to Curston Science Park.

The buildings there were not small industrial units. Serious money had been spent on this architecture. The park was occupied by three businesses, surrounded by woodland. As Ben took an initial ride through, he noted that there was a medical research company, a computer technology company, and a design engineering consultancy.

Riding back out and then pulling off the road into the woods, where he spotted a bit of a clearing which would do for his drone's home-point, he got on with his next inspection.

The computer technology and medical research companies both had active security with CCTV and guards at their entrance barriers. The computer technology building, Smythe Futures, was the most impressive, looking like something out of a Bond movie, with its cantilevered offices stretching out over the wooded bank, like a view point for Curston.

Ben began to wonder whether he was on a hiding to nothing. After all, whatever he did to try and locate Sven's next major target, Sven was bound to have already found it ahead of him, the police *and* GCHQ. *He* wouldn't have been using a drone. *His* tool of choice was hacking.

So if Sven already had the next target in his sights…what *was* he waiting for?

29

It was late evening on the Friday when Ben got his first break. The drone was picking up the sound of another motorbike. This was the third he had heard in the last couple of hours. However, the sound of this one was more like the one Sven had bowled Ben over with.

Ben turned the drone about, homing in on the sound and there he was. Sven was leaving a large housing estate on his Kawasaki Ninja, heading towards town. Ben's only aim now was to bring Sven down by Taser, as quickly and cleanly as possible. That meant with the minimum of collateral damage, avoiding drawing attention and in a quiet but accessible spot for Ben to apprehend him, while he was still in shock.

This was all a bit of an ask. Ben realised this would require no small amount of luck. Luck which Ben felt he was now due in spades.

Nevertheless, it was still going to take quite some physical effort on Ben's part to pull it off. Whilst the drone could keep up with Sven's bike, in practice, the drone's operational range was going to be limited by its distance from Ben. Since Ben was on foot, having parked his bike in a quiet area of an industrial estate, it meant he did not have much time to act. To add a further complication to the need to control the drone while he ran, the wind was now picking up.

The drone closed in behind Sven as the bike took a left and headed towards the bus station. Ben's task of steering while running became so much easier when the drone came close enough to get a 'lock on'. This meant the drone was now able to follow Sven independent of Ben. All that Ben needed to do was drop altitude to get within Taser range and then fire.

As luck would have it Sven was actually heading in Ben's general direction as he raced across Curston's market square and sprinted down a pedestrianised street, to head him off at the end. It was difficult for Ben to watch where he was going and to keep the screen steady enough to know where and when to fire.

Sven crossed a roundabout onto the high street and then things seemed to be falling into place for Ben as traffic lights slowed Sven down to allow three women to cross, as they headed for the Hot Spotted night club.

Ben stopped running to give the drone controls his full attention, dropped the drone further towards his target and as soon as the green light for Taser range lit up he fired.

The four Taser darts and wires chased up by their stun-pulse battery struck Sven on the left shoulder. The darts didn't penetrate the body armour but the battery impact did get Sven's attention. Sven glanced round then down. Seeing the Taser pieces he looked up, just as Ben fired again, this time aiming for the more exposed neck area. Seeing the drone, Sven twisted the throttle. The pull of the bike whipped Sven's head back, the Taser darts and battery bounced off the helmet and Sven raced across the Zebra crossing doing a wheelie.

'Wanker!!!' The women chorused in Sven's wake, barely half way across the road.

Ben was also cursing as he was off like a shot again. 'Fucking technology! If you want something doing well, fucking do it yourself!'

What happened next seemed to go in slow motion for Ben. As he got to the end of the pedestrianised street, onto the high street, Sven was still heading his way, and was glancing back and up at the locked-on drone. Ben jumped up onto the bonnet of a parked car, attempting to place the controller on the cars roof so as to be hands-free. Springing off the bonnet with Sven firmly in his sights, and unaware of Ben, Ben stepped on the roof of a passing car doing twenty miles an hour and went into a dive that was intended to take the vigilante down.

However, the parked car Ben had used as his first spring board set off its alarm, drawing Sven's attention. Sven leaned forwards and accelerated. Ben's contact with the passing car put a twist into his dive. So as he passed the space where Sven should have been he was upside-down arms outstretched. To add insult to injury, when Ben had dumped the controller on the car roof it must have fired the drone once more. Four Taser darts stuck in Ben's face and the battery smacked him in the left eye. His spin, now with added shakes, face-planted him on the opposite pavement, just as Sven took a sharp left off the high street.

It was the water in the face rather than the crowd of concerned people shaking him that brought Ben round. He could only see out of one eye, but didn't need two eyes to tell it was raining now. Trying to remember what had just happened, he noticed there was something over his face. He pulled it away and swore. It was the Taser wires.

Trying to sit up Ben found people were attempting to keep him down. They were telling him to stay calm and that an ambulance would be on the way as soon as they managed to guess all the answers to the questionnaire.

Ben was having none of it. Apologetically pushing aside people and their brollies, he looked across the road to the roof of the parked car for his drone controller. It had slid off the roof, down the back and was now on the tarmac half under another parked car behind.

Alert enough now to check the road for traffic, Ben dashed over to retrieve the controller. Luckily it was still working, and so was the drone, which had tailed Sven up the hill to the south of Curston. It seemed that in an attempt to lose the drone Sven had ridden into an area of woodland. This had slowed him down somewhat, which gave Ben a chance, however small, of catching up with him. Ben wished he had his own bike now, as he left the bystanders behind, to sprint on up the hill.

The rain seemed to get heavier the higher Ben ran, and the gusting was getting worse. He was starting to feel sick but fought on. He reminded himself this was nothing compared to the Fan Dance, then tried not to remember that he had failed the Fan Dance on his last SAS selection. Then the first flash of lightning lit the still darkening sky.

Puffing and panting, Ben felt the incline start to ease off as he got near the top, but *he* didn't ease off one bit. Guided by the GPS on the control unit he bounded off the road and into the trees. Blinking and wiping rain from his one good eye, the other now swollen shut, he realised he would have to go more slowly in the dark of the woods. He had no torch on him.

It also occurred to Ben that he had had quite a run of bad luck with his eyes of late. Holly, wire cutters, and now a Taser battery, what was that all about? Abandoning that train of thought as negative, he checked the screen once again.

'Oh that's fucking great!'

The trees were now swaying so badly in the worsening storm that the collision detection had finally countermanded the lock-on and brought the drone to a halt, unable to pursue Sven further. Sven had got away yet again.

'FOR FUCKS SAKE!!!' Ben almost threw the controller into the mud at his feet but stopped himself in mid swing.

All he could do now was set the drone down and go retrieve it.

If it wasn't for the GPS tracker Ben would never have found the drone in the dark, with one eye. The frequent lightning only gave him snapshots of his surroundings but finally he got to it and not a moment too soon it seemed. It had come to rest on a slab of rock at the side of a gully that had water in it deepening by the second with the worsening rain.

Lifting and folding the drone up to put it away with the controller, Ben reminded himself that whilst this evening had not gone at all well, this device was his only chance of getting even with Sven. For that reason he would be taking good care of it.

Still standing at the side of the dark gully Ben noted that that last rumble of thunder was sounding rather different and longer than the others.

It came roaring out of the dark like a train, lifting Ben off his feet and hurling him down the gully, tearing the drone from his grip. He fought in vain to regain his balance in the storm which now included whipping and scratching branches, as well as mud and stones.

Then he was hurled free, weightless for a moment. He caught a flash of his surroundings as he fell from the high bank into a swollen burn along with the sliding land. An angry thunder clap could be heard even below the cold murky water. As he fought to lift his head above the rapids for air, his arms and legs were striking rocks and debris. He tried to grab hold of anything he could to help himself up and out. But the few things he grasped for were torn from his grip on his flume-ride down into Curston.

He tried to remember the content of what he had sleep-read. This *thing*, whatever it was, needed to serve a purpose, not simply torment him.

Battered by the floodwater that he tried to rise above, Ben bobbed up and caught sight of a bridge during a lightening flash then he was under it, entering Curston's old industrial estate heading for the river and deeper trouble. Another flash, as his head surfaced momentarily for more air and he glimpsed the nearly choked culvert just up ahead. His fingers clawed at the stonework to the side, which proved as much use as grabbing for a grinder. It felt like nails were being torn free. Then he was into the dark tunnel which had no breathing space.

Trying desperately to recall, he did remembered something. He had to reach out to the left to grab the ladder he was rushing towards.

He couldn't afford to have that ladder torn from his grip as well, so when he felt it he reacted with a vice-like grip which almost tore his arm out of its socket. He yelled a stream of bubbles into the floodwater.

Fighting the pain from arm and lungs, he drew himself closer to the ladder, managed to grab a rung with his other hand then grabbed for the next one up with his now injured arm. Shortly he got his feet onto the ladder, fighting the strong current. He almost passed out before he got his head above the still rising water. Gasping for air, his mouth just above the floodwater, the torrent was still doing its best to tear him loose and away. Nevertheless, Ben's determination saw him through and he finally reached the hatch, where he breathed a sigh of relief.

This must have been how Sven exited the culvert unseen, he thought. Wouldn't be long now and he'd be on his bike home for a hot shower. But the hatch was locked. No amount of shoving shifted it and yet it clearly wasn't sealed air-tight, as the water was still rising.

30

The gap between the roof of the culvert and the ladder hatch was only a metre, so even though Ben tried to get his legs out of the drag of the floodwater he couldn't quite do it.

Hanging onto the ladder in a near foetal position, feet on a rung, he felt unknown *things* bumped into him on their race down to the river. Something sharp stabbed his backside at one point, possibly a splintered section of tree trunk, causing him to jump involuntarily and smack the crown of his head on the hatch. His skin was sore from all the cuts and bruises received on his journey down. His muscles ached from the strain, and he was getting cold. He didn't know how long he was going to have to hang on for, or even if he was going to be *able* to hang on.

He had tried his phone. Though it was waterproof, there just wasn't any signal down there.

The water continued to rise in the dark airless confines, over Ben's legs and torso, then up to his neck. He began to consider ducking down and trying to make it to the river, but couldn't remember quite how far it was, only that there was no grill across the culvert by the river.

As the water level reached his chin he had a thought. He wasn't sure whether it was logic or faith, but since the sleep-reading about the ladder *had* come true after all, then at some point the broken legs must also be true. While he did not wish that to be true it surely meant that whatever he did in this situation he would survive.

He tilted his head back and pressed his face against the underside of the hatch, adding a crick in the neck to his list of complaints in order to keep in the land of the breathing.

An hour later he realised, now shivering uncontrollably, the water level was beginning to drop. Provided he didn't stop shivering and suddenly feel that warm glow that comes before death by hyperthermia, then he was going to make good his escape.

However, by the time he did swim out, when sufficient air gap had returned to the roof of the culvert, his skin was like a prune. Still shivering he was spewed into the river. Struggling with the cold and cramping muscles he swam to the bank. He ended up on a pile of sticks brought down by the flash flood, caught in the riverside bushes.

It was way past first light by the time Ben got back to his bike. He wasn't really in a fit state to ride home but he had to have the store open at seven. He attempted to unlock his helmet from where he had secured it to the back bar. That's when he spotted his next problem. His electronic lock did not acknowledge his wrinkled thumb print, which meant neither would the bike's ignition.

Exasperated, Ben left the bike and jogged the best part of six miles back to Sevensands. At least the effort kept him warm. In his state of exhaustion though, he could feel he was starting to burn what body fat he had on him.

By the time Ben got back to the house he had only just over an hour before his seven hour shift at the store started. The idea of going in, in this state, was ridiculous. What was he trying to prove? That he still had what it took to keep going? He was just going to have to phone in sick. That was the sensible thing to do. Then he remembered that Harry was away for the weekend.

Removing his sodden trainers, he saw himself reflected in the door of the cooker he realised just what a dreadful state he was in. He needed to think of a solution quick. He wished his fancy dress costume had turned up on time. Then he had his *bright* idea.

He pulled the curtains closed tore off his tattered and filthy clothes and threw them in the washing machine, programmed it, switched it on then went for a shower.

After his shower he inspected all his cuts and grazes. He wasn't bleeding anymore but he looked like a tsunami victim. His left eye was still swollen shut though no longer quite as tight shut. There was a glimmer of vision returning. He went for his jungle cam box. For what he had planned he needed quite a bit of grey and some yellow.

Hearing the washing machine spin cycle finish Ben looked at his G-Shock watch and smiled with his cracked lips, he might just pull this off, to have his shredded clothing ready to wear for work.

As the washing went on to drying mode Ben considered having a full English fry-up but his inner craving disagreed, so he consumed three tins of salmon and a coffee.

Ben's first customer turned white as a sheet in the doorway, seeing him standing there at the counter.

'Jesus, Mary and Joseph, Chance! You look like you've been grave robbed, you do!' said the not so young farmer.

'Looks good doesn't it, Rod. I'm advertising the Film Theme Fancy Dress do, which's at the village hall tonight...Y'coming?'

'Not if you're dressed up like that. It's made us feel proper sick. What are you supposed to be?'

'One of the zombies from 24 Hours Later.'

'Well, if it's all the same with you, *I'll* be back twenty-four hours later.' Rod turned and left.

The next customer was Mikey.

'Bloody Hell, Chance? Is that for tonight's do at the hall?'

'Yes. What d'you think?'

'That is *absolutely* bloody *amazing* mate. You look dead on your feet...But why are you dressed up now? Surely they've not got you working here till seven? You'd have time to dress up when you get home.'

'No. Eddie is in at two. The idea is to get a few more tickets sold. After all, this is for a charity right?'

'Yeah, some kids thing.'

'So, are you going?'

'Are you kidding? Of course I am. I'm going as Captain Jack Sparrow. So people will think I'm just being in character when I have a skin-full.'

Two girls ran screaming and crying from the store. Ben and Mikey watched as they ran to a car on the forecourt and climb back in slamming the doors closed. Seconds later the mother was out and into the shop.

'Good God, Chance! What do you think you are doing, scaring my girls like that? You should be ashamed!'

'Sorry. I'm helping sell tickets for tonight's charity do.'

'Well that is a totally inappropriate choice of costume for the store. Does Harry know you're doing this?'

'No.'

'I thought not. I think I'll give him a call.'

'Give Chance a chance Brenda.' Mikey defended, 'He's been *dying* to do this.'

'He looks absolutely horrific!'

'I know, right.'

Brenda came closer. 'I can't even imagine how you can do that with make-up.'

'And you'd know a thing or two about make-up.'

'What's that supposed to mean, Mikey?'

'You being a woman and all.'

Brenda shook her head. 'Since you scared my kids off, Chance, I better get them their mix-ups.' She quickly grabbed the sweets, paid and left.

'What a moaner, eh.' Mikey turned back to Ben. 'You must have watched a lot of those urr *Making the Movie* bits at the end of the blue-rays to learn how to do that stuff so well.' He reached out to touch the cuts on Ben's arm.

Ben pulled back from the counter. 'Don't...It might...come off and leave a patch.'

'Right...Well I better get what I came in for,' Mikey turned towards the aisles.

By lunchtime Ben had eaten three of the hot pasties which could no longer legally be called Cornish. If he had been able to find the tin opener in the dreadfully untidy kitchen he would have been able to sort his still present craving for tinned fish too.

Word had got round the village about *Chance the Zombie* and the takings in the store had rocketed with the increased footfall. As an added benefit Ben did manage to sell more tickets to the charity do.

Ben half expected Jill to drop by, but she didn't. She must have been too busy to check her social media, he thought.

When Mikey returned for a late lunchbreak he wasn't so impressed. 'What's up with your make-up, Chance?'

'Why?' He looked in the mirror by the till. 'Oh...I see...It's...wearing off.' Ben's injured eye, although still grey and yellow with camo paint was almost back to normal now.

Mikey pointed at the cuts on Ben's arms. 'I'd have thought that those sorts of prosthetics would peel off rather than just fade.'

'Urr...well...they *were*...painted on. Maybe they are being you know...absorbed.'

'Absorbed? Who do you think you are, the Swamp Monster? No I guess they must be flaking off.'

'Right, sure.'

At that point the postman came in. 'Chance, you look like the walking dead...Oh and this is yours,' he handed him a parcel.

'Thanks. It's for the charity do.' A reply which could as easily refer to the parcel as to Ben's torn clothes and grey skin.

When Ben got home he showered again then lay on the bed but was only there five minutes before he remembered his bike. He thought of calling *Five* and asking someone to bring it across. He also considered pleading for a new drone. But he anticipated the earful he would get off Cynthia about budgeting when he still had not brought Sven in. So instead he phoned for a taxi to take him to Curston market square, where he walked down to where he had left the bike. He was glad to see it had not been tampered with and even happier that his electronic locks could now read his thumb.

Shortly he was home again, to try for that power-nap, having set his alarm for six, just in case he was out for the count. He certainly needed to get his head down after thirty four hours without sleep and an endurance test besides.

When the alarm woke him he was hungry again. Although there was meant to be food at the do Ben cooked a couple of salmon steaks and some veg and while that was cooking had sardines on toast.

Later, when he had washed up, Ben got into the Predator costume and had the forethought to try and drink from a pint glass through the mask. The array of teeth and fangs held the edge of the glass back too far from his lips. He pushed the mask in hard with his alien paw, made contact with the glass and tried drinking. The water dribbled from the side of his mouth and out the bottom of his mask, streaming over his chest-plating.

'Bollocks,' the synthesiser in the mask changed his voice to sound like a Predator swearing.

He might be able to shove small snacks into that opening but was going to need a straw if he was going to be drinking anything, which was highly likely as he was already quite hot under all that plastic. He started looking through the draws for a straw. Not one to be found. He thought about the store. They didn't sell them. Then he had another thought. He rummaged through the draw at the sink again and pulled out a biro. He took the cap, nib and tube out of it.

'This will have to do.' He looked for pockets. A Predator didn't have pockets. He shoved the empty pen under his left bicep plate.

All set he headed out, clunking his head of cable-like dreadlocks off the doorframe. To lock the door he had to use his left paw because he found the two long claws protruding off the back of his right wrist got in the way.

'What a phaff! Who designed this alien?' the Predator moaned, then growled as Ben had trouble lifting the alien over-trousers to put his keys into his trouser pocket underneath.

He stomped down to the village hall. Passing the house where two dogs always growled at him on his way to or from work, this time they took one look at him and ran away from the gate yelping, tails between legs.

At the hall Ben had to remove his left glove to find his ticket in his trouser pocket. This took a lot of pushing and pulling under his over-trousers to get at it.

Gareth, who was on the parish council, and in charge of collecting tickets, was not impressed. He had it in his power to say *not to worry* but instead pointed out 'That's really not a good look mate, at a kid's do. It looks like you're having a wank!'

Ben growled and slammed the creased ticket down on the table.

'What are you supposed to be anyway?'

'A Predator, Gareth.'

'You've got to be kidding. You *do* realise this charity is raising money to support children who have been victims of internet grooming?!'

'Shit!' It was all too late. Wishing now that the suit was realistic enough to have its cloaking system, Ben turned away to the bar.

At the bar Ben ordered a Guinness then attempted to retrieve his wallet.

Stevie watched Ben as he poured the pint and began giggling. 'Steady on, tiger, we have women in the room.'

Ben turned to see Gloria standing in the queue.

'I don't mind if he wants to knock one out,' she exploded with laughter.

Paid up, wallet back in pocket, glove back on, pen in mouth and glass to mask, Ben took four long gulps.

Gloria watched on with further amusement at the makeshift straw. 'Are you old enough to be drinking a Guinness?' She exploded again.

Ben stomped off into the main hall. The lead guitarist of the band was just explaining to the gathering crowd what was expected of everyone. When the band played the theme for someone's costume they were encouraged to take the centre of the dance floor and then strut their stuff. Ben felt relieved. They were unlikely to play the theme from the Predator movie, and even if they did he wouldn't recognise it.

The band launched into the James Bond theme and immediately two 007s were having a dance-off to cheers from the crowd.

Minutes later Ben saw someone who had to be Jill arrive on her own. She had an indigo wig and a dark brown leather bomber jacket over a gold swimsuit. She seemed to spot him straight away and headed across in her knee-high dark brown leather boots. As she got closer Ben could make out her red contact lenses, and eye-liner which made her eyes look *manga* big.

'Major Motoko Kusanagi I presume,' he greeted in his Predator voice with reference to the main character from Ghost in the Shell.

'Very good, Chance,' Jill nodded, knowing it just had to be him under that costume going by size alone. 'But what happened to the Zombie outfit I heard about?'

'Urr...well...I had sent off for this but it only arrived this afternoon. The zombie costume was just my attempt to sell more tickets at the store.'

'I see. But surely you could have stayed with the zombie and got your money back on the Predator costume.'

'You know, I hadn't considered that.' Ben took a long draw on his pint.

Jill grinned, 'The straw doesn't really look the part does it, Chance?'

'I know, it sucks.'

Later in the evening Captain Jack Sparrow staggered over to the Major. 'The twat...has stood you up has he?'

'Not at all.'

The Captain blearily looked past the Major and the Predator, swaying as he scanned the crowd. 'Well where is he? We've got two zombies in here and they are women, and I'm sure of that because I've snogged them both.'

'Maybe you should go easy on the grog Jack,' said the Predator. 'The zombie I'm looking at looks like Burt.'

'Juthinkso...?...If Chance was here...'

'I *am* here.'

The Captain turned to look at the Predator, squinting his eyes. 'Chance?...What the Fuck?!...What have you done?...You were a dead cert for the best costume award...I've been telling everyone to come and see your zombie outfit!'

'Well I...um...ran out of the make-up to do it again this evening, and this was what I had ordered off eBay for the do.'

With a wave of dismissal Mikey heard the theme to Pirates of the Caribbean and staggered towards the dance floor 'My audience…awaits.'

'He does do a good Jack Sparrow,' said Jill, taking Ben by the glove and pulling him away from the wall where they had been standing.

Ben thought she wanted another dance, so he put down his near-empty pint on a glass filled table and followed, but she was heading to the door. 'Where you going?'

'I thought I'd take my Chance…home.'

31

Ben had to leave Jill's early the next morning.

'Where are you going?' Jill mumbled.

He clearly wasn't nipping to the loo, hopping about the bedroom trying to put his Predator suit on quietly. 'I've got to open the store.'

'In your Predator suit?' Jill still sounded half asleep.

'No.'

'What time is it?' sounding more awake.

'Just gone five. I have to get home and change. No excuse for a second day of fancy dress at work.'

'How about...just one more time?' she asked seductively, not referring to his costume.

'Sorry...I can't...later.' Ben lent in and kissed her.

'Well, don't forget to pack your things when you get back from work.'

'Pack my things?'

'Yeah, well you have a full shift tomorrow don't you, and I'll be picking you up straight from the store.'

'Of course...The Edinburgh Fringe.'

It was a quiet morning in the shop with only three farmers coming by to fuel up their quads and cans before ten. Farmers didn't get the luxury of a break from routine, even if they could spare an hour or two in an evening for an occasional charity do.

Eleven o'clock seemed to open the floodgates to all those locals with hangovers. They arrived in droves, in need of bacon, eggs, sausages and other fry-up essentials. Some making requests for painkillers almost as an afterthought at the counter. Others however, preferred the alternative approach, requesting bottles of spirits, smelling like they still had the best part of a bottle in their blood system.

With a queue of never less than three impatient customers at the counter it was the wrong time to be ringing in but both the store phone and his mobile kept going for it. He ignored them both in his attempt to focus on the customers. However, the repeated ringing made him wonder if it wasn't separate callers but one *urgent* caller.

He started to get as impatient as some of his customers. He found it increasingly difficult to concentrate on putting all the food and drink through the scanner properly and give the correct change. His wandering mind began to catastrophize. What if something had happened to Jill? What if Sven had her?

The first chance Ben got to check his mobile for messages it was almost a quarter to twelve. It had been Cynthia. It must have been on repeat dial because as he walked outside to call her back, where there was better reception, the mobile rang again.

'Finally. Did I *wake* you McGregor?'

'No...I'm working...I'm on my *own* in the store.'

'Do I sense that you have more *loyalty* to that shop than this operation?'

'No, not at all.'

'Well you haven't been reporting in, so I take it you still haven't got anywhere with this Sven.'

'Well I haven't caught him no, but I came close, real close. I almost had my hands on him Friday night.'

'Friday? What about last night?'

Ben couldn't say he was in fancy dress. 'Look Cynthia…If you must know I got injured I've been trying to recover.'

'Well again, why didn't you report in?'

'I thought about it, but I'm so close now I didn't want you pulling me off this.'

'Well you're taking far too long.'

'It has been more difficult than we were expecting.'

'Never mind, McGregor. I've decided…'

'No wait I just need this evening to follow through on my plan.'

'Too late…I'm sending in support.'

'A new handler?'

'Not exactly no. You have a spare room in that house don't you?'

'Yes but…'

'Good. She'll be with you later this evening.'

'She?' Hell this could screw things over with Jill before he had chance to break up with her gently at Edinburgh.

'Agent Oakley.'

Back at the house he didn't waste any time. He had his lunch, packed a case for Edinburgh and then prepared for what was intended to be his final mission. He didn't want to have help from Agent Oakley. He didn't doubt her abilities. It was just that this had become personal between Sven and him, since Sven killed Aussie. Ben wanted this wrapped up before Agent Oakley arrived.

He went to the safe at the back of his corner cupboard in the kitchen, moving cleaning utensils out of the way to provide his thumb-print. He removed the Glock and all of its spare magazines. There was another with more magazines in the back of the bike. This time he meant business.

Ben would go to Curston and look to cross paths with Sven. He had a hunch that today was *his* lucky day and not Sven's. The plan had come to him by reframing what he was dealing with. The bike wasn't a pursuit vehicle, it was a *weapon*. The plan was now to *immobilise* with extreme prejudice. It would be Sven's turn to be patched up for a change.

Ben preloaded a nine millimetre round into the chamber of the Glock and stuffed it under his body armour. He was ready.

32

Ben stationed himself central to Curston, parked off the road behind the castle keep near the market square.

His heads-up was tapped into a *Five* satellite view of the town, which could even penetrate the layer of cloud above him. It did not give him the clarity or the freedom of control that the drone had provided but was better than nothing. The widest area he could cover without being too small-scale to pick out individual bikes fortunately managed to cover all five routes into Curston.

Surveillance was always a strain, having to concentrate for long often uneventful periods. Observation skills training helped, but it was never easy. It was possible to make some differentiation between bikes, to a degree, by their movements. Confident riders of bigger bikes tended to move more smoothly than newbies on small bikes. Newbies often had an element of sway or wobble, especially at slower speeds.

Nevertheless, in the three hours that Ben had already been on surveillance there had been two false alarms with potential matches entering Curston. Ben didn't let it get to him though. Each check made a good dry run, and it provided a break from the tedium.

Because he would not know for sure it was Sven until he had eyes-on, he had to make sure not to draw attention to his approach.

Otherwise he could have police interference once again. So he kept to the speed limit as he checked out each potential target.

The intention was not to come up from behind, which would result in a pursuit. Ben's plan was to blindside Sven by coming out of a junction, right onto him, torpedo style. To do that he needed to note Sven's route, to second guess where he was going, and get ahead of him. Wherever Sven would come from, and head to, there was one thing Ben knew. There would be purpose to Sven's actions. He would not be there as a Sunday driver.

Ben spotted another target. He wasn't too confident about this one because it had pulled out of the hospital car park and was shortly heading along the high street. Ben set off anyway.

He considered his options. The quickest route from the market square had been pedestrianised, so that was out. Parallel to that the end of the road was too open. He preferred a more concealed junction. The best option came out the other side of Wrap Park, much further along than Ben would have preferred. There were a number of side roads along the way entering housing estates which the target could turn off into. However, that would only mean having to work out a new blindsiding point.

The chosen point would have to provide for a split second positive ID of Sven and the Ninja without Sven spotting him in time to react. Ben knew his plan wasn't perfect but it was the best he had, presently.

The potential Sven moved along the high street at under twenty miles an hour. Ben set off down the hill towards the industrial estate which joined the road he wanted to be coming up to, ahead of the target.

As Ben drew close to the desired junction, he noted that the target bike had stopped on the high street, making it even less likely to be Sven. After a minute of waiting near the junction, pretending to check his mobile, he decided to risk a ride-by, just to confirm it was not the target.

He took a right and headed towards town. As he passed the police station he noted that the target had started moving again, towards him. This was not ideal. What he needed was a vehicle ahead of him, preferably a van, to provide some level of cover, but the road was clear.

The lights up ahead turned red. So Ben slowed to keep his distance a little longer. At the junction he saw a black Range Rover pull up ahead of the target which eased up on the inside. The car obscured Ben's view so he couldn't be sure of its rider as he closed in, until he noticed the suppressed weapon being drawn.

Two shots were fired through the back passenger window then the bike pulled forward for the rider to deliver a further two shots through the front passenger window, this confirmed it was Sven. Ben switched off the engine sound simulator, going stealth, and pulled back on the throttle. Leaning forward against the tremendous torque he aimed the bike for Sven's.

Sven didn't seem to notice until the last moment, Ben silently hurtling up towards him as he turned left at the still red light to leave his scene of crime. Ben was forced to cut the corner as Sven pulled away, still aiming for the centre of the Ninja. He narrowly missed a car coming through the junction at speed to make the lights. The car hooted angrily, but Ben ignored it, Glock drawn for plan-B.

Sven had put *his* weapon away. *He* was focusing on making good his escape, leaning into his own machine's acceleration, as Ben passed narrowly behind him, mounting the pavement at an angle. Ben almost lost control of his bike as the suspension did its best to cope with hitting the curb. With the Glock still in his grip at best it was like trying to steer with one and a half hands. A garden wall scraped at his boot while the hedge brushed aggressively at his arm, slowing him right down.

Ben got back onto the road but now he had been forced into chasing Sven. Not what he wanted at all, but he wasn't likely to get another chance to blindside him for now. He would just have to shoot his tires out from under him. Taking aim and firing at the rear tire Sven swerved as if he had spotted the gun in his mirror, but then Ben realised the swerve was to avoid a pothole. Ben bumped through it, further confounding his aim.

Sven heard the shot and now began snaking about erratically on the road. It was hard for Ben to make his shot. The rounds went wide. Ben needed to look out for passers-by. He must not hit an innocent party, which was why it was a good thing this street would become a sixty zone country road shortly.

However, with another of those cocky waves Sven enjoyed winding Ben up with he swerved and sped up a side road leading into a housing estate.

This further infuriated Ben, though he knew he must not let anger get the better of him. He had to stay focused. This could be his last chance. Ben could not afford to be shooting at Sven on an estate if he could possibly help it, so had to have a really clear shot before he loosed another round. Otherwise the police would be getting called in.

Ben sped round the corner and did his level best to close the gap. There wasn't so much space to continue erratic swerving with cars parked on both sides but Sven did his best to continue. Ben thought to get close enough to Sven's rear wheel that on a swerve Ben's front wheel would clip it and put Sven onto the tarmac. However, just as Ben was almost on top of him, trying to clip the wheel and take aim at the same time, Sven took a sharp left.

Ben tried to follow but collided with the side of a parked car putting a big dent in both doors. No alarm went off but it made quite a noise. He tore away from the scene, trying to close the gap once again.

It was too much to hope for that this road was a cul-de-sac. Going by the satellite map on his heads-up, which he was now on the edge of, he could see they were on a crescent which led back to the road they had just come off. The curvature of the road meant that parked cars were obscuring Ben's view of Sven, until he had almost caught him up. However, as they reached the end of the crescent Sven turned left again.

Ben turned and sped down the straight, only to see Sven re-enter the crescent again.

'What's he playing at?'

Round the crescent they went, the sound of the Ninja starting to bring people to windows to see what was going on. Not good. Then they were back onto the straight. Was Sven trying to run Ben's battery down? That wasn't going to happen any time soon. Ben noticed Sven look at his left arm as if checking the time.

Ben mounted the pavement. If Sven was going to turn down the crescent again Ben was going to cut across him. He pulled back on the throttle and hoped no one would come out of a garden gate to see what was going on. They would never hear him coming.

As Ben left the pavement at the corner, Sven braked this time. Ben tried to brake but skidded and went into the back of the car he had hit previously, scratching and buckling the boot.

'And *that's* why you shouldn't park near corners.'

Pulling the bike away and bringing it around, Ben looked to see Sven just sitting there revving his engine a few yards away. He gave that wave again and shot off.

'Cheeky fucker!' Ben raced after him closing the gap on the curve, but suddenly Sven veered to the left and mounted the pavement. Ben came up alongside and aimed his Glock. This required him to look forwards and sideways at the same time, a recipe for disaster. He couldn't get a clear shot at the tyres or a leg, he took aim at an arm, his finger tightening on the trigger then Sven was gone.

Ben hadn't fired. Sven had braked suddenly and taken an alley which Ben could see on the satellite's live feed. It led back to the other road. There was no point turning back. Ben continued on, expecting Sven to turn left again for another loop. Sven turned right.

'Yes! Now I have you.'

Ben tried to get his timing right this time to blindside Sven but as he came out of the crescent Sven swerved to the right, mounting the pavement, passing behind Ben. Ben slammed the brakes on, doing a front wheel wheelie, coming to a skid-marking halt on the driveway of the house opposite the crescent junction.

Ben back-footed the bike off the drive and noticed Sven waiting for him again, checking his watch.

'What the *fuck*?!'

Ben's anger was now being over-ridden by suspicion. Sven was definitely up to something. The hit on the Range Rover was clearly not the whole objective for Sven. There was something else in the pipeline.

Ben sped after Sven again, out of the estate onto the same road they had come in on then they went left heading for the country. But what was in that direction?

They were off the satellite view. Ben switched his heads-up to the ordinary sat-nav, just as Sven took another left. Ben followed. Now they were going uphill. He saw that this road ended up passing the back of Curston

Science Park so they were probably coming back down into Curston but to what end?

As Ben closed the gap this time, Sven drew his weapon and fired. The shot went wide. Ben swerved, slowing. That had to have been a warning shot. But why? Why now?

Sven slowed too and turned left, heading into the Science Park then raced down the street towards the Medical Research building.

'Of course. The research building will be where the drugs are being manufactured.' Ben knew he needed to call this in, but there wasn't time. He wanted to close the gap but his curiosity now made him unsure about immobilising Sven who still had his own weapon at hand but was not aiming it in his direction.

Two guards stood at a padlocked barrier, but not the barrier of the medical research building. They were guarding the Smythe Futures computer technologies building next door. They seemed oblivious to the sound of the Ninja racing towards them at first. They were looking back towards their building, and the unscheduled opening of the underground loading bay security door.

Sven leaned over left to line up with the barrier as he sped out of the junction firing twice. Both rounds dropped the guards with clean head shots as they started to turn.

As they dropped, so did Sven, bringing the bike onto its side. Bike and rider went skidding under the barrier, taking the feet out from under both dead men who then impacted Ben as he tried to replicate Sven's action close on his tail.

Sven was up again in what looked like a practiced motion and racing for the loading bay door which was starting to close again. Ben picked himself up off the ground and heaved his machine up then sped onto the down ramp. He had to repeat the side skid action to get under the closing door in time.

Inside, Ben saw Sven ride into a goods lift and close the door. He couldn't reach the lift in time to reopen the door. There was only one other lift, a passenger lift next to it. Leaving his bike by the lifts because it was unlikely to fit in the passenger lift, Ben stopped to think.

There was no indicator on the goods lift to say which floor Sven was going to, but why take the bike in? This had to be called in. Ben got his mobile out, but there was no signal. He ran back to the security door but couldn't get it to open up without a security card.

There was nothing else he could do but try and catch up with Sven. He went back to the goods lift and pressed the button to call it back.

At that moment the doors to the passenger lift opened and Ben turned to see a guard with a pump action shotgun. As the barrel rose in his direction he tried to warn him, raising his own weapon. 'MI5! Drop your weapon!'

Ben wasn't sure if the man heard him. The shotgun blast lifted Ben off his feet and hurled him backwards.

33

The guard came over to Ben's prone from, and kicked it hard. That movement hid the blur of Ben's Glock as it put a nine millimetre round through the guards right eye and spun him backwards.

Ben tutted as he got to his feet putting a fresh magazine into his Glock. He put the weapon away then removed his helmet which had taken some of the blast and no longer seemed to be in working order. Placing it by the body he removed the guard's security card, from where the lanyard attached it to the hip. Ben simply wound the lanyard around his left wrist for quick access. Then he picked up the shotgun and pocketed spare cartridges.

The goods lift arrived and as the door opened Ben held the shotgun at the ready but it proved to be empty. No guards, no bike and no Sven. Ben decided to get his bike in there in case he regretted not doing so later.

He looked at the floor numbers, three to minus three. The lift was presently on minus one. He listened for any sign of activity above or below but heard none. He pressed minus two. The doors closed but the lift did not descend. He swiped the card and tried again. Nothing. He tried the card and minus three. Nothing. So tried zero. The lift started going up.

When the door opened he was greeted by two guards with shotguns.

'MI5! Drop your...' He fired twice in quick succession because he could see from the rising weapons they were not prepared to drop anything but their bodies.

The second of the two men pulled his trigged before he died. The blast toppled Ben and the bike over to the back of the lift. Getting back to his feet it felt like some of the shot had got between plates on his left leg.

Ben picked up both shotguns, threw them behind the bike and took more cartridges from the bodies, placing what he could into the pump action magazine. Then he pressed on at a jog, leaving the bike in the lift, to check out ground zero.

There was no one at reception, and all the monitors were out, which meant none of the security cameras were working. He checked for spare security passes of a higher level in the draws, feeling like it was all becoming some real-life shoot-em-up game. There were no passes.

Heading back down the corridor, checking offices as he went, they were all empty, but then it *was* a Sunday, even if some places did keep running twenty-four seven these days.

He came to another lift, this one with a stairwell. He took the stairs but as he did so he heard people coming down. They would have the advantage of numbers and higher ground, so he had to make use of speed, aggression and surprise.

Lifting the shotgun, a round ready in the chamber, he was surprised to find the descending crowd was a group of men and women in white-coats.

'MI5…!'

They didn't look at all relieved to see him. There was no going back. Ben didn't see a weapon, so didn't fire on them. Instead he put the safety on and used the barrel and stock of the shotgun to brutally jab people in the stomach, sweep them off the steps, batter them around the heads, and generally immobilise them. People tried to defend themselves but within seconds the stairs were littered with unconscious bodies.

'What is the matter with you people?'

Ben pressed on up.

On the next floor he jogged down a corridor. As he came towards a junction he could see there was someone waiting in ambush. There was a shadow cast on the left wall from someone in hiding just round the corner on the right. No more warnings. Ben took out his Glock passed it to his left hand and as he slowed before the corner he fired round it blindly. A body slumped away. It was another guard.

The guard had the same security card Ben already possessed so he left that and he didn't need the shotgun but took extra cartridges. Then he turned the remains of the guard's head over. He hadn't seen radios on the guards but that was because they were wearing ear-buds and collar-mics. He pulled out the ear bud and lifted it to his ear. It was dead, like its wearer.

Moving on Ben almost reached a door when it opened towards him. Two guards were coming through, weapons raised. Ben fired as he shifted towards the wall that the door was opening towards. The first man went down spinning the second and both of their shots went wide. The second man tried to recover his balance but Ben saved him the effort.

Both dead guards had a higher security clearance card so Ben took his off for an upgrade. Then he considered heading back to the lift to try going down. He was convinced Sven had gone down because there was no sign of him upstairs. However, having started going up Ben was now curious what and *who* was up ahead. He pressed on.

He entered a windowed corridor with clean rooms, with people in white suits with masks. At first he thought this must be where the drugs were being produced, but as he looked through the corridor windows he made out electronic components on conveyor belts. This would be the cover operation.

He heard people coming and turned to see through the windows four guards were about to come round the corner. He turned to back-track and find a better fighting position, only to see another four guards in the corridor behind him. It was a pincer movement with no cover. He jumped sideways to smash through the glass but just bounced to the ground.

Though the guards were armed and could have fired they didn't. New orders must have been issued. They charged him from both sides as he tried to get up, giving him a taste of what he had dealt out to the white-coats.

The shotgun was kicked away from him. Ben delivered a punch between one man's legs, then an upper-cut to another's jaw, sending them both reeling backwards. He followed this up be kneeing a man in the pit of his stomach then back-kicking another off down the corridor. A rain of blows from shotgun butts were coming in hard and fast at his arms, legs and head, but he fought on. He reached for the Glock but it was gone, taken or lost somewhere on the floor. He couldn't see it. He felt teeth smash, nose break, and returned the favour twice over.

These guards were hard. They just kept getting back up for more.

Ben struck a guard hard in the throat. *He* didn't get back up. He twisted another's arm, feeling something in it snap just before he kicked the chin hard and snapped the neck. Another one wouldn't be getting back up.

Still none of the guards were shooting at him.

Ben could feel his head and limbs swelling under the blows. Another man down then another but then it was him. He tried to get up but then he felt his leg break. Someone had struck it very hard with their shotgun. Ben cried out, then a second time as they broke his other leg. A final blow to the head brought darkness with it.

He was brought round by a series of slaps to the face, to find himself bound to a chair in a rather plush office on what he assumed to be the top floor, with its big windows overlooking the valley and Curston in the late summer evening light.

Ben's body ached and burned all over. He struggled against his bindings. Immediate pain reminded him that he now had two broken legs. He couldn't think how he was possibly going to get out of this one. He tried to remember what he had sleep-read about the broken legs.

'So, what have we here? An MI5 agent?' inquired a tall thin man with a rather posh accent.

'Yes.' There seemed little sense in denying it now.

'I appreciate your honesty.'

Ben thought he detected a hint of sarcasm.

'...I am Terence Smythe...You seem familiar somehow. Have we already met? It is hard to tell with the state of you. Shame you didn't come quietly, really. The grind must be going rind and rind.'

Ben peered through his swollen eyes. Terence had once been a customer at the store but had never introduced himself. Ben recalled that he had been after a bottle of Jura single malt. 'I don't know. I don't think so.'

'Oh, no matter...I just hope you *can* tell me what your colleague has got planned. Surely this is not standard operating procedure for MI5? A two person attack, on an electronics firm?'

'He is not a colleague. I'm only here because I am trying to apprehend him.'

'Oh come now, I find that a little difficult to believe considering what you have done here already.'

'I identified myself but your people attacked, what else did you expect?'

'An approach through different channels, perhaps?'

'I didn't know I was coming, or I'd have let you know.'

'Really? So what is this person's name?'

'We don't know. He is a vigilante. His code name, if you like, is Sven.'

'Well I don't bloody *like*! So, if you didn't expect to be here this evening, I take it you have no back up coming.'

'No,' he shook his head with a sigh but found himself wondering about Agent Oakley and how far away she might be now. She couldn't possibly know where he was though.

'I believe you. We have your phone and you had no other communication devices on you r person. I took the liberty of using your thumbprint while you were unconscious to access your phone records. I take it this is not an MI5 phone. It seems to have a tedious number of texts to and from women, particularly one called Jill.

'I'll tell you what I think. I think you are bluffing. I think you and *Sven* are working together outside of MI5 operations. After all, what would MI5 want with us? However, you've clearly bitten off more than you can chew. So I'll ask you to be honest with me. Who is your partner?'

'Sven is not my partner.'

'I know you know about the drugs operation in the basement. Between the two of you, you've hacked into my system to compromise my security and killed a number of my people. I need to know who Sven is, since *they* are clearly the brains.'

Terence turned to the men who brought Ben in. 'You two stay here, the rest of you go and see what's keeping the others.'

Ben thought it quite obvious what must be keeping the others.

'This *Sven* has been picking off my employees for some time, a growing irritation. It would seem that I overestimated how secure this operation was here so I still believe you know more than you are telling me.'

Ben was tempted to make a facetious comment but kept quiet.

Terence went over to his desk and retrieved a small pack. 'One of the ingredients to our designer drug is a natural toxin. A saponin. In very small quantities it acts like a detergent. It helps the stimulant elements of our drug more speedily and deeply penetrate the tissues. Also ensuring it remains in the system for longer periods before the body can flush it out. This enables us to demand a higher price in the marketplace.

'However, in higher concentrations the toxin is quite lethal. I'm also given to understand it would be a most agonising and yet not instantaneous death. Now I'm not much of a chemist *myself* so I don't know what makes for a lethal quantity,' he waved the pack, 'but if I were you, I really wouldn't chance it...So who is Sven?'

'I don't know. But if you find out, let me know.'

Terence opened the pack, took out a syringe and a small bottle. He began to fill it slowly in front of Ben, to make him think about what was coming if he didn't respond appropriately. 'Are you ready to talk?'

'Okay, okay.' Ben spluttered as he struggled against his bonds attempting to lean away from the dribbling needle point that was closing in on his neck. 'It's Sven Gali.'

'Oh how tiresome.' The needle went in, followed by the fluid.

34

Ben groaned as he felt the toxin flood into him.

The men laughed.

Then as they watched, Ben's skin turned rosier and he began to blink.

'Ha. Look, I think his eyes are going to pop out,' said one guard.

'He was warned,' Terence added with a nod.

'No, I don't think they are popping out,' said the second guard, 'look, it's more like the swelling in his face is going down. And look at those cuts on his hands. They look like they're…'

'It's not possible,' Terence complained. 'He should be in agony.'

'What toxin did you say it was?' asked the first guard.

'A *saponin* that we use for the Liquid Crystal. You wouldn't understand. It's an extract from something called the Crown of Thorns.'

Ben began to feel better. A lot better. He strained against his bonds but they held him so firm the tubular steel chair began to buckle.

There came the sound of something rolling across the veranda and the men turned to see what looked like a grenade clunk against the large panes of glass.

'It's a…'

The explosion blew in the windows. Shards of glass flew at the men like a cloud of shrapnel. Some caught Ben.

A dark figure on the veranda passed from left to right incredibly fast, firing two rounds. Both guards fell backwards with large exit holes in the backs of their heads.

Then Sven was standing there by the glass door to the veranda, which remained in tack, watching Terence. The bike helmet was gone but a black balaclava remained.

Terence shifted his gaze to Ben's Glock on the desk. He wondered if he could get to it in time to at least shoot Sven as he shot at him.

Sven slipped into his cocky mode. He played mime artist pretending the window next to the door was still in place, shifting his hands over the imaginary surface.

Terence frowned thinking he must be dealing with a madman.

Sven's hand went to the door handle and tried it slowly at first. It appeared to be locked. Sven began to frantically rattle the handle.

Ben smirked. He could see the humour when someone else was on the receiving end.

Terence couldn't stand it any longer. He made a dash for his desk. He almost had the Glock in his hand but took a nine millimetre round through it instead. He screamed out, dropping the case of toxin from his left hand to hold his injury.

Sven was beside Terence in an instant, sweeping him from his feet to land hard on his hip and dash his head off the tiled floor.

Terence screamed again and then again as Sven trod on his injured hand while picking up the toxin case. He opened it. It contained one more bottle and syringe. He filled it with exaggerated actions like it was another mime act. Then as Terence began to struggle Sven knelt down and plunged the needle and contents into the big boss's genitals.

Ben watch on as Terence's screaming rose in pitch then changed to a gargle as his body went into convulsions. Sven's body language during these long seconds of vengeance conveyed neither remorse nor enjoyment.

As Smythe's body went limp Ben realised Sven's attentions had now turned to him.

As Sven came across to Ben, a number of things were to pass through his mind in quick succession. The question at the forefront was whether the clinic could bring him back from a bullet through the brain?

Finding he had the time, he then wondered how he was supposed to get from this situation to being under a load of rubble. Whatever was about to happen, two things were clear: He would not be getting the store open in the morning; and as for that trip to Edinburgh, well…Would Jill ever forgive him?

Should any of that really matter now, in the grand scheme of things?

Sven holstered the gun and stepped behind Ben to untie him, then stepped back.

'Urr…Thanks.' Ben frowned. This was the second time Sven had found him tied up and set him free. Was this supposed to be some sort of truce now? After all that Sven had put him through recently? The whole idea seemed even more ridiculous than that stunt Sven had just pulled with the door handle.

Ben tried to get up from the seat. Even with the curative property which the Crown of

Thorns venom had on him, his legs couldn't take his weight.

Sven realised Ben's legs were both broken, looked at his watch then came round in front of Ben to grab his arms. Ben launched himself up and out from the armrests. He wrapped his arms tightly around Sven as he made to step back, turning away. He brought Sven down hard on his front.

The next step was tricky for Ben. His weight was both his advantage and disadvantage. He was pinning Sven down but their combined weight was pinning Ben's arms to the floor like some slapstick accident.

Trying to push Ben's deadweight off with bound arms, Sven twisted to one side, looking to place a hand on the floor to push up. However, the twist released Ben's left hand and as quick as he could Ben went for Sven's neck and ripped the mask up and off for the grand reveal. Twisting Sven's head sideways for a clearer view, he peered round.

'…You…have *got*…to be pissing me!!'

Ben was stunned. He felt the body below him trying to buck free. He could *not* make sense of what he was seeing. Then he was struck hard on the back of the head and the lights went out.

Ben coughed the choking dust from his dry mouth and as he did so he realised he was in an enclosed space. He also noted the tickling trail moving across his forehead that meant he was either sweating or bleeding. Since he was not overly hot it was most likely blood.

He tried to move. There was a lot of weight above him and it shifted. Dust trickled into his left ear and over his neck, but not before he heard the scraping sound of rock or concrete. Trying to control his breathing in the dark he had to think about what had happened to him, to better understand his situation.

He remembered trying to tackle Sven...and then this. But there had to have been more in between. Had there been another explosion? It would seem so.

He tried moving his arms. Only his left arm was possible to move. He worked his hand up towards his face then pushed outwards. He felt a large lump of rubble fall away to provide some dim light and fresh air. He shifted more rubble away and tried to pull himself towards the hole he had created.

Then he remembered...His legs, they were broken.

He listened again and thought he could hear someone approaching. He was unsure whether to call out before he understood the situation better, but then a torch-light was on him and he heard a welcome voice.

'I've found him.' It was Gina Oakley.

Epilogue

Ben wasn't sure whether this room in the clinic was ever occupied by other agents but it was getting to feel more and more like *his* home from home. Unfortunately, he would rather have been elsewhere, and under different circumstances.

His legs were each in a scaffold brace of pins, holding his bones in place, just for a day or two. All of his injured bones had had to be re-broken and realigned since the starfish venom had accelerated his healing while he was buried.

The venom, in less concentrated form, was core to the clinic's secret regeneration process for those given the experimental gene-splice. It was still under review whether there were going to be others.

Ben moved his tongue round his mouth and could feel new teeth coming through where he had lost others in the beating, as if the previous ones had only been baby teeth. He was marvelling at the medical technology when the door to his room opened.

He had been expecting a visit from Cynthia. She would have been informed that he was now well enough for a debriefing. However, this was the more pleasant appearance of Agent Oakley.

'How are you, Ben?'

'Oh you know...Feeling a bit *pinned down*, Gina.'

'Cynthia sent me.'

'I guessed as much.'

'The thing is…'

'You're working for Section 13 now and She's passed the operation on to you.'

'Yes. She believes I will be able to track Sven more effectively.'

'Well I *can* understand that…How you managed to find me, when even I don't remember where I ended up, *is* kind of amazing…And thanks for that by the way.'

'No problem.'

'So how did you do it? I remember my phone was taken off me. Was there some other tracker on me?'

'Nope…As I arrived in Curston the sky lit up to the south, like a volcano. I assumed that could have had something to do with you, or Sven, or would certainly soon get your attention too.

'So I went to investigate. There was no sense going towards the epicentre of the blast. If you had been involved *and* survived you would most likely have been on the edge of the blast zone. Since it was hillside and much of the debris had come down into the valley it made sense to search down there first.'

'How long did *that* take you?'

'Well, the woods were pretty thick there…I guess about ten or fifteen minutes.'

'Amazing…How did you say these thoughts come to you again?'

'Images mainly.'

'Do you ever read books in your sleep?'

'What?...You mean like sleep walking, you wake up to find you've been holding a book in the dark?'

'No. Like you can see a book and you just start reading it in your dream.'

'I don't think so. Why?'

'Oh nothing...Just wondered.'

'Right...Well *I* was wondering if you could tell me what you now know about Sven. No trace of his body has been found yet, and while he *could* have been vaporised in that explosion, I really don't believe he has been.'

'No?' Ben tried to decide how much he should say. He liked Gina but the whole *Sven* thing was still something he was wrestling with. 'Sven is certainly a very tricky character. A highly skilled killer but you know all that. I tried to apprehend him after a shooting in Curston but he led me into a trap in the Science Park...Sven used me...'

'Go on...' Gina encouraged, sitting down on the edge of Ben's bed.

'Used me, to draw some of the heat off him. Maybe I wasn't thinking clearly. I didn't know what was going on, what I was getting into. I tried to report in but there was no signal and the building was by then in lock-down. I tried to take control of the situation but it all blew up in my face.'

Gina gave a sympathetic smile but said nothing.

'With overwhelming odds I was captured and taken to the guy in charge, Terence...Smythe. He tried to get me to tell him who Sven was. When I couldn't tell him anything he tried to force it out of me by injecting me with toxin.'

'Did you tell him anything?'

'How could I? I didn't know.'

'*Didn't*? Or *don't*?

'I got hit on the back of the head and woke up where you found me in the rubble. There's clearly a whole lot I have no memory of.'

'Did you, at any time, see Sven with a bomb capable of destroying the whole building?'

'Not at all...Hand weapon and grenades maybe. No pack. Not even any paniers on the bike.'

'Right well that may confirm the theory that the Smythe operation was supporting terrorism and may have been stock piling explosives or even producing them. We'll have to wait on forensics for that one.'

'I see.'

'Okay...I'm going to let you rest now but if you think of anything call me...Okay?'

'Okay Gina. Will do.'

The book seemed to float over Ben's bed like a paperback for a giant, threatening to fall at any moment and leave him crushed with its words. Surely the story of this op was over and yet he could see by the way the pages hung there that there were a few more pages left.

Sven jogged towards the industrial unit in Strawford, opening the roller door using a remote under the trouser belt. Rolling under the door it was closing again after barely a metre of travel.

In what passed for the office the body armour was stripped off and discarded. Then the chest compression was removed to reveal breasts.

Zoe Innes sat down in front of her make-up mirror and went to work. There was no time to waste, though much had already been prepared for her bugging-out back home to Cambridge with her dash-bag of essentials.

As she worked on her next disguise, part of her mind went over the last few days with something akin to self-congratulation.

Zoe had been tying up some loose ends prior to the main op and doing so in a way which would lead to the desired finale.

On the Friday evening she had gone to the house of one of the loose ends, a Sean Dent, disguised as a rather androgynous pizza delivery guy. The target had been identified not only as one of the main drug-runners for the Science Park operation but a member of the tight-knit Dent family who had the serious crime connections she had been tracing.

Zoe had found herself moving from loan sharks to more serious criminals since her brush with Jerry Atherton. Her hacking skills had recently led her to Terence Smythe.

Sean had not been expecting a pizza nor the nine millimetre slug from the content of the box. The bullet had immobilised him in his hallway. Zoe, as opportunistic as ever, went inside, checked Sean's condition and then investigated his home for anything of interest, of which there was little.

On leaving she had called the police pretending to be a concerned neighbour who thought they had heard a loud bang like a gun shot.

When the Dent family came for a return visit to Curston Hospital on Sunday, Zoe had also returned. Disguised as a nurse she had entered Sean's room, interrupting a hushed discussion about whether Sean remembered any more about the man who had shot him.

With a smile Zoe had looked at her watch, pretending to take Sean's pulse, then administered a capsule promising that these anti-biotics would soon deal with the infection causing his raised heart rate and would take away the pain.

The family had smiled their thanks, quite unaware of Zoe's play on words. As she closed the door she heard a warning to Sean not to say anything to the police.

Outside the hospital, a little later, in her body armour and sitting on her Ninja, she waited for the Dent family to leave. She also watched the phone-tracker app on her mobile, which showed Ben stationed by the castle keep, less than a mile away.

Ben was the wild-card in this plan but nevertheless a crucial one. The floor plans of the Science Park target suggested there would be overwhelming odds. Zoe could over-ride the security but Ben was needed as a distraction, while she placed her bomb.

Through regular use of the Dark Net she had learned, sometime ago, about a duel-solution explosive. This explosive had resulted in the sinking of the Wave Forge under the Queen Elizabeth II Bridge, and later the crater left in the Chilterns. In both cases it had involved Gina Oakley who ironically was also nearby when Smythe Futures became past tense.

With the chemical formula Zoe was then able to use her trusted contacts to produce these two solutions in separate labs. Taking delivery of both solutions and storing them apart until needed, Zoe had pumped one load into the front tyre and the other into the rear tyre of her Ninja. All that was needed then was something guaranteed to bring the two solutions into contact. For this she used C4 surrounded in ball bearings, with a proximity detonator. Once the sensor on her belt got half a mile away from the bike it would explode. The aim of the bomb was not to kill people. If everything went to plan she and Ben should have done that before the bike went up. The bike was to destroy evidence of her presence but more importantly to be a distraction to the services while she ran back to Strawford.

Sitting on that bomb at the hospital Zoe waited for the Dent family to exit after visiting time then she followed their Range Rover. A half hour later Sean's digestive juices would have penetrated the capsule and released the cyanide, but he got to live longer than his family who died at the traffic lights.

The incident worked like a dream for Zoe. Ben was on her tail. She just had to make sure they did not get to the target before the security cameras shut down. That's when the loading bay door was timed to open, all down to a computer virus she had placed on the Smythe Futures system.

Once they were inside, Zoe loaded her bomb bike into the goods lift and with the security card she had had forged using security information she had hacked. She went down into the basement and began her killing spree.

Things only went awry when Zoe came back up and found Ben had been captured. The intention was to get him to chase her out of the building, to safety. However, as she rescued him she found that he was not going to be chasing anyone anywhere, and time was of the essence. Zoe didn't want the police turning up and getting caught in the blast, so had to get Ben out of there the only way she could. Drag him.

Even that didn't go to plan as his near dead-weight fell on her. Then the very thing she never wanted to happen happened. He revealed her identity. Arching her back as he sat back astonished, she managed to get a leg free around his side and delivered a contorted back kick to his head and knocked him out. Then he really was a dead-weight. She struggled to get out from under him then struggled to drag him. She didn't want to leave him, but now he knew her identity.

There seemed to be only one solution. Put it down to chance.

She dragged Ben across the shattered glass onto the veranda, to the glass fencing and heaved him up, then over. She saw him fall down into the trees, not far below. She heard the branches shake as he crashed through. Then came what sounded like rustling undergrowth as he tumbled on down the wooded hill. He no doubt came to a sudden halt against a tree trunk.

Zoe knew all about Ben's gene-splice. In fact, being the opportunist, on top of dealing with Smythe's criminal operation, Zoe had also been testing out Ben. She was very interested in his ability to recover from injuries, from cuts to lost limbs.

So she was reasonably confident that Ben had survived her dropping him over the edge. If she was wrong then that was her identity compromise dealt with through bad luck.

Zoe picked her section of canopy and dived over the edge. There was no way to simply catch an upper branch and swing down like a monkey, when coming from that height.

The human form was too tall and heavy, making the forces too great, even with Zoe's strength and fast reactions. This sort of jump was a last resort. The trick was to use the branches to slow the fall to the point a grip and twist could be sustained for a more controlled descent. It didn't always work well and Zoe had often hurt herself practicing this in the past. Nevertheless, she managed to survive, which was quite something in the near dark.

Reaching the ground where it was even darker, Zoe followed the trail of destruction to Ben who was, as anticipated, wrapped around a tree but still breathing. Taking his arms she had pulled him off to the side and down until the ground started to level out and his body refused to slide easily anymore. Then she left him there, and ran off through the woods to the west.

Half a mile away Zoe heard the explosion. It was much bigger than she had expected for two motorbike tyres of liquid explosive. She saw the flash from behind light up the wood ahead of her and the ground trembled. She didn't turn back. She would know soon enough whether Ben survived when she hacked back into Section 13.

One thing was for sure, Zoe thought as she finished working on her appearance, she would definitely be investing in the Crown of Thorns gene-splice with the money she had taken from the Smythe operation. Zoe could get almost any product or service she wanted through the Dark Net.

There were a couple of things she had left to do before her vanishing act. She took a burner phone from the dash-bag and transferred a file to it from her active phone.

This was a report detailing what she had found out and done whilst tracing and terminating the Smythe operation.

Importantly this report included evidence proving that Veronica Caultard was on the Smythe payroll and had been required to turn 'Sven' over to Smythe once located, not bring 'him' in to MI5. This was then sent to Cynthia.

The pay as you go sim was then removed and destroyed along with the card from the active phone to prevent tracing or connection of previous calls.

Zoe's whole body language was different now as she changed clothes then picked up the dash-bag and turned away from the desk. In her sleeveless leather waistcoat and jeans she strode out of the office to her Ford Focus, sporting her transfer-tattooed arms and untidy mop of black hair.

Throwing the dash-bag onto the back seat and activating the industrial unit's roller door she took one last look over the interior to check there was nothing she had forgotten to do then got into the car.

Her clean-up team would empty the place in the next few hours and dispose of all the evidence, just as the removal firm would deal with the house and contents.

Zoe looked over her shoulder and reversed past the Honda Civic she had been driving as Jill Selkirk.

**Other titles by
Kevin H. Hilton**

Breakfast's in Bed

Possession

Afterlife

Singularity

Northern Darks

Dark Net

Misadventure

Printed in Great Britain
by Amazon